CW00865191

Chasing Georgia

Chasing Georgia

The Georgia Series, Book 2

June V. Bourgo

DEDICATED TO ALL THE CHILDREN IN MY FAMILY CIRCLE
Adam, Aiden, Braelynne, Brenden, Brody, Callee, Deklan, Desiree, Emily,
Haley, Jayden, Jennifer, Jessica, Josh, Kaylyn, Logan, Maya,
MacKenzie, McKenna, Nathan, Samantha, Shayla, Teagan, Zach
and one who remains forever in my heart

IN MEMORY OF MY FRIEND AND NEIGHBOUR

SHARON MARIE MARCHANT
1951-2013

Sharon left us on July 1st, 2013 for her next big adventure.
Her zest for life, enthusiasm, caring and intelligence touched all who knew her.
She devoted her life to her family, her pets and her gardens.
She was also a special mother, mentor, friend and grandmother to her blended family.
Sharon, I miss seeing you working in your garden and hearing the squeak of your clothesline!

PART 1

Bitter are the tears of a child: Sweeten them.
Deep are the thoughts of a child: Quiet them.
Sharp is the grief of a child: Take it from him.
Soft is the heart of a child: Do not harden it.

Pamela Glenconner

Chapter 1

The lock on the door slipped into place, shutting out the world and securing his privacy. A few steps took him across the room to his desk. One flip of his finger turned on the desk lamp. *Finally, some peace and quiet,* he thought. He settled back into his leather chair, retrieved a key from its hiding place and unlocked the bottom drawer. A thick blue folder sat on top. He picked it up and ran his hand over the front cover, then dropped it onto the desk top. A cloud of dust blew up into his face.

"Damn..." he sputtered, wiping his face with the sleeve of his terry cloth robe. A glance around his study confirmed the room needed a good dusting and sorting out. Books from the bookcases were scattered around the room on any available surface; a small table in the corner by the couch, on chairs, and piled in the corners of the room. Newspapers and magazines cluttered the desk top. A direct result of the fact that he now locked his study door to keep out intruders. *Perhaps I should take the time to tidy up.*

His eyes hardened and a sneer played at the corners of his mouth. "So...did I ever say I was a good housekeeper?" he said aloud, with a shrug of his shoulders. He didn't mind the disarray. A room that housed his secrets and a sanctuary to express his inner thoughts gave him control and a power without criticism or disapproval. The sneer grew into a sinister grin and he pushed the chaos from his mind.

His attention returned to the blue folder. The routine was always the same. He'd stare at it with great anticipation and feel the quickening of his pulse in sharp contrast to the slow methodical opening of the folder. His hands shook as he spread the pictures over his desk and savoured the face that met his admiring gaze.

The eyes that stared back at him held a mystique, innocence, yet a sensuality that drew him in: a rich, dark brown pool of warmth and an invitation that spoke to him in volumes. The fullness of her lips and her devastating smile were not lost on him. The initial stirrings of lust warmed his body.

Sweaty hands shuffled through the pictures until he found the one that took his breath away. A full-length photo taken at a movie premier. He'd cut out the part of the companion standing beside her, dismissing his insignificance and annoyed that this man believed himself to be worthy of her company.

She wore a mauve evening dress; a scalloped beaded bodice that accentuated her ample breasts. Fitted beneath her bodice in an empire style, the slim-fitting fabric flowed in a soft silk over her curves to her mid-calf; a side slit opened the material exposing her left leg all the way up to her mid-thigh. Her hair fell in a cluster of auburn curls spreading over her bare shoulders. Always amazed at the effect she had on him, a shudder coursed through his body. His right fore-finger traced her cheekbone all the way down the side of her face and he imagined the softness of her skin. He placed his hand over her breasts and closed his eyes, imagining he was stroking her, hearing her purrs of enjoyment as his hand moved down her body and slipped inside the open dress slit, moving up her leg onto her silky thigh. His body responded to the fantasy and he placed his other hand inside his robe to touch his nakedness, releasing a deep sigh.

A sudden knock on the door broke through his flight of erotic imagery. "Dammit…"

The moment was gone.

Chapter 2

Georgia Charles opened her eyes and stared into the darkness of the room. Tilting her head, the red LED lights on the alarm clock showed 4:00 a.m.

Apprehension filled her to the core. She threw the covers aside and sat up.

Shaking off the memory of a bad dream, she left the bedroom and settled into her father's favourite armchair in her parents' living room. Dawn broke through the last remnants of night with the promise of a bright, spring day. Georgia smiled, remembering the rainstorm she'd travelled through the day before on the ferry from Gibsons to her parents' home in North Vancouver.

Five years previous, a cheating husband, who'd left her for his pregnant mistress led her to the Yukon to spend time with her best friend, Marion. Her own pregnancy had come as a shock a few days before she was to return home. She thought back to her last day in Whitehorse when she'd been kidnapped by bank robbers. Georgia had escaped her abductors and spent the winter lost in a cabin in the remote wilderness of northwestern British Columbia, where her daughter was born. Colin, her ex-husband, became the father of two baby girls born a mere two weeks apart. In the spring, Sean Dixon, an author and owner of the cabin she'd sought refuge in, rescued her. Books, and movies touting her a heroine, brought an unwanted notoriety to her life. The past few years, she'd travelled extensively with her co-writer and boyfriend, Sean Dixon, promoting their book and movies. Her daughter, Kaela, travelled with her and Sean when it was feasible or stayed with her parents while she was away. When at home, she shared a house with her grandmother in Gibsons on the Sunshine Coast peninsula, accessible only by ferry.

And now her ex-husband was dead. A sudden heart attack.

A voice broke into her muse. "Can't sleep?"

She turned to see her mother standing behind her. "Not much. Too many dreams. You wake up knowing you were dreaming but can't remember them." She frowned. "Except the last one."

Sandra Carr sat on the couch facing her daughter. "Want to tell me about it?"

"It's hard to explain." Georgia hesitated. "You know those dreams where there are bits and pieces and it doesn't make much sense? There were woods all around and I saw Kaela's face. Her eyes were huge and full of fear. The scene changed to fast, swirling water. She was bobbing around in it. It was so noisy—the water I mean. Then there were two of her. One in the water and one on the shore. They were both really scared. I woke up after that. Weird."

"It's upsetting when we have bad dreams about our kids. But it's only a dream," her mother said, "Colin's passing at such a young age is a shock to us all. You have a big day tomorrow with his funeral and more than likely your worry over Kaela is praying on your mind."

"You're probably right. I was thinking about all that's happened since the kidnapping. I can't believe five years have passed."

"I can't either. The years just flew."

"And now Colin's dead," Georgia said. "He missed so much of Kaela's first years. It's brought home the fact that time is precious, and I've missed some things in my daughter's life too with all this notoriety."

"You've always been there when it counted. You're a great mother to Kaela. Don't ever doubt that."

Georgia stared into her mother's face. "Now that Kaela is starting school in the fall, it's time for me to think about staying home more. She needs stability."

Her mother smiled. "Things should settle down now. You'll have more time to think about your personal life. You're becoming yesterday's news."

A giggle turned into a laugh, and ended with Georgia's infamous snort. "Thank God for that."

She stood and gave her mom a hug. "Thanks you. I feel better now. Let's go back to bed."

The next day, Georgia walked across the parking lot to the concrete sidewalk that led to the funeral home. A shudder passed through her body, but it wasn't from the cool June breeze. She glanced down at her five-year-old daughter and held her hand a little tighter. The narrow walkway led them to a white single-story building, half-hidden by flowering shrubs and rose bushes in full bloom. The California-style dwelling with its beckoning façade of warmth and comfort reminded her more of a yacht club or golf course clubhouse.

Passing through the open doorway, Georgia took a deep breath and let out a long sigh. She and her daughter stood on a green marble floor in a foyer lined with tall white pedestals housing pots of trailing multi-coloured flowers. The warm air hung heavy with their fragrance. She breathed in the moist pungent odor and that coupled with her nervousness, left her feeling nauseous. Her hand went to her stomach. *Be strong.*

The mirrored walls projected the appearance of a much larger room. The half dozen doors leading to other areas of the home were closed. An archway with white ornate iron gates centered the back wall and standing by the open gates was her ex-brother-in-law.

"Hello, Steve," Georgia said, as she lead Kaela across the room. Her high-heeled shoes echoed in her ears. She concentrated on their clicking-clacking across the floor to calm her nerves.

The man in the black suit ignored her. His eyes, wide-open with amazement, were focused on Kaela.

"Steve?"

"My God, Georgia…it's been a long time."

He took a hold of Georgia's free hand, letting his gaze slide back to Kaela.

"This is my daughter, Kaela…Colin's daughter."

"She certainly is," he said.

"Did you know my daddy?" Kaela asked, shyly.

"Yes I did. I'm married to your father's sister and that makes me your Uncle Steve. It's nice to meet you, Kaela." His large palm swallowed up her little hand as he shook it in greeting. "Come with me, ladies. I'll take you to your seats."

They followed Steve through the archway into a room set-up with jade green velvet chairs. As they moved up the centre aisle, the low hush of voices rose to a higher pitch. They passed rows of people from Georgia's past. Work colleagues, distant relatives and mutual friends of Colin's strained their heads sideways to catch a glimpse of them. The group of people standing by the altar, adorned with more floral displays, turned to stare blankly at them.

Kaela tugged at her mother's sleeve. "Mommy, why's everyone looking at us?"

Georgia was angry at their blatant curiosity. She hadn't expected to attract so much attention. In truth, they were looking at Kaela more than her. She placed a protective arm around her daughter's shoulders and drew her closer to her side.

"They're curious, sweetheart. They haven't seen me for years and they've never met you. It's okay."

Steve led them towards the seats reserved for Colin's family, but as his ex-wife and given the fact that they had treated her badly in the past, she wasn't comfortable with that. She stopped him and pointed to the second row on the left. He seemed to understand and nodded. Georgia looked at the group standing up front. She recognized Colin's parents, Alice and Frank Charles. Alice turned her back to her, but Frank gave a nod and a weak smile. Mary, Colin's sister, pretended to ignore her, but Georgia caught the furtive glances from beneath her hooded eyelids. She took in the erect pose of her body, chin thrust out and her haughty stare. *The same snotty bitch she's always been.*

She glanced away from them to take in the long thin table set up beside the pulpit. Floral vases lined the floor in front of its white clothed drapery. An urn containing Colin's ashes sat in the center, framed with pictures of Colin—his first birthday, school pictures from primary grades to law school. The tug of Kaela's hand, vying for her attention, brought her back to the present.

"What is it, sweetheart?" she asked, looking down at her daughter.

Kaela was staring at the first row to the right of the aisle, her expression frozen, and her face pale.

"Who is that, Mommy?" she whispered.

Georgia followed her stare, only to gasp. *Oh my God.* She found herself staring into the face of a five-year-old girl—a girl with Kaela's face.

The child was staring back at Kaela with equal surprise.

"Mommy...?" Kaela asked, again.

"That must be Shelby, your half-sister."

"But...she looks like me," she said with awe.

Georgia shook her head in silence as she studied Colin's other daughter. Shelby's hair was longer and her nose a little thinner, but the straight blond hair, full lips and bright blue eyes were identical. The two girls were so much alike there was no question they were sisters.

"Now we know why they were staring at us, honey. You two could be twins."

"That's weird!" Kaela said with finality. "I wish she'd stop looking at me."

Georgia glanced down at her daughter. Her face was clouded over and her lips were pursed into a pout. "You mean like you're staring at her? Don't you think she must be feeling a bit strange about you too?"

"Yeah…but I don't like her having my face." Kaela crossed her arms across her chest and stared at the floor.

She placed an arm around her daughter's shoulders, feeling the confusion her daughter was experiencing. Turning her attention back to Shelby, Georgia let her gaze slide to the woman sitting next to her and made eye-to-eye contact with Julie, Colin's widow. She was shocked at her appearance. Her thinness and pallor suggested more than that of a grieving widow. The last time she'd seen Julie was six and a half years ago at the office Christmas party. That was about six months before Colin had left Georgia for a pregnant Julie. She had been a well-proportioned, vibrant young woman who sparkled with life, the obvious envy of other women, including Georgia. The frail woman before her was aged beyond her years.

None of them knew at the time that Georgia too was pregnant. Georgia thought back to that brutal winter she'd spent lost at the cabin and her ordeal of giving birth to Kaela alone. When Sean rescued her and brought them both back to civilization, the Charles family had snubbed her. They hadn't believed Colin was her daughter's father. Looking at the two girls now, it was obvious they shared the same dad. Colin had fit Kaela into his life on her birthday, Christmas, and the odd visit or two during each year. And now he was dead. A week ago, he'd passed suddenly of a heart attack at the age of forty.

Julie's eyes fell to Kaela and after a few moments came back to rest on Georgia. Her eyes searched Georgia's and after another quick look at Kaela she turned her back to them; but not before Georgia caught sight of the tears sliding down her cheeks. It was hard to read her expression, but something in her eyes caught her off-balance. *Compassion? Don't go there*, she thought and brushed off the feeling. She didn't want to examine her feelings where Julie was concerned.

A soft note from the organ announced the start of the memorial service.

"Today, we gather together to pay tribute to the short life of one of our loved ones," the minister said, "Colin Alexander Charles—son, brother, father, husband, colleague and friend—taken from us far too quickly, shall be missed by all who loved him."

A young woman sitting in front of Georgia with Colin's work colleagues began to whimper. His secretary, sitting beside the girl, leaned close to the girl.

"Stop that!" she whispered firmly, loud enough for Georgia to hear. "Control yourself, Beth. Do you want Julie to hear you?"

A smile tugged at the corner of Georgia's mouth. She hated to be presumptuous, but it appeared what goes around had definitely come around. Instinctively, she knew the girl called Beth was Colin's mistress. *Nothing has changed there either.* The service continued with Colin's brother-in-law, friends and law partners paying homage. She found herself tuning them out, lost to her own thoughts. Grief was a strange thing. Colin was a cad when he was alive but now he was gone; all these people who knew him had selective memory in regard to his life.

Am I grieving Colin's passing? Yes … yes I am… grieving the loss of my daughter's father and the loss of the man that Colin could have been.

The voice of the Minister broke through her thoughts.

"…and now let us pray."

A quick glance around the room revealed bowed heads and Georgia quickly closed her eyes, chiding herself for her thoughts. Such a disrespectful reaction on her part surprised her. Suppressing a nervous giggle, she turned a snort into a series of forced coughs, hoping no one would notice. *What is wrong with me?*

The service ended and the Minister gave directions for all present to file row by row past the altar to view the pictures before proceeding out of the room. At that moment, Beth broke out into loud sobs. The row of work colleagues began to squirm in their seats. The woman became the focus of attention and that broke through the nervous hysteria Georgia felt. Back in control, she walked her daughter past the pictures. She had read that people experienced grief in different ways–hysterical laughter being one way. Still, she felt terrible about her horrid reaction. Kaela stopped to look at a picture of her father with her half-sister, Shelby.

"Come along, dear. Others are waiting," Georgia, said softly. *Why did I let her talk me into bringing her?*

They were led into the back gardens to a section consisting of memory walls. There were three marble walls set in a horseshoe, with a marble bench centered in the middle of them. Plaques were set in place covering the opening of each interment box. A small vase sat beside each plaque to house flowers left by family members and visitors.

The minister said another prayer and Julie placed the urn in an open box. The service was over. People moved forward to pay their respects to the family. Georgia stood back with Kaela and watched. She leaned down to Kaela. "We'll come back in a day or two when the plaque has been placed and bring some flowers, okay?" Her daughter nodded and held onto to her mother a little tighter.

They followed the group around the gardens to the front of the home and stopped to look over the cliques of people scattered around the front lawn. There she saw Julie looking toward the parking lot where Colin's secretary was leading the woman named Beth to a car; Georgia noticed the subtle tightening of the woman's shoulders—a change of body language so slight that no one would have noticed unless they were studying her as she was.

Julie knew.

Georgia's emotions were mixed. She felt a sudden compassion for the pain Julie must be feeling; yet, she felt an overwhelming compulsion to ask her how it felt to know her husband was cheating on her. Under the present circumstances, Georgia felt a lack of smug satisfaction in having gained this knowledge.

"Georgia, how have you been?"

She spun around to find Frank standing behind her. "Very well, thank you. Please accept my condolences," She drew Kaela in front of her. "This is your granddaughter, Kaela."

"Hello, Kaela," he said softly, touching her cheek gently with two fingers.

"Hello, Sir," she replied, her fluttering eyelids not quite meeting his gaze.

"I'm sorry for the loss of your father, child. You are much like him, you know…and your sister, Shelby."

"Uh, huh…" Kaela whispered.

Georgia felt uncomfortable and decided they should take their leave.

"We must be going, Frank. My thoughts are with you and the rest of your family."

"People are coming back to the house. You're most welcome to join us."

Georgia searched the group for Alice and caught the woman glaring at her. *Certainly not by Alice.* "Well … I don't know … I mean … I hadn't planned on it." Georgia fumbled for words. "The truth is the timing may not be right."

"Your daughter gives you the right. However, I understand," he said, turning to Kaela. "It was nice meeting you, Kaela. I hope to see you again."

Kaela gave him a shy smile and nodded.

As they turned toward the parking lot, Frank stopped her. "Georgia ... this family owes you an apology."

"Thank you. It means a lot for me to hear you say that."

Frank reached out and took her hand. "Today isn't the time to discuss it, but I hope one day soon you and I could talk. And I would love to see my granddaughter again."

"You're right, it's not the time. Perhaps soon. Take care." She ignored his reference to seeing them again. *Why now? After all this time?*

Georgia sat quietly in the car before driving away, trying to sort her jumbled thoughts. *Frank looked so sad. Death always brought out regrets.* She couldn't help but wonder if Alice had any.

"Oh, boy... there I go being waspish again."

"What's waspish mean, Mommy?"

Georgia was startled by her daughter's question. "I didn't realize I said that out loud. It means I had unkind thoughts about someone."

"Who?"

"It doesn't matter, sweetheart. Funerals put people on edge and bring strange emotions to the surface. Forget I said anything."

Kaela stared at her mother for a moment. "Maybe that's why I was so mad at Shelby. It's kind of cool to have a sister who looks like me." Suddenly, her face clouded over and she started to cry. "But why did Daddy love her more than me?"

Her stomach rolled over. "Oh, baby..." She undid her seat belt and put one arm around Kaela, wiping her tears with the other. "Your Daddy loved you the same as Shelby."

"Then why wasn't there a picture of me and Daddy on that table?"

Georgia cursed Alice Charles under her breath. "Because your father's passing happened so quickly, it caught us all off guard. His side of the family haven't any pictures of you, sweetheart, and with all the grief, no one thought to ask me for one. But that has nothing to do with your Daddy's love for you."

Kaela sat up straighter. "I could have given them the one in my bedroom of me and him flying my kite in the park. They could have put it beside the one of him and Shelby on the beach."

A sigh of relief was followed with thank God for the innocence of children. "Yes, it's a beautiful picture of the two of you. Now, how about you and I stop at that new ice cream parlour on the way home to Nana's?" *Here I am, rewarding her daughter's sadness with food.* She had tried consciously to avoid that trap, believing it was a bad habit to teach a child, but these were exceptional circumstances.

Kaela gave her a semblance of a smile. "Can I have a double fudge chocolate chip cone?"

"You sure can. That's my fav too." Georgia turned away from Kaela and fussed with her seat belt. She didn't want her to see the tears she held back in her eyes.

Damn the Charles family.

Chapter 3

Three days later ...

"What's *she* doing here?" Alice demanded.

Ignoring her, Georgia stared straight ahead and followed Derek Connor's secretary into the conference room to join the rest of Colin's family, law partners and a few of his closest friends.

"She's named in the will, Mrs. Charles. She has the right to be present," Derek said, motioning Georgia to a chair. "As you all know, we're here for the reading of Colin's will. Let's begin."

"I, Colin Walter Charles, of the city of Vancouver, in the Province of British Columbia, do make and declare this to be my Last Will and Testament. I hereby revoke all Wills and Codicils heretofore made by me."

The lawyer shuffled the papers, cleared his throat and began again. "The foregoing instrument, consisting of six typewritten pages, this included, was at Vancouver, British Columbia, signed sealed and declared by the testatrix—that's Colin—to be his Last Will and Testament, in our presence, and we, at his request and in his presence and in the presence of each other, have hereunto subscribed our names as attesting witnesses." Derek Connors looked up at the people sitting before him. "Colin has appointed me as his personal representative and estate trustee. That gives me the power to execute his testament and control over all trust accounts. All debts, expenses, encumbrances, and taxes are to be paid from his residuary estate."

Georgia narrowed her eyes and tried to focus her attention on Derek, listening as he dealt with each item one by one. Being enclosed with these people in such a small room made her squirm and her stomach rolled over, leaving her nauseous. She glanced sideways. None of them meant anything to her anymore.

Nevertheless, here she was, sharing the intimacy of their grief. She assumed of course, that Colin's Will had nothing to do with her, but everything to do with their daughter. Derek dealt with the legacies to friends and colleagues first.

"Well, that covers it except for the immediate family and Georgia," Derek stated, "The rest of you are free to leave. Once we're through with probate, you'll be contacted. Thank you for coming in."

Derek rose to stand by the door, shaking hands with all who left. Resuming his position at the table he continued with the reading.

"To his sister, Mary, and brother-in-law, Steve, he leaves his BMW and his boat. Should his parents survive him—and with this being the case—he leaves them the house he inherited from his grandmother in Maui..."

Finally, Derek mentioned Kaela's name.

"Colin set up a trust fund for each of his two daughters, Shelby & Kaela. When they are nineteen, they can draw from the trust to continue their education and will be given living expenses. The terms of the trust are clear. They must be working and self-sufficient by their twenty-fifth birthdays. At that time, the remainder of each of the trusts will be transferred in a lump sum to each of them. If the trustees deem either one unable to manage money prudently or in the case of mental incapacity, the monies will remain in trust with the issuance of a monthly stipend.

As for Georgia, Colin has increased your child support to fifteen hundred dollars a month to more than cover Kaela's care. Should the occasion arise where there are unusual expenses, for example medical or dental bills, you can apply to the trustees and they will be covered by the child's trust." Georgia heard a gasp, no doubt from Alice.

"The rest—company shares, bonds, personal belongings, cash, jewellery and the residual home—go to Julie. That about covers it. Any questions?"

The first one to speak was Alice.

"I'm assuming Colin has a clause in the will, where a blood test is required to prove paternity for the child, Kaela?"

Georgia stiffened. *Here we go.*

Complete silence filled the room. She glanced around and wasn't surprised to see the dropped eyes of all present. No one looked at anyone else, least of all her. Their embarrassment was obvious.

"Alice...you only have to look at the child," Frank chided.

"There's no such clause. Nor is one required," Derek counselled, "If Colin chose to recognize Kaela as his daughter and include her in his will, that's his right."

"We can contest..." Alice began.

"Alice, shut up," Frank boomed.

The air hung heavy, as silence once again prevailed.

"No one will be contesting Colin's will," a small voice challenged, "These are the final wishes of my husband and they will be respected by all of us in this room."

Georgia looked at Julie in surprise. Julie gave her a thin smile; an unspoken bond of motherhood passed between them.

"Alice, our son is dead. I agree with Julie. We must respect his wishes," Frank said, firmly. It was as much a plea as it was a declaration and Alice fell silent.

"As for the trust funds," Derek began, clearing his throat uncomfortably, "I'm accountable to both Julie and Georgia until the girls are of legal age. The court does not supervise these funds and I was required to take out a bond to protect you both from wrong doing. You'll both receive an annual accounting. My fee is 5% and I will be handling the investment personally. I'm available to you at any time to discuss our investment policies."

Derek stood up for a second time and addressed Georgia directly.

"Georgia, trust funds are exempt from probate. You can expect to receive your increased support cheque the first of the month. If you have any questions at all, please contact me at any time. Good luck to you and your daughter."

Georgia rose and shook hands with Derek. "Thank you, Derek." She nodded to Julie and Frank. Ignoring the others, she held her head high and strode out of the conference room. As she waited for the elevator, someone called her name. To her surprise, Julie approached her.

"I was hoping you and I could meet soon and talk. There are things that should have been said years ago and things that should never have been said. I understand if you say no. I only ask you to consider the girls..." Julie paused.

"The girls?"

"They both lost their father and ... I think it might help them both if they spent some time together."

Georgia was taken aback by her suggestion. The only one in the Charles family that accepted Kaela was Colin.

Julie continued. "They're children, free from the mind restrictions we grown-ups place on ourselves...and they're sisters. They should be allowed to know each other."

"Even if I agreed, there's Alice to consider. She knows Kaela is Colin's daughter, but she won't acknowledge it. I don't need or want her wrath."

"This is my decision as Shelby's mother. Alice has no say in it. Please think about it?" Julie implored.

"Alright, I'll consider it."

Julie started back to the office, when Georgia stopped her.

"I'm sorry about Colin, Julie. I know how hard this must be for you."

"Yes, you do," she responded, softly, "Thank you."

Georgia drove to her parent's home in North Vancouver, relieved she could put the events of the past few days behind her. Seeing Colin's family took more of a toll on her than she realized. Julie's words echoed over and over in her mind.

They are children ... they are sisters; they should be together... they need each other.

It gave her lots to think about. Georgia felt happy that Colin gave Kaela what was rightly hers.

Too bad he had to die before he fully accepted that responsibility ... and it's only money. Kaela needed him in her life more than the couple of times a year he gave her. Still, he'd been more than generous with the child support and the trust fund. Reflecting back, Georgia thought that Julie's acceptance had come too late. *How sad that it always seemed to take something tragic to show us the errors of our ways. Still, maybe Julie's right that the girls should meet.*

On the other hand, sometimes when the grieving ends, some people selectively forget their new-found vision. They return to their old way of thinking in self-defence to hide their guilt. First Frank expressed an interest in Kaela, now Julie. Can I trust them? Should I trust them? I sure as hell don't want Alice in my daughter's life.

Georgia vowed to protect her from any outfall that might occur from that kind of situation.

By the time she reached her parent's home, her head pounded. She sat in the driveway with the engine running, staring at nothing. She had mixed feelings where Julie was concerned. She leaned back against the headrest and scrutinized her belief that she'd dealt with all the negatives in her life the past five years. She'd learned a lot about herself the winter she was lost and about her marriage. It occurred to her that perhaps she'd never examined her feelings towards Julie because the woman had never been in her face. She couldn't blame the woman for her marriage break-up from Colin. Their affair had merely been the straw that broke the camel's back. Georgia knew that. Still, she resented her and the whole Charles family. *Showing up alive the following spring with my baby, had thrown Alice into a tailspin.*

She drummed her fingers on the steering wheel. *Time, that's what I need. It's not crucial to make a decision so soon. Kaela's needs are foremost and dealing with the loss of her father paramount.* With a sigh, she turned the motor off and stepped out of the car.

That night replicated the previous one. Sleep came sporadically, full of dreams and restlessness. Georgia gave in and went into the kitchen for a hot cup of tea. She sat on the love seat in the picture window of her childhood home and stared at the city lights across Burrard Inlet far below. Over the years much thought had been given to the rudeness of her ex-mother-in-law. *Deep down Alice Charles knows Kaela's her granddaughter. Why has she rejected her?*

The only conclusion Georgia reached was the fact that Alice was a complex and private woman: the matriarch who controlled her family. Georgia hadn't allowed her to control her life or Kaela's and all the publicity surrounding her disappearance and her heroic survival seemed to embarrass Alice. Position, wealth and privacy were foremost for Colin's mother.

Somehow she blamed it all on Georgia. *Alice probably blames me for his death too.* She finished her tea and padded back to bed.

Chapter 4

Georgia placed her face against the cool tiles of the bathroom wall and closed her eyes. "Ahh..." It felt good to escape into the confines of this room, alone and quiet, shutting out the loud music blasting through the prestigious mansion. Her pounding head eased a little.

She'd flown back to Vancouver from Britain the previous evening with Sean where he'd received a literary award for his latest book. Tonight they were attending a post-production party at a house rented by the Director, celebrating the conclusion of the filming of a mini-series based on Sean's latest suspense trilogy. Sean had spent the past sixteen weeks as a consultant and doing rewrites on the screenplay.

Famous faces, great music, plenty of food and drugs of choice. The party became crowded and noisier as the evening wore on. A fun night but not a lifestyle Georgia would be comfortable with on a regular basis.

She opened her eyes and stared at herself in the mirror. There were dark circles under her eyes. *Thank God for make-up.* She ran her fingers through her curly hair, gave herself a nod of approval and rejoined the others.

"Having a good time?"

Spinning around, she found Trent Matheson, her agent, standing behind her. Trent represented Colin as well, and over the years they became close friends. "It's been a great night. I can't believe I'm still on my feet."

Trent looked at the stemmed glass in her hand and chuckled. "Are you talking about the champagne or your jet lag?"

"Both. The bags under my eyes are growing bigger."

"Preparation H."

Georgia looked at Trent puzzled. "Excuse me?"

"The secret of the stars. They use it under their eyes. Try it—it works."

Georgia laughed. "Okay … maybe I will."

"You two have come a long way since Sean found you five years ago in his cabin."

"Haven't we though? Speaking of which, have you seen him? This place is a zoo."

"Last time I saw him, he was in the garden. Let's go find him and breathe some fresh air." Trent steered her through a set of open French doors.

They wandered along interconnected paths lighted with solar lamps through different landscaped sections of the small acreage. Flowering shrubs and bushes impregnated the warm air. The scent was intoxicating on this warm June night. They entered a series of waist-high rock walls with water fountains and ponds filled with Japanese Koi. They stopped to admire the lights of Vancouver far below them. This property was set on the North Shore Mountains across the bridge from Stanley Park. Freighters sat off the shores of English Bay.

Georgia turned and stopped in her tracks. Sean sat on the ledge of a rock wall, his back against a cedar lattice panel covered with ivy, legs dangling apart with his hands resting on his thighs. Between those legs stood a woman with long blond hair and a killer body.

Trent whispered, "Oh, shit."

Georgia ignored him and watched the woman stroke Sean's cheek with her fingers. She wasn't at the right angle to see Sean's face to read his expression, but he appeared to be staring into her face, listening intently to her talk. The woman slipped her arms around his neck while pressing her ample breasts against his chest. Her face wore an expression of seduction, her eyes fixated on Sean's face. In the next moment, she lowered her face and locked her lips onto his. The kiss seemed endless.

Georgia stiffened and her chest constricted. She couldn't think. Didn't want to. The long kiss ended and the woman lifted her head and turned towards Georgia. A look of recognition crossed the woman's face and a crooked smile played at the corner of her mouth as she tossed her long hair back.

Sean followed the woman's gaze and locked eyes with Georgia. Her expression remained frozen while Sean's eyebrows rose in surprise. Their silent stare lasted as long as the kiss. Finally, Georgia gasped, turned on her heels, and marched back towards the house.

Trent ran after her. "Let me drive you home. I'm ready to go anyway."

"No, I'll drive her." Georgia turned to see Sean right behind them.

"I'd rather go with Trent," she said in a croak, her throat constricted.

"Don't be ridiculous. Let me explain." He reached for her arm but she pulled away.

"There's nothing to explain. I know a passionate kiss when I see one."

Trent backed away a short distance, looking uneasy.

Sean began again: "Look, it was nothing…" Georgia glanced around; people had begun to stare.

"I don't want to talk about this in public." She looked at Trent. "If you don't want to drive me home, I'll call a cab." Georgia turned and started for the patio doors.

Sean grabbed her by the arm and steered her around the side of the house, leading them to the large circular driveway out front. "We came together, we go home together. We can talk in the car." He pressed his lips into a firm line.

Not wanting to draw any more attention than they already had, Georgia pulled her arm from his grasp and marched along side of Sean. They walked across the grass and through the iron gates to the street beyond. They never spoke a word until after Sean started the engine and slowly edged his way around the parked cars.

"I'm sorry you saw that. But there is an explanation. Laura…"

"Laura? You know her?"

"Of course, I know her. I don't go around kissing strange women."

"Oh that makes me feel so much better."

Sean gave her a quick look. "Sarcasm doesn't become you. Anyway, I didn't kiss her, she kissed me."

"Oh really? It was a passionate kiss and you didn't appear to be resisting. In fact you didn't pull away. So who is this Laura person?"

Sean glanced at her sideways and with a slight hesitation his voice dropped. "My ex-wife."

Her head jerked backwards and she sucked in a breath. "That Laura? What was she doing here?"

"I have no idea."

Her mind filled with a hoard of thoughts. Confusion followed. "Did you invite her?"

"Why would I do that? I haven't seen her since the day she walked out on me."

"So she shows up nine years later at a private party and comes on to you?" The moment she said those words she regretted them. She was beginning to sound like a shrew. A part of her wanted to believe Sean, but another part wouldn't let her.

"Pretty much."

She fell silent, trying to make sense of it. An overwhelming sense of exhaustion overtook her. Georgia put her head back and closed her eyes. "I can't deal with this right now."

"You're making way too much of this. I didn't know she was going to kiss me, okay?"

Georgia opened her eyes and stared at Sean. "She was snuggled between your legs stroking your face long before she kissed you. There was lots of time for you to push her away."

Sean said nothing.

"Take me to my parents' house."

"I'd rather you came to the condo with me so we can talk this out."

Georgia knew she was shutting down. "No, I want to be there when Kaela wakes up. She's missed me."

They drove to her parent's home in silence. He stepped out of the car and walked her to the door. Georgia unlocked it and turned to face him. She remembered when her ex-husband walked out on her for Julie. She wouldn't set herself up again for that kind of hurt again. "I saw what I saw."

A frown creased his brow. "You saw what you think you saw. We have to finish this."

"Not tonight. I'm way too tired. Good-night." She stepped through the doorway and closed the door.

The next afternoon, Sean showed up at the house. Georgia led him through the house and out to the patio.

"I've been trying to reach you on your cell. When I called the house, this morning, your mother said you were still sleeping."

"Jet lag and my cell was dead."

"Oh…" he said, not sounding convinced. "You know I'm going to Dease Lake for a few days to open up the cabin for the season. I don't want to leave without clearing this up. Can we please talk?"

Are you going alone? Georgia pushed the thought from her mind.

She thought about the cabin and all it meant to her. It had been her salvation after she escaped the clutches of the bank robbers five years ago and the place of her encounter with her native spirit, Nonnock. She thought of the cabin as hers because it signified her child's birth and Georgia's rebirth. She'd done a lot of thinking since last night about her relationship with Sean. Georgia realized she needed to re-examine his role in her life and assess her wants and needs.

She sat opposite him in a lawn chair. "We do need to talk," she said. A gut-wrenching feeling in the pit of her stomach made her nauseous.

"Yes, about Laura."

"No … yes. I mean about her and other things." She squirmed in her seat. "Will you see her again?"

"No, I told you that last night. Anyway, we have plans for you and Kaela to join me at the cabin for the summer."

Georgia studied his face. That had been the plan. She'd so looked forward to some time for them. He seemed sincere; still … "I don't think it's a good idea for Kaela and me to be at the cabin this summer."

"Why not? We already planned this."

"I need some alone time."

Sean's look of sadness mirrored her feelings, but she knew she must stay strong to convey the things she needed to say. She stood and used her nervous energy to weed the hanging baskets mounted on the gazebo. Silence hung heavy between them.

Sean spoke first. "So you're going to let last night ruin everything we planned?"

Her back stiffened and she turned to look at Sean. "I need to spend some time alone with my daughter. I want to be a full-time mother for awhile."

"I get that. You've missed a lot with our hectic schedule. But you can do that at the cabin."

Georgia sat down again on the edge of her seat. "And I think we need some time apart."

He looked like she'd slapped him in the face. "I thought we had something strong between us. All was fine until Laura showed up."

"Was it? We did have something going on but I'm not sure what it was. Ever since you rescued me at the cabin, we've been thrown together, living in a dream. Our book about my kidnapping, the tours, the movie and then your mini-series, interviews, all the fame and travel ... now it's back to reality. The past five years we've been living a whirlwind and it's been fun ... and comfortable. I need a normal life and at the moment I don't know what that is ..." Georgia paused to take a breath, "... and you have unfinished business with your ex-wife."

"That's not true. Look, I told you that she came on to me. Kissing my ex-wife was the furthest thing from my mind. To have her suddenly appear after all that time, so obviously trying to seduce me ... well, I was amused and curious. When she kissed me, I let it happen because I wanted to be able to say to her without any reservations, 'Hey Babe, it's over'. But then I saw you and the devastated look on your face. I'm so sorry it hurt you."

Georgia considered his apology, wanting to believe it. "And what if she calls you out again?"

"She already has."

Her head jerked around. "What? When?"

"This morning to apologize for causing a problem last night. Then, she asked me if I would meet her for coffee."

"What did you say?"

"I told her that I was in a relationship and it would be unfair to you, then said, I saw no reason to meet with her as we had nothing in common anymore. Afterwards, I wished her all the best."

"... and she said?"

"She was sorry to hear that and she was in the phone book under her maiden name if I ever changed my mind. Feel better?"

Georgia felt the tears sting her eyes and she blinked to hold them back. Her mouth opened to say something but her throat was too constricted to talk. Tightness welled in her chest. She waited for Sean to say something first.

Sean leaned over and took her hand. "Do you realize that this is the first summer we've had off since we met? I was hoping we could spend time at the cabin and move forward in our relationship."

She sat back in her seat. *Move forward? What did that mean?* Her brain fired in all directions. She hadn't expected the conversation to go this way, nor did she know how to address it. "I ... don't know."

Sean's face darkened.

She continued. "I learned a lot about myself that winter at the cabin, but I never had the time to test out my new-found independence. It took last night for me to realize I'm not ready to do the couple thing."

Sean studied her face for a long moment. "You're afraid I'm going to be another Colin."

"I know you're not. But I'm not supposed to be a fearful, little girl who's heartbroken because the man I care for cheated on me either."

"Say again?"

Georgia slumped down in her chair, stared up at the sky and let out a big sigh. "I reacted like a jealous wife."

"Rightly so ... and I love you for it."

She jumped up and threw out both her arms. "That's my point. I don't love me for it. Suddenly, I was right back being that insecure, snivelling little girl I was with Colin. I hate it." Sean knotted his brow. He stood up and placed his hands on Georgia's shoulders. "I'm not sure what it is I'm supposed to say here to make this right. I do know that we care for each other. So we've had a little hiccup. Now we move forward."

Tears bubbled up inside her. She pursed her lips together and whispered. "I can't."

Sean stepped back from her and let his arms drop to his side. "So you want to be free to see other people?"

A knot twisted in her stomach. Georgia thought she would vomit. The last thing she wanted was to see other people. "This isn't about that." The image of Laura's face was etched in her mind. Sean had been hurt badly by his ex-wife. She obviously wanted back into his life. Georgia didn't have the right to ask Sean to put his life on hold when she asked for her independence. Tears filled her eyes and in barely a whisper, she answered him. "I want to be alone."

Sean face turned a vivid red and his right eye twitched as he stared at her. A trait she recognized whenever he struggled with something. His face contorted as he jumped to his feet. "Goddamit woman. You want alone? Let me show you alone."

Georgia watched him turn and stomp towards the side gate to the driveway. She wanted to stop him, but she couldn't. Her feet wouldn't move. She was unable to reverse what she'd just set in motion. The side gate slammed hard against the fence as he left, causing her to wince. Once he was gone, she slumped into the lawn chair and sobbed.

Colin's unfaithfulness and death coupled with the betrayal of Laura and Sean's kiss, unleashed pent up tears no dam would hold. She cried for Kaela, who didn't have the opportunity to know her father; for Colin, whose life was cut short; but most of all, she cried for herself.

Once again, she felt she'd lost her way.

Chapter 5

A small, weak voice, barely audible, came from the other side of the door. "Honey? Are you in there?"

He gathered up the loose pictures and documents and shoved them back into the blue file. His upper lip curled back as he spoke in a silky tone. "Hold on a minute." Anger filled his whole being as he stood and strode to the door with a glare. Even at 3:00 a.m. she wouldn't leave him alone. *Why wasn't she sleeping?* Her cloying and possessiveness of late tested his patience.

The loud click of the lock as it snapped open echoed throughout the room. He opened the door to a petite woman wearing a pair of oversized flannel pajamas, and a hair net over her head. *Rose doesn't have a sexy bone in her body.*

"What are you doing in there at this time of night?" she asked.

He forced a smile. "I couldn't sleep. Thought I'd do some reading to make myself relax. Why don't you go back to bed? I'll be up shortly."

"Are you sure you're okay?"

"I'm fine."

Rose stared at him for a few seconds. "I'm awake now too. Why don't I make us some tea?" She tilted her head and looked beyond him to his desk. "Maybe tomorrow I'll clean this room up for you."

Infuriated with her, he stepped forward in the doorway blocking her view and his feelings. "No need. You know how I feel about my space. A cup of tea would be nice. I'll join you in the kitchen in a minute." He stepped back, shut the door in her face and threw the latch.

Turning on his heel, spite fueled his movements. He yanked the drawer open, threw the blue folder inside, locked it and hid the key once again. *Bloody interfering cow.*

He'd married her right out of high school with him five years older. A red head whose beauty caught his attention, he soon realized it all stopped right there on the surface. To his mind, her personality matched her lack of intelligence. She told him once that she couldn't believe that a handsome guy like him would want her. All of this supported his belief that he could control her and use her as a cover. But after fifteen years together that seemed to be changing. Rose had developed an inquisitive demeanor and became more demanding of his whereabouts. *It was time, once again, to emphasize her place in their marriage with a lesson or two in subservience.* He smiled, remembering her pain during the last lesson. With the study door secured, he hid the key over the molding.

Chapter 6

Frank Charles eyes moved slowly around the room, taking in the empty built-in mahogany bookshelves and his high backed leather chair behind the desk. A black leather love seat, set on the braided oval rug he bought on a trip to New Mexico, was flanked by the tiffany floor lamp he inherited from his mother. He smiled at the thought of Alice's frustration with his hodgepodge of furniture and his apparent lack of decorating style. The door to his study was always kept shut to protect her from embarrassment in front of her haughty friends. A fact that both amused and pleased Frank, as his study was the one area of his life Alice knew better than to meddle in. This was his man room.

Tell-tell imprints showed where pictures once hung on the now faded walls. Boxes were piled against the far wall in front of the picture window that faced his beloved gardens. Frank ran his hand over the surface of the red mahogany desk. His thoughts were of past memories spent in this room. Many business and personal resolutions had been made whilst sitting behind this desk. The most recent would prove to be his most courageous and undoubtedly, the most life-changing decision of all. He sighed. They'd been through a lot together.

The sound of the doorbell brought him out of his muse and he left the study to answer the door. Two young men stood on the doorstep in coveralls.

"We're from the moving company, sir. I'm Chad and this is Logan."

"Please, come in." The front foyer was filled with boxes. "You can take these first." They were filled with personal effects and treasures retrieved from the attic. Next, he led them into the study. "Take it all, except the desk."

They moved to the upstairs landing and Frank took them into the master bedroom. "All of these boxes and the tall boy dresser please."

"Is that all, sir?" Chad asked.

"That's it for up here, son. Next, we'll go into the garden for my power and gardening tools."

Ninety minutes later, all of his things were in the moving van. Frank verified the address of the storage locker with the young men and followed them in his own vehicle. It was noon by the time he returned home from the locker. He opened the foyer closet and retrieved a packed suitcase, a shoulder bag of personal effects and toiletries, along with his briefcase and placed them in the trunk of his car.

Frank wandered through the house, room by room—one final check. He stood in the doorway of the now empty study one last time, expecting to feel depressed. *Only an empty room.* His memories were locked in his mind forever. He closed the door and went out to the garden to sit and wait.

Thirty-five years he'd spent in this house, almost half a lifetime.

However, there would be no missing the house. Home is where the heart is. *Did I ever feel comfortable in this place? Alice never let me forget she was born and raised here ... it's hers.* He stood and wandered the paths. Now the gardens were a different matter. These were his pride and joy, his hobby, and his salvation since his son, Colin, had passed. Alice hated gardening, deciding it was beneath her. Not him. Frank loved to kneel down and dig in the earth and see the fruits of his labour.

He'd taken a leave when Colin died and Alice expected he'd return to his law practice in due course. But instead, he'd retired and let the gardener go, preferring to spend his time puttering in the garden. A smile lit up his face at the memory of Alice and her latest tirade.

"Oh, Frank, why do you insist on grovelling in the dirt like a common gardener? It's so embarrassing in front of my friends."

"Let it go or I'll give you something to really be embarrassed about," he'd said.

Alice's head had shot back. "Like what?"

"Like gardening in the nude."

Frank chuckled and leaned forward to take in the pungent scent of the rose bushes in full bloom. Memories of playing in the gardens with Mary and Colin when they were children brought a lump to his throat and tears filled his eyes. "Oh, sweet Jesus." He placed his hands over his face and let the tears fall. *Where had the time gone?*

After a time, he wiped his eyes and sat quiet in thought. It had been years since he'd cried, not even at Colin's funeral were there tears. *That's it, the death of my son and nostalgia for the innocent years.* It certainly wasn't because he was leaving Alice. In fact, it was Colin's passing that forced him to take a good, long look at his own life. Today, he'd finally faced his grief and made peace with himself over the loss of his son. There were regrets.

Colin had been as driven as Frank when it came to their respective law practices. A family thing passed from father to son for the past four generations. *It should have been my death that taught Colin to live in the now and recognize when having enough was enough. I guess it was my lesson to learn, not his.*

His thoughts turned to his daughter. *Dear Mary, who takes her mother's word verbatim. It's Alice's fault the kids grew up to be rival siblings in the truest form. She played them against each other and against me. I tried for years to live up to her expectations, along with our children. But I let it happen and fully accept responsibility for my part.*

His decision to leave as Senior Partner of the prestigious Vancouver law firm was the right one. Remembering how furious Alice had been about his decision made him smile. All part of his plan to take control of his life and live each day to the fullest.

Voices from inside the house interrupted the stillness. A glance at his watch showed three o'clock. *They're back.* Alice and Mary left three days previous on a shopping spree in Seattle. Frank spent that time packing his things. He could have left without telling Alice, but after forty years together she deserved to hear it face to face. She had no idea leaving her was part of his life-changing plan. No point discussing it with her as they were miles apart in their thinking. Any shared common ground disappeared years ago.

"Frank? Are you out there?"

He sighed. *Here comes the confrontation. Best to be done with it. Once out that door, I'll never return.* Frank stood, stretched, and with one last look at his gardens, headed into the house.

They were both in the family room surrounded by bags and suitcases. Mary walked over and placed a kiss on his cheek. "Hi, Dad."

"Hi, sweetheart. Did you have a good time?"

"Super. The weather was great. We found a new restaurant with delicious food and spent oodles of money."

"I can see that," Frank said, sardonically. "Why don't you make your mother a cup of tea? I'm sure she could use one after that long drive." He watched Mary head to the kitchen. He wished she'd dropped Alice off and continued on home. However, nothing would deter him from talking to his wife at this point. The need to leave as soon as possible overwhelmed him.

Alice opened her parcels and laid the contents across the couch. "Come and see my treasures."

Frank ignored her request. "We have to talk."

"Not now, I want to show you this. I bought the cutest little …"

"Yes, now," he insisted, a little harsher than intended.

Alice turned and gave him a scathing look. "Aren't we in a mood? What it is that can't wait five minutes?"

He hesitated a moment, not sure where to start. *There's only one way, out with it.* "I'm leaving." *Okay, maybe a bit blunt.*

"Leaving? What does that mean? Leaving for where?"

"Not for where, whom. I'm leaving you."

Alice stared at her husband with disbelief. She backed up to the couch and sat down with her mouth open. "You're not serious."

Whatever that cutest little thing she wanted to show me was, she just sat on it.

"The most serious I've ever been."

"Where would you go? We've lived in this house for thirty-five years."

"I have somewhere to go. There's a whole world out there."

Alice stood up and held herself erect. Her eyes hardened. "Who is she? Who's the bitch you're moving in with?"

Frank shook his head. "For God's sake, this isn't about another woman."

"Then what is it about? Honestly, Frank, I don't understand you. First you give up your partnership at the law firm, and then you spend your time cavorting around the garden in the dirt, now this. I think you need to see a shrink."

"What's wrong with a man deciding to retire in his sixties? I don't need any more money."

Alice gave him a haughty stare. "Senior partners don't retire in their sixties. Peter is in his late seventies and hasn't even slowed down."

Frank lost his temper. "Peter Martin has nothing in his life but his work. There are other things I want to do with mine and I have the financial stability to live my life as I see fit. Perhaps if our son realized that, he wouldn't have worked himself to death before his time."

A crash in the doorway ended their argument. Frank turned to see his daughter staring at him with a look of shock on her face. The tea tray lay at her feet.

Alice yelled, defiantly. "That's cruel. Colin had a weak heart and you know it."

Keep telling yourself that and let yourself off the hook. Frank walked over to his daughter and led her around the spilled tea and broken china.

"Daddy, I don't understand. Why are you doing this?"

"Sweetheart, I'm sorry you witnessed this. I should have waited until you went home."

Mary stared at her father with tears in her eyes. "Maybe you should see Dr. Sims."

"This is something I should have done a long time ago."

Alice sneered at him. "Like, you've had it so hard."

"But you've been acting so strange lately, since we lost Colin. Maybe you need to talk to someone," Mary said.

"I did talk to Dr. Sims. He told me some changes needed to be made if I wanted to be happy again. I'm sorry if this hurts you, but one of those changes is leaving your mother."

"But, Dad …"

"Oh stop begging, Mary," Alice interjected. "I've never begged anyone for anything in my life and I won't start now, especially with your father."

Poor Mary. She looks more confused than ever.

"I better find the mop," she whispered, and left the room.

Frank sat on the arm of the chair. *Let her complain about weakening the arms.* But Alice didn't seem to notice.

"How could you be so selfish? Leaving me at a time like this. I'm a grieving mother for God's sake."

"Alice, losing our son is one of the reasons I'm doing this. His death woke me up. Yes, I'm being selfish, for the first time in all the years we've been together. If I stay here, I'll die."

She walked closer to him and crossed her arms over her chest. "I'll only say this once. If you go out that door, you'll never step back inside this house."

"I don't intend to. I'm sorry things turned out this way. After thirty-five years, the decision didn't come lightly." Frank stood. "I have to go."

"What about your things … your clothes?"

He turned back "All my things are gone. The movers took them this morning."

"Movers?" Alice parroted. A wary look came over her face and her eyes darted around the room.

"Don't worry. I only took my personal effects and clothes, everything in the den, except your father's desk, and the tall-boy in the master bedroom. The rest is yours."

"What do you mean the tall-boy? You can't take that."

"And why not? You don't have any use for it."

Alice shrieked. "Because, you idiot, it's part of a set and can't be broken up."

Frank felt weary. *Time to end the arguments and banter.* "Well, it's already gone, so sorry. There are papers in the den on your father's desk. The rest is yours, the houses and contents, your car, your money; except my investments and private accounts, and my car. It's more than generous. Let's keep it simple, shall we?"

He walked out of the room into the hallway. Mary came running towards him. He took her in his arms and held her tight. "Once I'm settled, we'll meet for lunch and have a talk."

"Okay, Dad," she said, sadly. He kissed her on the forehead and backed away. "And Mary, go home and take care of burning fires. The apple doesn't fall far from the tree."

Alice called out from the family room. "Mary?"

His daughter looked at him in confusion. "Bye, Dad. I love you."

"Love you too, sweetheart."

Frank crossed the foyer to the door that led him into the garage. He could hear the women talking behind him.

"Hmm, I suppose the suite could go into the guest room ... yes. I've been meaning to replace the furniture in that room and it doesn't need a tall-boy ..."

"Mother? Dad has walked out the door and you're talking about furniture?"

"Oh don't be so dramatic, dear. He's going through a thing. He'll be back with his tail between his legs."

"Mom, I don't think ..."

"Hush up, now. Tomorrow we go shopping for a new bedroom suite."

The door to the garage shut automatically behind him. With a smile, he slid into his car and hit the garage door opener. *It'll take her a while to realize her take is wrong and she can't control me any longer.* He backed out of the driveway and headed towards the highway without as much as a glance back. Once on the Sea-to-Sky Highway that took him north of Vancouver to Horseshoe Bay, he heaved a deep sigh. Frank knew he hadn't handled it as well as he should have. And, he felt bad for Mary. Still, a load had been lifted from his shoulders. A sense of freedom took over. His soul felt free.

Eventually, Alice would realize it was best for both of them. Yes ... definitely the right decision.

Chapter 7

Derek Connors stared across the desk at Julie Charles completely dumb-founded. The frail woman sitting before him stared back expectantly. Feeling the fool and totally unprofessional, he composed himself. "I'm sorry. I wasn't expecting this."

Julie gave him a wry smile. "None of us ever do. Now, can it be done—legally I mean?"

"Absolutely."

"How long will it take to do the paperwork? I don't need to tell you time is essential."

Derek glanced at the piles of folders on his desk, but this needed his imme-diate attention. "A couple of days would do it. Is that okay?"

"That's fine."

He watched as she stared down at her hands in her lap, stretching out her long fingers and examining her painted fingernails. She quickly looked up at him. "What about Alice?"

His eyebrows shot up. "Alice? What about her?"

"She won't like this. Can she contest it?"

"Yes, she can. Anyone can contest anything they don't agree with." Derek let out a sigh. "I think we can safely assume she will."

"But can she win?" Julie's eyes filled with tears and he heard the plea in her voice.

"Probably not, as these are your legal wishes and you present valid reasons. But there are never any guarantees with these things if contested."

She stood and walked to the window. He felt her pain, but steeled himself. *Stay professional.* A new thought came to mind. "There is another consideration we must address. What if Georgia doesn't agree? I mean this should be settled now, not later ... if you understand my meaning."

"I've given this a lot of thought. She *has* to agree." Her shoulders slumped with resignation.

"Would you like me to approach her? If she says no, we need to consider other options."

Julie returned to her chair and sat straight and rigid on the edge; her chin thrust forward, her resolve fixed. "There aren't any other options. I'll talk to her, one mother to another. Tomorrow, I plan to go to Gibsons."

Derek let out a low whistle. "It won't be easy for either of you. You're a brave woman."

She gave him a thin smile. "I don't know if brave is the right word; desperate maybe. Are we done?"

"For now."

Julie stood and retrieved her purse hanging over the arm of the chair. "We never know what we're capable of until circumstances like these motivate us."

Derek rose and walked her to his office door. "Would you like me to wait until you've talked with her before I draw up the papers?"

"No, please proceed. I'm determined to make this happen. No is not acceptable."

"If I can be of help in any other way, please don't hesitate to ask," he said.

"Thank you. I'll be in touch."

They shook hands and Derek watched her walk through the outer office to the hallway. He walked to the window and stared out at the traffic without really seeing. As the Charles family lawyer, he'd seen them through a lot of issues over the years. But this past year, they'd lost Colin; Frank left Alice, and now this. It was a lot to handle in a short time. *A complicated issue with an even more complicated family. This will turn their lives upside down and against each other.*

A bad feeling passed over him. Derek knew he'd be caught in the middle.

Chapter 8

"Frank?" Georgia stopped on the sidewalk at the railing around the outdoor patio of *Just a Cuppa Coffee* in lower Gibsons. She lifted her sunglasses onto the top of her head and stared at the two men seated in front of her. She was shocked to see her ex-father-in-law here in Gibsons relaxing and laughing with a friend.

Frank looked up in surprise and stood up. He grabbed her hand. "Georgia ... so good to see you. Join us?"

She glanced at her watch. "I only have about twenty minutes before picking up Kaela. Then I'm off to Vancouver for the night."

"Then join us until you have to leave."

"Alright." Georgia entered the coffee bistro a little unsure of the situation and ordered an iced cappuccino. When she approached the table, Frank rose and pulled a chair out for her.

"Let me introduce you to an old friend, Bill Truscott. Bill, this is Georgia, Colin's first wife."

She nodded and shook hands with the old gentleman, who suddenly stood.

"It's really nice to meet you, my dear. Please forgive me for running away. I have an appointment down the road."

"I'll wait here for you, Bill." Frank turned to Georgia and smiled. "I'm so glad we ran into each other."

"Are you here on business as well?" she asked.

"Oh no, not me. I've retired you see. And according to Alice, became a bum."

Georgia couldn't believe what she was hearing. ""I never would have thought you'd retire so soon. What about your partnership in the firm?"

Frank's face clouded over. "They bought me out. When we lost Colin, I took a long hard look at myself and my life. Some changes were in order."

"Loss can do that," she said. Frank appeared to retreat into himself. "So are you visiting your friend here?"

Frank looked startled at her question, and then he started to laugh. "No, I live here. Actually, in Halfmoon Bay at the moment. I'm staying with Bill."

Georgia was really confused and suddenly uncomfortable. The thought that Alice lived so close to her was disconcerting. "Oh? I wouldn't think Alice would like it over here away from her friends and her club."

Frank laughed again. His face lit up, and took on a stress-free boyishness she'd never seen in all the years she'd known him. "Alice would never live away from the city and certainly would never leave her family home. I left her, my dear. We 're legally separated, pending a divorce."

Georgia spit out her iced cap, almost choking. "You left Alice? When?"

"Two months after Colin died. It's been a month now."

Georgia couldn't believe what she was hearing. "And she accepted it?"

"I didn't give her a choice. I took my things when I left so there was no room for debate."

"You were married a long time. It must have been a difficult decision for you."

Frank looked out towards the water in the bay. "It was. I mean thirty-five years is a long time. I miss some things about the old boot, but we hadn't been good together for a lot of years."

"Wow, I'm in shock." She wasn't surprised that they had separated. Alice wasn't an easy woman to live with. But Georgia was more impressed that Frank had found the courage to leave such a strong, controlling woman who had worn the pants in their marriage since day one.

"Not as shocked as Alice. But we grew apart and have different values now. I wasn't willing to admit that until Colin's passing forced me to examine them. And after a month apart, I think she's starting to understand that too."

"I must say, I've never seen you look so young, or so relaxed."

"I'm feeling really good about my life. Bill is a recent widower. We've been keeping each other company and renewing an old friendship. Eventually, I'll buy my own place here."

Georgia suddenly felt at ease with Frank. "I'm glad you're happy. But now I must leave and pick up Kaela."

Frank stood with her and without warning gave her a hug. "One thing I've learned through these past months is that family is most important to me. I hope you will allow me to visit with you and Kaela. I really would like to spend time with my granddaughter."

"I'd like that, Frank. Call me." As she hurried away to her car, Georgia was surprised she had opened up to Frank so easily. Admittedly, her problems had always been with Alice, not him. Still, he'd let his ex-wife get away with her nonsense. But that was all in the past.

An hour later, as she and Kaela rode the ferry to Vancouver, she thought about how her daughter could benefit by having another grandfather in her life. *That would make two, and one great grandfather.*

By the time Georgia arrived at her parents' place, showered and dressed for her evening out with her agent, Trent, her mind was made up. Frank could be a grandfather to Kaela if that's what he wanted. She wouldn't stand in his way.

A couple of hours later, Trent lead her up the stairs and into the old Strand Theatre to attend a movie premiere. The only reason she'd agreed to come was because Sean and her had written the script together for this movie, based on one of his novels. Trent pressed her to come because it was her first scripted movie and she deserved to bask in it.

Georgia stumbled mid-way up the long staircase. "Oops..." She grabbed onto his arm to steady herself and clung to him tightly for reassurance.

He squeezed her hand on his arm. "You alright?"

"I'm fine."

"You're trembling."

Her hands felt clammy and she was shaky. "My first screenplay. It's exciting and scary." All true. But that wasn't the only reason. She wanted to see Sean so badly, but didn't know what she would say when she did. She knew she'd panicked over the incident with his ex-wife and then again when Sean wanted to 'move forward' with their relationship. There was no doubt in her mind that she loved the man and sorely missed him. Perhaps their encounter tonight would open the door she'd closed. *Perhaps ... maybe.*

They stood with a group of movie insiders they knew and fell into their chit chat while waiting to go in. A buzzer sounded. It was time. *Where was Sean?* Inside and seated with Trent, Georgia laughed inwardly. All the trouble she'd gone to pick a dress for tonight, the bright turquoise sun dress that fell short of her knees, accentuating her long legs, the plunging neckline that revealed her ample cleavage and equally plunging backline all for naught. Not to mention the new hair cut and make-up blended with her dark tan. She looked and felt good, and he wasn't coming.

The lights dimmed and the music started. Two latecomers mumbling excuses pushed their way down the row. A young woman in her early twenties stepped on her toes as she passed.

"I'm so sorry." Even though it was slowly darkening in the theatre, Georgia could see she was beautiful. An indigenous girl with long black hair, she wore a red tube top that tightly covered her ample breasts, ending just above a jewelled diamond in her belly button, exposing her tiny bare waistline. Her red and white floral skirt started at her hips and flowed to her ankles with a long split up one side. The air filled with a perfume fragrance that was unfamiliar to Georgia, but wafted a succulent sweet scent.

The man following her eased passed Georgia in the now full dark theatre, but she knew that manly scent so well. It was Sean. Her heart sank knowing he was with the beautiful and much younger woman. He didn't seem to notice Georgia. It was too dark. This she told herself.

She lost herself in the movie, not wanting to spoil her pleasure at seeing something she had written with Sean being acted out on screen. But it was hard to forget his intoxicating scent of the woman he was with.

After the movie ended, she and Trent exited through a different door than Sean. But they all came to stand together in the same group in the lobby. While the others gushed about the movie and congratulated her and Sean on the script, Georgia turned and came face to face with Sean. She knees wobbled in the warmth of his dark eyes staring back.

"Hello," he said.

Tongue-tied, she could only muster one word. "Hey."

"How are you?" he asked.

As if they were the only two people standing there, Georgia could only see Sean bigger than life, talking to her. "I'm good." *How lame. Say something.*

"It's good to see you, Georgia," Sean said.

"You too." *So he could gloat with his girl toy.*

"Georgia, this is Serena Thomas. Serena ... Georgia."

The moment was lost. The noise and the people returned to Georgia's senses. The girl called Serena, gushed on about how great it was to meet her and how much she looked up to her. *Oh great, make me feel like your mother.* She listened politely with a smile on her face but inwardly wished the girl would shut up and go away. She was even more beautiful in the light of the foyer and appeared even younger. Serena rambled on about how wonderful Sean was and how they were flying to L.A. in the morning ... together. Georgia's stomach rolled over. She felt like someone had punched her in the gut. *Kick me in the head and put me out of my misery.*

Trent grabbed a hold of her hand. "We're on our way to the party. We'll see you there." He steered Georgia towards the door.

She gave them all a wave and a big smile that she didn't feel and let Trent lead her outside.

"You're in pain." Trent held onto her hand while they walked to the car park.

"No."

"Then why are there tears running down your cheeks?"

"Oh shit, if you saw it, everyone else must have." Georgia wiped her face with the back of her hand.

"Nah. I didn't see it, girl. I sensed it. You were a great actress back there."

"She's so beautiful, so bubbly ... so young." Georgia blew her nose with a Kleenex Trent pulled out of his jacket pocket.

"I thought we were talking about, Sean? Who are you talking about?"

Georgia stopped walking and gave him a long stare. Men could be so clueless sometimes. "We *are* talking about Sean ... and his half-his-age date. Come on, even you couldn't take your eyes off of her."

"Oh ... right. Georgia you're a very beautiful woman yourself and you look extremely sexy tonight."

"At least someone noticed. Thank-you." She let out a deep sigh. "It's all my fault. I sent him off to date other women. What did I expect? He'd mope around the cabin? Instead he's keeping company with a beautiful 'younger' girl. They've probably been running barefoot up at the cabin all summer."

Trent chuckled. "That's pathetic."

Georgia punched Trent on the arm. "You're laughing? The love of my life is with a beautiful woman who's young enough to be his daughter and you think it's funny."

"I'm sorry but you're only antagonizing yourself."

"Tonight, I intend on becoming completely, disgustingly drunk."

"Something tells me we aren't going to the after party." He opened the car door for her and let himself in the driver's side.

"Would you be disappointed?"

"Hell no. I've been to too many of these events lately. You hungry?"

"Starving, I didn't eat dinner." *Anything to avoid that party.* "Does Sean have business in L.A.?"

"Not that I know and I'm his friend and agent. Last I heard, he took the summer off and was going to start writing in the fall."

Georgia let out a depressed sigh. "Probably a pleasure trip with his 'adopted daughter'."

Trent backed out of the stall and straightened out the car. He put it in park and turned to face her. "Stop torturing yourself. I've never heard her name before so he can't have known her long. I'll see what I can find out when he returns, but you should call him. You need to settle this thing between you two."

"What about him? He never tried to call me."

"Pride ... in all its stubborn, egotistical glory on both sides. But you're the one who sent him packing."

"I know that. And I hoped tonight might get us talking again." She threw the hanky on the floor beside her with a vengeance. "But if he wanted to get back together why would he bring a date?"

"You came with one."

"No I didn't."

Trent's eyebrows shot up. "Oh? What am I, chopped liver?"

Georgia's face turned red. "Of course not. Sorry. It's just that ..."

Trent laughed and shook his head. "No need to explain. Your heart belongs to another. Call him."

"Well, that'll depend on what you find out about his travelling companion. Right now I could eat a horse."

"Let's go to that great Greek restaurant in Kitsilano. We'll gorge ourselves on souvlaki and red wine."

Georgia perked up. "Yes, please. You're a great friend, Trent. Thank-you."

"Hey, what guy wouldn't want to wine and dine a beautiful woman, even if she is in love with another man."

She looked Trent up and down. "You're a very handsome man you know. You could have been out with any woman you wanted tonight, instead of babysitting me."

"I'm not a great catch for any woman. I love my work and travel too much. They never stick around for long."

"That's because you haven't found your soul mate yet. You are a great friend though and much appreciated."

"Well friend, let's get this pity party going and turn it into a wine party, shall we? We'll leave the car at the restaurant and taxi home."

Chapter 9

The man slipped quietly in the front door and tread softly towards his study. His hope was to lock himself in his private world before Rose knew he was home. He was halfway down the hall before noticing the light shining across the floor in front of the study door.

He stopped in his tracks. Something wasn't right. The light could only mean one thing. His study door was open. He flew down the hall in an instant.

His wife sat at his desk with the blue folder wide open. She was so engrossed with the contents that she didn't see him standing in the door frame. Anger built so quickly that it spread through his body igniting a rage that shook him to his core. "Bitch," he yelled.

Rose looked up defiant. She held up a picture from the folder. "Who the hell is this woman? What's this all about?"

In an instant, he was across the room, pulling her by one arm across the desk and onto the floor. Papers flew in all directions.

Rose yelled out and tried to curl into a ball, as he kicked her wildly. "Please, no … stop."

He stepped back from her, but no less angry. "What are you doing in here? You know this room is off limits."

His wife tried to crawl away from him but he cut her off. Using both hands, he pulled her onto her feet and pushed her onto the couch. Holding one arm, he shook her as she cowered into the cushion, "Answer me." He twisted her arm until she screamed out in pain. He let go and waited.

Rose whimpered. "I saw that blue folder before. I wanted to know what was in it."

Enraged even more, he back-handed her so hard, she fell off the couch onto the floor. *How dare she question me about my business? What other secrets had she discovered?* His eyes swept the room. Rose lay crying in a heap on the floor.

"How'd you find the key?" he demanded.

Between sobs and gulps for air, she pushed herself up into a sitting position. "I saw you hide it over the door."

"And then you went snooping through my personal things in here until you found the desk keys. Didn't you?" The man bent over, grabbed her shirt with one hand and balled the other into a fist. "Answer me."

Rose cringed. "Yes," she whispered.

He pulled her up and pushed her back onto the couch. "This is my room and it's off limits. You violated my private space and my trust. Why?"

She swallowed hard and thrust her chin forward. "I'm tired of your secrets."

One balled fist landed hard in her face … not once but twice. Blood spurted out of her nose and Rose fell backwards with a moan. But this time she didn't cry.

So she was only concerned with the blue file. He glanced towards the bookcase. All was intact. *She didn't find any of my other secrets.* His emotions and anger were back under control. "You'll know what I want you to know. The only rights you have are the ones I allow you," he said with a firm, menacing tone.

She stayed quiet, stared at him for a long moment, and then stood on unsteady feet. In a quiet, reserved voice, she spoke. "I'm done."

Leaning back against the desk, his eyes followed her every movement, amused by this sudden change in her demeanor. He knew his job was finished. The old indentured Rose was back.

She limped past him to the doorway, turned and spoke in barely a whisper. "I'm going upstairs to pack a bag. I'm leaving and you'll never touch me again."

He couldn't believe what he was hearing. "What?"

Infuriated, he closed the gap between them. He'd mistaken her passiveness for subservience. "You stupid bitch." He pressed himself against her, pinning her to the wall and wrapped his hands around her neck. As he watched her eyes bulge in fear he squeezed tighter, felt the surge of power rush through him. *You've pushed me and now you're going to pay. No one fucks with me!*

Rose reached up and grabbed his hands. She tried to pull them away from her throat, but he was too strong. Gasping, she grasped at his hair and pulled hard. He yelled out in pain as her hands dug into his scalp and came away with tufts. Furious, he rammed his thumbs down on her larynx and pushed with all his might, saw the desperation in her eyes as her hands flew at him in all directions, scratching his arms, neck, and chest. In a matter of minutes, her will and strength ebbed, and she went limp in his hands. Letting go of her, she dropped hard to the floor. A few raspy breaths escaped her open mouth, followed by a rattle from deep in her throat. It was over.

His wife lay sprawled before him. Adrenalin pumped through his veins and he took deep gulps of air to stop his body from shaking. The man stared at her for a moment, leaned down and searched for a pulse. He stood, sneered down at her and stepped over her lifeless corpse. "Now you're done."

Later that night, he carried her body into the garage and placed it in the trunk of his car. A two-hour drive took him far into the desert where he dug a hole and buried her. There was a full moon that lit up the landscape. He leaned back against the bumper of the truck and stared into the dessert. His eyes followed the contours of the land in a semi-circle from left to right. "You've got lots of company, sweetheart. You won't be lonely." His laugh echoed from one rock face to another. "Here that, all you bitches?" he yelled out. "I'm back. Dearest Rose is one of you now."

He was home before midnight. By morning, his study was tidied and his secrets locked away. A suitcase packed with some clothes and a briefcase containing the blue folder sat by the garage door. The morning was spent cleaning out the fridge and putting out the garbage. They had no close friends, but he did call his next door neighbour, telling them his wife had left him and returned to her home state. He was going away for awhile to think things through. No one would question his story as they were private people and had little to do with the neighbours. They knew nothing of his or Rose's past. As a freelance journalist, he answered to no one.

The house was locked and it soon disappeared from his rear view mirror as he drove into town to the bank and then to the post office to have his mail held.

It was a beautiful summer day as he headed north towards a new beginning. He thought of the past fifteen years with Rose. *You were a good wife until lately, kept a clean house, cooked and laundered for me. The perfect decoy to hide my other life. Too bad. I'll miss the old Rose, but there are no regrets. She'd fulfilled her purpose and I don't want nor need her anymore. I never loved her, anymore than all the others.*

The image of his mother and father came to mind, reminding him of a childhood filled with beatings and rants. His parents were alcoholics. Domestic abuse was a common factor in their lives. He heard a dog barking in a field as he drove by and relived the moment his father shoved his mother's head against a concrete wall, all because the family dog peed in the house and she'd tried to stop him from beating the dog.

Love's a beautiful thing until the bitches piss you off. Then, they need to be put back in their places. His father taught him that. But love had eluded him—that is, until he'd found his sweet Georgia peach.

Johnny Cash and June Carter sang 'Going to Jackson' on the radio. His fingers tapped the steering wheel in rhythm to the music. Suddenly, he burst out laughing, realizing the verity of his freedom. "It's our time now. I'm on my way."

Chapter 10

Julie sat in the park opposite Georgia's house and watched her walk down the street holding her daughter's hand. The two were chatting and laughing. A pang of jealousy at the obvious bond between them tugged at her heart. Her vision blurred. She couldn't believe how much their daughters looked alike. Wiping away the tears only strengthened the belief she was doing the right thing.

Mother and daughter disappeared into the school on the corner. It was mid-August. Frank had told her Kaela attended the summer school fun day program four mornings a week. She deliberately picked today, knowing Georgia would be alone. Julie waited, taking in the beauty of the little park. It was a beautiful sunny day, and she watched the squirrels running up and down tree trunks. They stopped to chatter at her, making it clear they weren't impressed with her sitting so close to their home.

Georgia emerged a few minutes later and stood talking with a group of mothers before starting back up the street. *What a lovely neighbourhood to raise children in.*

She left the bench and walked towards the other woman. At one point Georgia glanced her way without recognition. It was understandable. Julie had her hair pulled back in a pony tail, wore dark glasses and a ball cap pulled low on her forehead, a deliberate attempt to hide her face. Georgia turned up the driveway to her house.

Julie came up behind her and took a deep breath to steady her nerves. She removed the sunglasses. "Georgia?"

The other woman spun around with her hand on her chest. "Julie? You scared me."

"I'm so sorry ... I didn't mean to."

Georgia looked wary. "What are you doing here?"

"I ... I know I should have called first, but I didn't think you'd let me come. Can we talk?"

"Uh—yes, but you should have called. Look, if this is about the girls ... "

"May I come in? Just for a few minutes?" Julie needed some time with her and didn't want to be left out in the driveway before she had her say.

Georgia hesitated. "Since you came all the way from Vancouver, come in." She led them into the kitchen and pulled out a stool from under the island that separated the kitchen and dining room.

"Sit," she said, indicating with her hand. "Coffee? It's fresh."

"Yes, please. Black's good." Julie watched her pour the dark liquid into two cups with shaky hands. She noted that Georgia must be feeling as nervous as her.

Georgia sat down on the other side of the island across from Julie. "I don't understand why after all these years; you suddenly want the girls to be friends. Yes, they're half-sisters, but they don't know each other. The Charles family turned on us after Kaela was born, and questioned Colin's paternity. We didn't deserve that."

"Alice was the only one who did that ... no wait." Julie put her hands up, palms facing towards the other woman. "I admit, at first I thought you were trying to entrap Colin by saying the baby was his. I mean, no one knew about the pregnancy until five months after he'd left you ... "

Georgia cut her off. "And neither did I. There you go. Because Colin's dead, what makes you think I want to be your friend? Why would I want anyone in the Charles family back in my life?"

Julie took a deep breath and started again. "I'm not asking you to be my friend."

Georgia stared hard at her in silence. "How can you expect our kids to form a relationship if their mothers don't have one?"

Fair question. Julie opened her mouth to talk, but shut it again. *Not yet, too soon.*

Georgia picked up the conversation. "I protected Kaela from Colin's family these past years. How do I know Alice hasn't poisoned your daughter's mind against her sister?"

"Alice is a manipulator. We both know that. As she played Colin and his sister against each other and their father, she did the same with you and me." Julie paused as a wave of nausea hit her. *Not now, please.*

Georgia stood, nervously. "Another coffee?"

"No, thank you. The truth is I was young and naive and bought into Alice's silliness. But not for long. Don't you think I had to struggle against her demands like you? I've had to protect Shelby against her games too."

Georgia sighed. "I never thought of it like that. I guess no one is immune to her manipulation." She sat back down on her stool. "You came with money and I didn't, so I believed you were accepted by her."

"Oh, please. Alice is motivated by money and status but her agenda's really about control."

"Okay, I understand that. So we were both victims to Alice. But what about the girls and their father? Do you know how hard it was to explain to a child why her father only saw her twice a year, but spent more time with his other daughter?"

Julie studied Georgia's defiant expression and thought carefully about her next words. "Colin may have lived in the same house as Shelby, but he didn't spend a lot of time with her either. His law practice came first and then his ..." Julie faltered. "... his playtime."

The two women locked eyes in understanding and remained silent.

"So because Colin wronged us both, you think we should band together and bond?" Georgia asked.

"No, I don't expect so. I wronged you, too. I may have been naive but I was also ambitious. When Colin came on to me, I dismissed you, thinking only of myself. I was a bitch. Reading your book opened my eyes to a lot of things."

Georgia raised an eyebrow but said nothing.

"It forced me to take a long look at myself." Julie stood and stretched her aching limbs. "All that you went through—the trip to the Yukon, the kidnapping, escaping into the wilderness, lost at the cabin, childbirth alone—all that happened because of me. I played a role in it, and believe me; I'll always carry that guilt."

Georgia looked confused. "Then, I really don't understand what you want from me. Is it forgiveness?"

Julie shook her head and sat down again. "No, I owe you an apology, but words are hollow. I'm not looking for forgiveness."

Frustrated, Georgia threw her arms up. "Then, what?"

Julie noted the exasperation mirrored on the other woman's face. *The moment has come. No more stalling.* With a deep breath, Julie tried to steady her nerves as she organized her thoughts. She had rehearsed this moment over and over in her mind, but now that it came to it, the practiced lines fell apart. She cleared her throat. "I want you to become Shelby's guardian, and eventually, adopt her."

"What?" Georgia jumped up from her stool, knocking her empty cup onto the floor. They both jerked back when the mug crashed and splintered. Julie watched as Georgia opened her mouth to speak, but nothing came out.

Finally, Georgia spoke. "Excuse me a minute." She disappeared into a small room off the kitchen and returned with a broom and dust pan.

As awkward as it felt, Julie decided to say nothing, remembering an old saying, *He who speaks first loses.* She watched her clean up the mess, dump the broken china into a garbage can under the sink, and return to the little room. With no idea as to what would happen next, she braced herself and tried to calm her nerves by admiring the old country kitchen.

Georgia returned, grabbed the coffee pot and a new cup for herself, poured them both a coffee and sat back down. She stared right into Julie's eyes. "Why?"

"There's only one way to say this and since subtlety isn't my strong point today, here it is … I'm dying."

She watched the other woman's face blanch. Georgia looked as if someone threw cold water at her. "Dear God."

"The medical term is *Diffuse Brain Stem Glioma.* In layman's terms, high-grade, inoperable brain tumour."

"Are they sure?"

"First, second, and third opinions—all the same diagnosis."

The colour started to return to Georgia's face, but she still looked grave. "What about treatment?"

Julie sighed. "I was diagnosed and started treatment two months before Colin died. A combo of chemo and radiation appeared to be helping until now. The cancer has moved to grade four, I'm afraid."

Georgia faltered. "Have they said … uh … you know … how long?

Tears welled in Julie's eyes. *Stay in control, focus.* "Four months tops. It's in the brain stem. So you can see the need to move quickly for Shelby's sake."

She watched the woman before her shrink into her seat, her hands covering her mouth. "Dear God, poor Shelby. Does she know?"

"Only that I'm ill. I'll tell her soon, but not until her future is set."

Georgia picked up their coffee mugs, took them to the sink and dumped them. She placed her hands on the sink and stared out the window.

Poor woman, Julie thought, with a wry smile. *She's really rattled. We haven't had a sip of that coffee.*

Georgia turned and leaned against the sink and crossed her arms. "First, please know I'm truly sorry. As a mother, I feel your pain. But why me of all people?"

"Because Kaela is her sister and you're the closest thing she has to an immediate relative."

"Don't forget Alice. She's a blood relative and I'm not. You know she'll fight this."

"I won't let that happen," Julie said, quietly.

"Can you stop her?"

"Derek Connors thinks so. After all, I'm Shelby's mother and it's my decision what happens to her after I'm ... after..." She fought hard to hold back the tears but lost the battle. Once the tears came, the nausea she felt took over. She vomited on the kitchen floor.

Georgia ran around the counter to her. "Are you all right? What can I do?" Julie looked up through bleary eyes and saw a face full of genuine concern.

"I'm so sorry. Can I use your bathroom to clean up?" Georgia's arm slipped through hers and she allowed her to lead her to the bathroom where she was given a fresh towel, a washcloth, and mouthwash. Georgia left her.

She stared at her face in the mirror. *Damn. Why did you let yourself lose control?* She applied fresh makeup which added some color to her white pallor. By the time she returned she was feeling better and her composure was back. The kitchen was spotless and Georgia was perched on her stool looking worse than she did.

Julie apologized. "I'm so sorry for springing this on you all at once." She swept her arm towards to the floor. "And for that."

Georgia stood. "Please, let's sit in the living room where it's more comfortable." She led them into the living room and sat down in the armchair.

Julie chose the loveseat and started the conversation rolling again. "I have two thoughts on this. First, Alice is too old. Second, she'll ship Shelby off to boarding school like she did Colin and Mary."

Georgia nodded in agreement. "You're right there."

"Shelby lost her father, and soon her mother. She's needs people around her who will nurture her. That's not Alice or a dormitory."

"What about Mary and Steve? They're her legal aunt and uncle."

"They chose a life without children. I trust Steve, but Mary lets Alice manipulate her."

"Right again. What about your side of the family?"

"I'm an only child. My parents were killed in a car accident when I was a teenager. My Aunt raised me and she's gone now. It's you or Alice." Julie gave her a pleading stare.

Georgia shifted uncomfortably in her chair. She felt cornered. "What makes you think I'm the right person for Shelby? Maybe I'd find myself resenting her because of what she represents from my past."

Julie shook her head no. "Uh-uh, not you. I read your book, saw the interviews, and watched the movie. That's not who you are."

Georgia laughed, which turned into a snort. "The movie and articles are a little Hollywood. They made me out to be Mother Teresa, which I'm not."

Julie laughed with her and felt for the first time that the two women were relaxed in each other's company. "Well, your book showed you for who you are, written in your own words. You're the chosen one and there isn't anyone else."

Georgia became sombre. "You certainly seem sure of yourself."

"I am and there's something else too. You're the only one who can win against Alice."

A frown creased Georgia's forehead. "I'm not sure I'm up for a fight against that woman."

Julie's heart skipped a beat. "If it means anything, you won't be alone in that fight. Frank thinks you're the best person to adopt Shelby and he would back you up one hundred percent." She watched the other woman stand and pace the room.

"He said that?"

Julie nodded.

"I hope you aren't expecting an answer right now. This is a life-changing decision, not only for me, but for Kaela and especially for Shelby. I need time to think this through."

Julie rose. "Of course. Only don't take too long."

Georgia winced.

The two women walked to the front door. "I can't promise anything," Georgia said.

Julie stood in the open doorway. "That's all I can ask."

"And if I say no—what's Plan B?"

Julie let out a deep sigh. "There is no Plan B. Alice will win." The two women looked deep into each other's eyes.

Georgia blinked a couple of times, pursed her lips and said, "No pressure there."

"One last thing, Derek Connors is the executor of my will. The child support Colin set up for Shelby would be transferred to you. Her trust fund works the same way as Kaela's. My estate will be liquidized, split evenly between the two sisters and added to their trust funds.

Georgia tried to speak. "But ... "

"No buts. I insist the girls be treated equally. They're both Colin's daughters and that way it should eliminate any resentment between them when they're older." Julie put her hand out and they shook hands. She reached into her pocket and pulled out a piece of paper. "Here's a number where I can be reached."

"Where's your car?"

"Across the street in the park."

Georgia shook her head. "Are you sure you should drive?"

"I'm fine. I'm only going up to Frank's in Halfmoon Bay. Shelby and I are staying with him for a few days. That's his phone number."

Georgia turned the paper over and over in her hand. "We'll talk soon."

As Julie drove to Frank's, she tried not to second guess what Georgia's decision would be. Forty minutes later, she pulled into the driveway. Frank came out to meet her.

"Well? How did it go?"

"She listened to me. At least she didn't throw me out." Julie shrugged. "Who knows?"

Frank looked concerned. "Maybe, I should talk to her."

Julie shook her head. "Not now. Let her digest it all. Where's Shelby?"

"Down on the beach with Bill. The tide's out. They're looking at starfish." Frank took Julie's hand and led her around the corner of the house.

Shelby's squeals of delight filled the air. She and Bill were bent down looking at something in the wet sand. Her daughter looked up and when she saw her, jumped up and down, clapping her hands. "Mommy ... Mommy, come and see."

Julie laughed. These moments spent with Shelby were so precious and she intended to enjoy every one of them.

Chapter 11

Georgia adjusted the receiver as she sank into an overstuffed chair. Talking to her best friend always had a calming effect on her frayed nerves. Their friendship since childhood never wavered, despite the fact that Marion lived a couple of thousand miles north in the Yukon.

"You're kidding." Marion's disbelief mirrored her own.

"Afraid not," Georgia said.

"Have you talked to anyone else about this?"

"No way. I need to get my head around it first. I called you because I knew I could count on you to be impartial. My family'll probably go on tilt if I even consider this." Georgia sat on the love seat and stared across the street at the park bench where Julie had sat this morning.

Marion let out a whistle. "How weird is that. It must have been strange sitting in your kitchen drinking coffee with her."

"That's an understatement. I've been thinking about it all day and came to realize it didn't matter anymore. Colin's dead and she's about to die. What possible good would it do me to play the martyred woman on her?"

"Some women would still want to tear her hair out."

"It's not like this all happened recently. It was years ago. Besides, it would be my ego rising up. This isn't about Julie and me. It's about a little girl who's going to become an orphan." She thought of Alice. "Well, not technically."

"Well said. So what's your initial take on this?"

"Initially, my paranoia kicked in. What with seeing Frank awhile back and now Julie's visit, I wondered if this was a plot to draw Kaela back into the Charles family. Of course, I realise that's ridiculous. Julie wants to give me her daughter, not take mine away."

"Hey, kiddo, it's understandable, given how that family treated you. What's Julie's prognosis?"

"Four months tops. My God, Marion, she looks terrible. I remember how she looked a few years back. Women really felt threatened by her beauty. Illness is so devastating."

"This may not be appropriate, but addressing your paranoia, at least you know she really is ill."

Georgia moved the curtain to see parents and kids playing together in the park. She felt sorry for Julie. Thank goodness Kaela was at a play date today. Her playmate's mother picked the girls up and took them to her house after school. It gave her time to think.

"I really am confused about this. I'd take her in a heartbeat. But I don't want to do it out of sympathy. It's a huge responsibility and it affects other people's lives too."

"It's a biggie. What's your main concern if you decide to do this?"

She took a moment's pause to think about it. "Having to deal with Alice. Julie did say Frank would support me on this."

"I don't think you need worry about that. You'll have Julie's last wishes and the law on your side. Certainly Shelby couldn't have a better guardian than you. I remember before the kidnapping when you worried about being a single mother to Kaela. Look at you now. You're super mom."

"Thanks for that." Georgia moved to the kitchen and retrieved a bottle of water out of the fridge. "It did pass my mind that I might resent her because of where she came from, but children are innocent. Rethinking this, Alice would be my second concern, my first worry is Kaela and how she'll react to an instant sister."

"Hmm … could be some sibling jealousy. But children are so much more resilient than adults. She could come to love having Shelby around, especially since they look alike."

"Do you think we could become a cohesive family?"

"Absolutely. Sure there's going to be some hiccups, but you have a gentle, loving soul and I know you can overcome any adversity." Marion paused. "Speaking of cohesion, have you talked to Sean at all?"

"Oh, Marion, you're so obvious. The answer's no. And if I decide to go through with this, it puts my life in a different light."

"How so? Sean loves Kaela, he would love Shelby too."

Georgia collapsed into the arm chair and raised her feet up. "It's one thing to take on one of Colin's children, but expecting him to take on two? I don't know. Let's be realistic."

"Okay. I'll say this once more. You're throwing away a great man here because you're too scared to make a commitment. You of all people know that life isn't always fair, and that there's no guarantees. So don't you dare use this child as another excuse to push him further away."

"Have you forgotten that he's with another woman? You're talking about this like all I have to do is pick up the phone and he'll come running."

"You don't know that. She may have been his date for the evening, like Trent was yours. How do you know he didn't take her to make you jealous?"

"If that were the case, don't you think he would have called me when I didn't show up at the party? And are you forgetting that they went to L.A. together the following day?"

"You'll never know if you don't try to talk to him. You hurt him by sending him away. You have to take the first step back. And people don't fall out of love in two months. If that were the case, he didn't love you in the first place and we both know he did..does."

This conversation made Georgia uncomfortable. "Heard you. Thanks for letting me run this whole Shelby thing past you. It really helped. Gotta go." She sighed heavily, realizing the truth in her friend's words.

"Go ahead and run away, I know where you live, kiddo. And remember, you're supposed to be the great master of conquering all your fears. So live up to your reputation, girl. Call me back if you need to talk."

Marion was right about so much but right now she had enough to deal with. *Sean would have to wait. Am I copping out?* She headed to the laundry room to fold clothes and clear her mind.

That night, she tucked Kaela into bed. "Tell me something? Have you ever thought what it would be like to have a sister or brother?"

"A brother? No way. Boys are buttheads." Kaela looked around her room. "A sister might be nice. We could share my room and have sleepovers each night." She giggled.

Hearing that, Georgia decided to test the waters a little. "What if we invited your half-sister over on a play date. Would you like to spend some time with her?"

Her daughter screwed up her face. "I don't think her mommy would let her come here. Besides they live too far away."

"Actually, her mother and I had a lovely visit here this morning. They're staying for a few days at Grampa Frank's. We both thought it would be nice for the two of you to meet and spend some time with each other. Would you like that?" She held her breath while she waited for Kaela to think it over.

"I guess so. It's weird though, 'cause we look alike."

Georgia let out her breath. "Okay. I'll arrange it for tomorrow after school."

The next morning she called Julie. "Hi, it's Georgia. I spoke to Kaela last night and she'd like to meet Shelby." She heard the woman suck in her breath. "We wondered if the two of you would like to come over after play school today and stay for dinner."

Julie's voice came in barely a whisper. "We'd love to. Thank you."

Georgia felt her guard go up. She didn't want to mislead Julie. "I really can't make a decision about this until we see how the girls feel about each other." She hesitated, then added, "And I'm not even sure if this is the right thing to do."

"Let's take this one step at a time, okay? This is the first step." Julie sounded confident.

"It's this damn time thing. I know you need a fast decision and I'm feeling pressured," Georgia blurted out, then, catching herself, added, "I'm sorry, that sounded insensitive."

There was a silence at the other end. "I understand. We'll see you about three thirty."

"Let's meet in the park across the street. The girls will have the park to play in and it's neutral ground for both of them."

Georgia hung up the phone. *What am I taking on here?*

Chapter 12

Georgia sat on the bench and watched Kaela swinging on the monkey bars. She checked her watch constantly. They were late. Maybe Julie changed her mind. Life would be easier if she had.

Her heart sunk when she saw Julie's car pull up to the curb. Georgia drew in a deep breath ... *no way to avoid this*. A shy Shelby stepped out of the car staring at the sidewalk as she waited for her mother to join her. Georgia's heart went out to the little girl.

"Shelby, this is Georgia ... Georgia, my daughter, Shelby."

Georgia gave Shelby a big smile. "Hi Shelby, welcome to Gibsons." She turned to call Kaela over, but her daughter had already seen them. She walked slowly over; her eyes on Shelby. "Sweetheart, this is your sister Shelby."

The two five-year-olds stared at each other in silence.

"Say hello, Kaela," she prodded her daughter, sensing her sudden shyness.

Kaela glanced up at her mother with nervousness in her eyes. She turned back to Shelby. "Hi."

"Hi." Shelby echoed.

"Sorry we're late," Julie said. "There was an accident on Rat Portage Hill."

Nodding her head, Georgia added, "Not surprised. There's always accidents on that hill. People drive it too fast."

Georgia looked back at the two girls, who were definitely showing discomfort with each other. "Kaela, maybe Shelby would like to play in the park with you."

Her daughter's voice returned and she smiled at Shelby. "Do you like the monkey bars?"

"Uh-huh," Shelby whispered.

"Let's go."

Shelby looked at her mother, "Can I?"

"Of course, go have fun," Julie replied.

The two mothers sat down on the bench in silence and watched the girls run off. Before long, the sisters were chatting up a storm and giggling like the kids they were as Kaela showed off her swinging routine.

"So far so good," Georgia mumbled. The park was unusually empty. It would give the girls a chance to become at ease with each other, with no explanation needed as to who the new girl was who looked like Kaela. She turned to Julie. "How are you feeling today?"

"Better. As each day takes me further away from the Chemo treatments, the nausea lessens. Yesterday, I was upset and lost control. The nausea took over."

"I'm glad you feel better." Not sure what more to say on the subject of Julie's illness, she changed the conversation. "So … what do you think about Frank leaving Alice?"

Julie smiled. "A definite shocker, although, I've never seen him happier."

"My thoughts exactly. Frank indicated that Alice was moving on too."

"I'd say. She's already seeing one of the senior partners at his old law firm. Can you believe it?"

Georgia chucked. "Nothing keeps Alice down for long." Silence. She grabbed at straws for something to say. "How long are you staying at Frank's?"

Julie looked startled. "I … I'm not sure. I guess it depends on what happens with you and me. I mean school starts in a couple of weeks. Should you decide to go ahead with this, we'll stay on the Coast."

A feeling of panic coursed through Georgia. She felt her face heat up. "Forgive me. You're not here on a vacation." She let out a sigh and ran her hands through the sides of her hair. "Wow … a lot depends on my decision, doesn't it?"

"I'm sorry you're feeling so pressured."

"One day at a time, like you said."

Their conversation didn't come any easier than yesterday's. The two women sat silently watching their daughters, who by now were playing like old friends. Georgia didn't think it was possible for her and Julie to ever be that comfortable with each other.

After a time, the two girls ran up to them. "Mommy, can we go home and play in my room?" Kaela asked.

"Sure. Time for me to start dinner anyway."

After eating, the women sat in the living room sipping coffee as the sisters watched a video in the bedroom.

"This is a wonderful neighbourhood for raising kids," Julie said.

"Yes, it is. Kaela and I are very lucky to be able to live in my grandmother's house. With all the travelling I've done and she's been doing, we hardly see each other. But once she's back next year and Kaela's in school full-time, I'll have to consider buying my own place."

"Will you stay on the Coast?"

"Oh yes. I hope to stay in this area too. I love the city but that short ferry ride keeps this coastal community rural and countrified."

"The girls seem to like each other." Julie ventured.

"Yes, they're easy together." Georgia added.

"Not like you and me." Julie said, with a slight smile.

"There is an underlying tension between us."

Julie started to talk but faltered. She took a deep breath and started again. "If I were your best friend, what I'm asking of you would be huge and a major expectation on my part. So given our history, I do understand the added tension here and the emotional conflict you must be experiencing. I'm sure you've spent a lot of time hating me."

Georgia stared hard at Julie. "Hate? That's a strong word. The one thing I learned that winter in the cabin was that hate is a wasted emotion. So is blame. I've given a lot of thought to this the past twenty-four hours since you appeared back in my life."

"And?"

"I disliked you because I felt threatened by your beauty and delicate demeanor. You were that little girl-woman that men fall for. Worse still, you weren't even aware of it."

Julie looked surprised. "I don't know about that. I was young, ambitious and in love. It was easy to believe the things you want to hear and wasn't hard for Colin to convince me there was no intimacy between the two of you anymore."

"Colin had a seductive charm that was hard to resist."

"I'm so sorry for all of it," she whispered. Tears formed in her eyes.

Georgia was at a loss for words. She stared at the floor embarrassed. *How can I respond to that? My whole life changed because of Julie's affair with Colin, albeit for the best. But at the time it was devastating and here we are exposing our inner selves to each other. Emotional conflict? Absolutely.*

Julie spoke softly. "Yes, I fell for Colin's charm. When we learned you were pregnant, it was easy to believe Alice's accusations that it couldn't be Colin's. I needed to believe it because I was about to give birth to his baby myself. And you weren't around to dispute it, at least until you turned up alive at the cabin."

"A shocker," Georgia mused.

"At that point, it was even more important to believe Kaela wasn't Colin's. If she was, then all that Colin told me about your relationship was a lie. Then there was the media storm rehashing all our business publicly. Colin finally admitted to me that Kaela was his and told me about the final weekend you spent together at Harrison Hot Springs; the weekend he was supposed to tell you about our affair and my pregnancy. Our relationship changed after that."

"But you married him anyway," Georgia said.

Julie shrugged. "Foolishly, I'd given up my career, had a new born baby. It wasn't until the cheating started that the trust broke down completely."

For the first time, Georgia could objectively see the whole picture and understand Julie's perspective. Colin was a charmer and a cheater and Julie found out the truth the same way she had. "I can't condone affairs, especially when children are involved but I reconciled the fact a long time ago that Colin and I were different people who shouldn't be together."

"I don't think Colin knew who he should be with. He was searching for something that all his affairs couldn't give him," Julie said.

"His mother's approval probably."

Julie nodded in silence and the two women fell silent.

"Look ..." Georgia shifted in her seat, "I'm not going to sit in judgement of you, especially now. Both of our situations have changed drastically, especially yours. All of which puts a new perspective on this. The past is the past. It is what it is. None of it is really about you and me, but about Shelby and Kaela, and they are innocents. They must be nurtured and protected."

Fresh tears flowed down Julie's cheeks. "You know, you're everything I thought you would be and more ... so much more. Thank you."

"Perhaps you and I can find common ground as mothers who want the same things for our daughters," Georgia smiled, "… who happen to be half-sisters."

She took their empty cups back into the kitchen. She stayed away a few minutes to let Julie regain her composure. Before she returned to the living room, she went down the hall to check on the girls. Shelby and Kaela were laying side-by-side on their stomachs on the bed, leaning on their elbows. Both of them were giggling at the antics taking place in the animated movie.

Julie stood with her back to her when she returned, looking out the front window towards the park. The ill-fitting t-shirt and skinny jeans accentuated her thinness and vulnerability. A shudder passed through Georgia as she took in her frailty. She couldn't help but feel compassion for her past nemesis. "Julie?"

The other woman faced her with a quiet reserve. "Yes?"

"Since things seem to have gone well with the girls today, perhaps we should spend as much time together as possible. The only way to know how the girls will be long-term or how Shelby relates to me is to throw us all together."

Julie sighed and threw her a big smile. "On that note then, Frank and Bill are having a barbeque for Shelby and me tomorrow afternoon. Frank asked me to invite you and Kaela, if things worked out today."

Georgia recognized a little of the old Julie in her smiling face. "We'll be there."

Chapter 13

A cool breeze came up from the beach and pushed Georgia's hair back off of her face. She stood on the deck of Bill's house in Halfmoon Bay with Frank watching the girls, Bill and Julie gather firewood for a bonfire. The afternoon went well. The kids were happy and played together on the beach, gathering shells and rocks. She and Frank finished cleaning up the kitchen.

"Thanks for coming Georgia. You don't know how good it feels for me to see my two grandkids together."

"Thank *you*. You still can barbeque the best New York strip steak in the west," Georgia quipped. She noted Frank's long stare and knew he had more to say to her.

"I know you haven't made a decision about all of this as yet, but I want you to know the fact that you've accepted Julie and Shelby into your life at this point and are considering her request, shows what a wise and compassionate woman you've become. Whatever your decision, I'll always respect you. Know too that should you say yes, I'll support you one hundred percent."

"That means a lot to me. Thank you."

"Let's join the others on the beach, shall we?"

The evening passed quickly as marshmallows toasted and songs were sung around the fire pit. They all returned to the house when the fire burned down and the breeze turned to a cold wind off the water.

Georgia headed to the bathroom before leaving for home. She stared at her-self in the mirror, deep into her eyes, searching for something from within, but not really sure what that was. *Inhale, exhale. Inhale, exhale. Shoulders straight.* She gave her reflection a nod. Goodbyes were passed around and Julie walked Georgia and Kaela out to their car.

Once Kaela was buckled in and the door shut, Georgia leaned against the front fender , crossed her arms across her chest and ran her hands up and down her arms, glancing everywhere except at Julie. "So ..." *Am I really going to say this?*

Julie stood in silence, her eyes never leaving Georgia's face. "We only have two weeks before the girls go to school. I've made a decision." She noticed Julie's eyebrows rise up, otherwise she remained poker-faced. "Uh ... not *that* decision, but *a* decision. This situation needs to be met head-on and dealt with forthright. My suggestion is that tomorrow the two of you move into the Gib-sons house with us."

The other woman's face blanched. Her mouth dropped open. She stood in a zombie state for a long moment, then her hand flew to her mouth.

Concerned, Georgia leaned forward. "Are you all right?"

Julie came to life. "Uh...I'm okay. I didn't expect you to invite us into your home. Is there enough room?"

"Believe me, I'm as surprised as you. And yes, there's lots of room. But if we're spending time together, you don't want to be driving back and forth from Halfmoon Bay each day. It makes sense we live together to see if this is going to work or not." Georgia prattled on in her nervousness. "Kaela finished her summer program yesterday, so the girls will have lots of time together. I'll probably have a hundred questions while the next fourteen days play out. And, if I agree to your wishes, you need to know you've made the right decision in choosing me. So what do you say?" She took in a deep breath and waited.

A long sigh escaped from deep inside Julie's chest. "Yes," she said decisively.

It was an emotional drive home to Gibsons. A dark and winding road that kept Georgia on her toes. *What am I thinking, extending an invitation without first discussing it with Kaela?*

She cast a quick glance at her daughter in her booster seat in the back."Honey? Are you awake?"

"Yup. Wasn't that fun today, Mommy? I really like Grandpa Frank and Uncle Bill."

"It certainly was and I'm glad you had fun. I want to discuss something with you about Julie and Shelby." She hesitated, knowing that Shelby wasn't aware of her mother's fatal disease, she had to be careful about what she said to Kaela. "Julie isn't well at the moment and she could use some help with Shelby. As good as Grandpa Frank and Uncle Bill are with Shelby, she could use someone her own age to play with."

"Shelby told me her Mommy is sick. She's really worried about her. Will she be okay?"

Georgia sucked in her breathe. "At the moment, she's fine. Honey, how would you feel about them staying with us for awhile?"

"Really? That'd be cool! Shelby and I can have sleepovers *every* night."

"That's right."

"When are they coming?"

"Tomorrow."

Kaela threw her arms over her head and pumped the air with her little fists. "Yay."

The next day their guests arrived at noon, with one suitcase each. Georgia took them down the hall to their rooms. "I moved Kaela into the guest bedroom so she and Shelby can share the double bed. I've moved into my grandmother's room and you can have Kaela's room with the twin bed. Her dresser is empty so you can unpack. So's the closet. The girls are using the tallboy in the guest room, so my things can stay in the dresser. That way I don't have to disturb Grammy's stuff."

"Thank you. We'll be more than comfortable. You're grandmother won't mind?"

"Absolutely not. She's in New Zealand at the moment and then off to Arizona for the winter."

Kaela grabbed hold of her sister's arm. "Let's go to our room, I'll help you unpack."

They watched the two girls head down the hall arm in arm.

"Thank you so much. I can't tell you what this means to me."

A slight choke could be heard in Julie's voice. Before things became awkward again, Georgia changed the subject. "Come with me and I'll show you the bathroom."

"Four women and one bathroom? This will be interesting." Julie quipped.

"I have an en suite with a shower in my room, so it'll work. And if the girls have the other one tied up, feel free to use the en suite."

In no time, they were settled in and the four of them sat in the kitchen eating a tuna salad Georgia had prepared earlier that morning.

"I thought after lunch we could go out and buy a few things. If you need anything, please say so. Are you on a special diet? We should make up a list of groceries."

"Okay. There are foods I need to avoid and yes, some foods I need to eat. How do you want to work this? I could buy my own food if you like or contribute for us both."

"Why don't you make up your list and we'll decide after I see if they are foods we all can eat."

"Sounds good. Then I need to go to the Pharmacy."

"Done."

The first week passed and the four of them fell into a routine. Julie's nausea disappeared and she seemed a little healthier. They spent the last days of summer visiting the beach, driving up the peninsula to tourist sites, and took the ferry to Powell River to attend the Jazz Festival. To the kids, it was one big vacation and they loved it and each other. Kaela called Julie Auntie J, and Shelby called Georgia Auntie G.

Life fell into place for the kids but not so for the mothers. And while the two women tried to keep their conversations light, their words often bumped into each other as they tried to avoid the pending decision looming ever so near.

Chapter 14

The start of the second week found Georgia alone for the day. Julie had gone to Vancouver. Grampa Frank accompanied her with the two girls. After dropping Julie off for a series of Doctor appointments, he planned to take the kids to a movie matinee.

She spent the morning reading snail mail from readers. Most of them sent emails through her blog site, but some still relied on the old fashioned mode of communication, using her agent's address, which were then forwarded to her. Sometimes she sent a reply if she felt it was warranted. Her attention to them was long overdue. One typed letter took her by surprise. Short and to the point, it left her with an uneasy feeling.

My Dearest Georgia,

You don't know me, but soon you will. You are the most beautiful woman I have ever seen. My admiration for your strength and intelligence makes my love for you grow stronger each day. One day when we are together, you will be my sweet Georgia Peach.

Until then.

All my love,

A Distant Admirer

Shivers ran down her spine and she shuddered. She would have chalked this up to a lonely man crushing on her, except for two lines in the letter. Georgia repeated them out loud. '*You don't know me, but soon you will*' and '*One day when we are together*'." The word ominous came to mind. A quick search through all the other letters confirmed this was the only one. She felt beside herself. "Dear God ... what should I do?"

She punched Trent's office number with trembling fingers. It seemed like an eternity before his secretary put him through.

"Hey Georgia, what's up?"

"Umm ... maybe I'm overreacting here. I'm a little freaked at the moment."

"I can hear it in your voice. What's the matter?"

She hesitated, feeling a little silly. "Have any of your clients ever had to deal with a stalker?"

"Uh ... an overzealous fan perhaps, an actual stalker ... no. What has you so tense?"

"I received a typed letter from a guy who signed as an admirer. It came through your office. The envelope is dated two months ago and it's pink. The stamp is from Nevada. No return address."

"Do you want to read it to me?"

She re-read the letter to Trent. This time her skin crawled. "It's the lines about soon you'll know me and one day when we are together that scares me. Not if, or I wish, or can we meet ... it's so decisive."

Trent let out a whistle. "Wow. I can see why you're upset. Look ... let me go through our latest batch and see if there are any more here. I'll call you right back."

Georgia paced the living room while she waited for Trent to call back. Finally the phone rang and she grabbed it on the first ring. "Trent?"

"It's me. Now stay calm. We have another letter here." he said.

Georgia gasped and her hand went to her heart.

"Before I go on, I called the Gibsons RCMP. They're sending an officer over to pick up your letter and I'm on the next boat over with this one. I'll be there shortly after two o'clock."

"I don't want to keep you from your work. I know this is a busy time for you."

"Don't be silly. Friends are there for friends or they aren't a friend. See you in a couple of hours."

Georgia held back and then asked the one question she really didn't want to ask.

"Trent? What does the second letter say?" She waited, dreading his reply.

"I haven't opened it. I put it in a baggie for the police. Oh ... which reminds me, put the letter and envelope you have in a plastic bag in case it has finger prints on it."

The dial tone echoed in her ear. Fearing the worse, numerous thoughts fired through her brain as to what the second letter might say. The mention of finger prints on the letter, hit home. *This is really happening.*

A couple of hours later, a police car pulled into the driveway and a young officer stepped out. Georgia watched him walk up to the door and before he could knock, opened it.

"Good afternoon. I'm Constable Denning. Are you Georgia Charles?"

"Yes, Constable. Please, come in." She led him into the living room and they both sat.

"I'd like to ask a few questions first; some background information about yourself if that's okay?"

"Certainly."

"How long have you lived here in Gibsons, Ms. Charles?"

"This is my grandmother's house and I've lived here off and on for five years. Do you know anything about me? I mean, my past?"

"If you mean about your ordeal five years ago when you were kidnapped and lost for the winter up north … yes. Mr. Matheson filled me in." A smile played at his mouth. "And my girl friend read your book and we saw the movie made about your experience."

"I've been travelling a lot the past four and half years, on book tours, talk shows, working on movie sets, etc. My daughter and I have spent time living with my parents in North Vancouver and staying here. My grandmother will be away travelling for about a year and I'm living here full-time so my daughter can start school."

"So it's the two of you in the house?"

"Yes … uh … no. I have guests staying with me at the moment."

"May I have their names?"

That question certainly made her feel uncomfortable. *He saw the movie; would he recognize the name?* "Julie Charles and her daughter Shelby."

"Relationship?"

Guess not. "She's my ex-husband's second wife."

Constable Denning looked up at her from his notes. His face didn't register what he might be thinking, but she felt sure he knew.

"His previous mistress?"

She nodded.

"I didn't realize you and she were …" he hesitated, "acquainted."

"My ex-husband recently passed from a sudden heart attack. Our daughters are half-sisters and are spending some time together." That was all she felt he needed to hear and left it at that.

"I see. So, the letter in question … is it the first one you've received?" he asked.

"Yes it is."

"May I see it please?"

"Of course." Georgia went to retrieve the letter and handed it to the officer with a shaky hand.

He retrieved plastic gloves from his jacket pocket and opened the baggie. Once the letter was read, Constable Denning wrote some notes and gave her his full attention. "Do you have any idea who this person may be?"

"Absolutely no idea. And it's post-marked Nevada. If that's where he lives, I don't know anyone in Nevada."

"So all your reader mail goes to your agent's office in North Vancouver and they forward it to you?"

"That's right."

"And how often does it come?"

Georgia rubbed her forehead. "I guess it depends on the volume. Probably a couple of times a month. But this batch sat here for a few weeks until I had some time to deal with it."

"Has there been any other contact, such as phone calls or unexpected gifts?"

"Nothing."

"Is it public knowledge that you live in Gibsons, Ms. Charles?"

Georgia had to think about that one. "Nothing is registered in my name since I've been staying with family." A frown creased her brow. "Having said that, I've had so many interviews over the past few years, I may have revealed that I was commuting back and forth from the Coast to North Van."

A knock at the door interrupted their meeting. Trent Matheson stood on the stoop when she opened the door.

"Trent, come in. Constable Denning is here."

They exchanged a hug and Georgia introduced the two men.

The officer continued with his questions. "Are the two addresses, your parents and your grandmother's, listed or unlisted, Ms. Charles?"

"Please, call me Georgia. They're listed."

The constable asked for the address and phone numbers of both homes and turned to Trent. "Mr. Matheson, do you have the second letter?"

"It's Trent, Officer." He handed him the letter which was inside a plastic freezer bag.

Officer Denning examined the second letter for what seemed like an eternity and wrote more notes. Georgia watched as he compared the notes and the envelopes.

"I think it's safe to say that he doesn't know exactly where you are at the moment. However, I must caution you, because of the references to being together, we can't assume anything. We need time to set up an investigation and process these letters. If he intends to live out what he suggests in the letters, he could pose a threat to your safety."

Chills ran up Georgia's spine. "And because my parents and grandmother are mentioned in the media, he only has to look them up and sooner or later he'll find me."

"If he's serious about finding you, it's probable. I think you need to take this seriously and be aware of your surroundings. Keep your doors and windows locked ... and look out the window first before you answer the door. You should also consider having someone stay with you until we sort this out."

"Would you read the second letter to me, please?"

The Constable and Trent exchanged looks.

"If I'm to take this seriously, I need to know what to expect."

He opened the letter carefully with gloved fingers, holding it up for her to read. It was on the same pink paper as the first.

My sweet Georgia Peach,

Our time together is nearer than I first thought possible. I never imagined I would be heading north to finally meet the woman of my dreams. We will be together soon, my love.

With a growing love,

A Closer Admirer

Georgia rose from the chair and walked to the window, staring blankly at the park across the street. Every bone in her body ached, and she felt chilled to the core.

Trent came up beside her and placed a hand on her shoulder. "Are you all right? Oh shit ... of course you aren't." She turned and he took her into his arms and held her while she shook.

A few minutes later, she was back in control and re-seated. She turned to Constable Denning. "So what's next?"

"Assuming he's planning to make contact at some point, keep a log of any phone calls, keep any voice messages or emails sent, any gifts delivered, log dates and times, pay attention to barking dogs, and if you notice anyone loitering in the park or outside your house, please report it to us at once."

Trent addressed him next. "Will your detachment handle this or will it go off coast?"

"We'll handle it on a local level, co-ordinate with the Integrated Unit on the mainland, as well as consult with our Criminal Investigative Analysis Services in Ottawa."

"So what will happen if you find out who he is?" Georgia asked.

"Well, we can't arrest him for sending you notes. But if you have a name, you can get a restraining order against him. We can check him out for any priors and have a chat with him to let him know we're watching him," Constable Denning said as he stood and handed two cards to Georgia. "One of these cards is mine. The file number is on the back of the card. The other one is for Victims Services. They'll be in touch with you tomorrow. I suggest you talk with them. They can offer resources and support to you and your family members."

As Trent and Georgia walked him to the door, he added, "One more thing, I suggest that you install a panic button to be on the safe side. Your address will be tagged in the computer so officers on patrol can keep an eye on your house and the park. Please don't hesitate to call if you have any questions or anything more to report. I'll be in touch."

Chapter 15

Trent headed to the kitchen and started a fresh pot of coffee. Georgia joined him at the counter on a stool.

"I'll stay here tonight, while we figure out something so you aren't alone here," Trent said, "or maybe you should come back to Vancouver with me and stay at your folks for a few days until you can find someone to stay with you."

"Nix to Vancouver … I don't want to worry my parents. This guy may be living a fantasy in his letters with no intention of ever coming here."

Trent stood, walked around the counter and placed his hands on her shoulders. "Now you listen here, that Constable told you to take this seriously. Yes, your parents will worry. But they need to know about this guy. Family and friends close to you need to know so they can keep an eye open for strangers hanging around their homes, searching for you."

"Oh God …" She put her hands over her face and shook her head. "You're right."

"That's better." He sat down again and spoke in a softer tone. "You have to think about who can stay here with you."

Georgia put her hands down and stared at Trent. *Time to tell him about Julie.* As she was about to speak the phone rang.

Trent stood and nodded towards the phone on her counter. "I'll leave you to your call. I need to check in at the office and my cell is in the car."

Stretching across the counter, she grabbed the receiver. "Hello?"

"Hello, stranger. Do you realize it's been ten days since we talked? I need to know what's happening down there, girlfriend."

A sardonic laugh that turned into another one of Georgia's infamous snorts echoed through the phone. "Hi, Marion. Got a few hours? What's not happening."

"Give it over then and don't leave out any details."

"Umm ... first, Julie and Shelby came over for dinner last week and all went well, albeit a little awkward. The kids act like they've been together their whole lives. Saturday we all had a barbeque at Frank's and Bill's ..."

"What? As in your ex-father-in-law Frank?"

"Uh ... yes, we had a wonderful time." Georgia was having a hard time focusing on the conversation. Her mind kept wandering back to her stalker and who in her life could be in danger.

"Georgia ... you still there?"

She pulled her thoughts back to Marion. "Frank was so good with his grand-daughters. You should have seen him. I decided that if I only had two weeks to make a decision about Shelby, we better all be together and not waste time. On Sunday they moved in with me and Kaela."

"Whoa! Back-up! Who are they?"

"Julie and Shelby."

"Excuse me? They moved in?"

Georgia couldn't help but grin. Under all the negativity, Marion could always be counted on to raise her spirits. She waited, while her best friend digested this newest information.

"Are you telling me that the two of them have been living with you a whole week and you never called and told me? Oh ... now I'm angry, no ... hurt." Marion had a real pout on.

"Look, it's been a really strange week for us all. I know I should have called but it was a spontaneous act on my part and I needed to be sure I'd done the right thing before telling anyone."

"Humph ... so did you do the right thing?"

Georgia hesitated. "In the beginning, yes. Now, maybe not."

"Why? What happened?"

"Nothing to do with them. It's ... well ... it gets even weirder."

"Oookay. Take your time." Marion sounded a little confused.

No wonder. Where do I start? Georgia composed her thoughts. "The RCMP just left ..."

"Oh, my God. What's going on down there?"

77

"It seems I have a stalker. So far he's sent two letters." Another long silence.

"Do you know who he is?" Her friend's voice, barely audible, had dropped a couple of octaves.

"Only that he may be from the States, and I'm his sweet Georgia Peach." she replied.

"Jesus, that's creepy. What are the cops doing about it?"

"They gave me a lot of advice about how to handle the situation and how to ensure my safety. They really don't have much to go on."

"I'm coming down to stay with you. You shouldn't be alone."

"Julie and Shelby are here. Where would you sleep?" Georgia realized something else in that moment. "Marion this puts things in a different light."

"How so?"

"Given what's going on in Julie's life right now, how can I ask them to remain here? How can I consider her request? I may be putting their safety at risk."

"I see your point."

Georgia placed her head on the marble counter. "Urrgh ... how did my life suddenly become so complicated?" she said with exasperation.

"I can come down you know. Maybe I can be of some help."

"No. As much as I'd love to see you, hold off until I figure out my situation with Julie. Trent is here right now. It's overwhelming but it's something I need to sort out on my own. Besides, we have no idea how long it will take to resolve this stalking situation. You can't put your life on hold babysitting me."

"I'll stay away for now but you promise to call me in a few days. I'm here for you and will be there in a heartbeat if you give the word. Okay?"

"Promise. Talk to you soon."

"One more thing." Marion said. "The police will take care of this. Count on it. So listen to what you said to me. You can't put your life on hold either. Don't let this stalker thing stand in the way of making the right decision where Shelby and Kaela are concerned."

"I'll think on that and thanks. Bye."

Georgia replaced the receiver and turned to find Trent leaning on the door-frame. "How much of that did you hear?"

"All of it."

She smiled at him. "Then pour us a cup of coffee and I'll explain why my ex-husband's widow and daughter are living here with me."

Twenty minutes later Trent knew the why of it. "You really are an incredibly strong woman."

Another snort. "Right about now I feel like a wet dishrag."

"Here's my summary of this whole mess," Trent began. "Julie's counting on a positive to her request regarding Shelby. You've been leaning towards a yes until this stalker thing turned up. She's, also, another adult who sounds like a strong woman, who at this point, isn't going to go away without an explanation."

"You're probably right there," Georgia said and squirmed on her stool.

"When they return from Vancouver, how about asking Frank to take the girls to his place tonight. You know he'll love it. I'm here until we sort something out. Your couch has my name on it. You and I will sit down with Julie, tell her what's happening, and ask for her take on this."

She let out a deep sigh. "It sounds like a plan but I hate to dump this on Julie right now. She doesn't need it."

"None of us needs it. But it's your reality for the moment and if Julie wants Shelby to be a part of your life, she'll deal with it. The cops may resolve this thing quickly anyway. Let's give them some credit here."

"That's what Marion said. Okay. Let's do it."

Georgia pulled Frank aside when they all arrived and explained the situation, while Trent amused the kids and Julie in the living room. Frank was more than happy to take the girls home with him, but not before he voiced his concerns for her safety.

"Trent is staying for a couple of days to help me secure the house. Then we'll see where we're at. With everything else that's going on right now, let's just take it a day at a time. I do appreciate your concern and I'm glad you're here for the kids."

"If you need me for anything, call me."

"I will. Let's keep this between us adults, Frank. I don't want the girls to know."

"Absolutely not."

After they left, Trent and Georgia sat with Julie.

They filled her in on the day's events and Georgia voiced her concerns for the safety of all of them.

Julie's reply was quite blunt. "Let's lay it out right here, I'm dying. This stalker doesn't scare me. My safety is quite irrelevant considering my circumstances. As for the girls, he isn't interested in them or me, it's you he wants. But if at some point we feel the girls aren't safe, we can send them to stay with Frank and Bill. The main thing here is to keep you surrounded with people and not give in to the fear."

"Are you sure? With what's on your plate right now, I hate to involve you in this."

"Absolutely. In a crazy way, it's nice to have something else to worry about besides myself."

The next day Trent arranged for motion lights to be installed on the front and back doors. Secret cameras were placed to cover the walkways, along with a panic button with an alarm system. Georgia and Julie met with the woman from Victim Services. The woman's caring and supportive manner made her feel that she wasn't alone.

Trent stayed for two days and finally said his goodbyes. He was needed at the office. As he turned to leave, Georgia had a sudden thought. "Did you notice the stamp on the second envelope?"

"It was also mailed from Nevada, but a town further north from the first letter. It was dated a week ago."

Her body turned icy cold. A feeling she felt a lot lately. "Promise me you won't tell Sean about this or about Julie." Trent hesitated. "Please Trent."

"Why?"

"My life is complicated enough right now. I can't deal with my relationship with Sean or lack of right now."

"Remember what Constable Denning said. Those around you should be aware. What if the stalker tries to use Sean to get close to you?"

Georgia let a long sigh. "But he isn't close to me right now. Can we just leave him out of it for the moment?"

"All right. I don't agree with it, but I promise to say nothing for the moment. But, if he gets wind of anything, I won't lie."

Frank brought the girls home and that night after Kaela and Shelby fell asleep, the two women sat in the living room.

"I don't mean to pry but I thought you and Sean were together. He hasn't been around and I heard what you said to Trent," Julie said.

"We broke up two months ago. Does that make a difference to you."?

Julie looked confused. "I don't understand."

Georgia wrapped her hair around her finger searching for the right words. "If I take Shelby in, I'll be a single mother of two, not a family unit with a mother and father."

"No, it changes nothing. Can I ask what happened?"

They were moving into uncomfortable territory and Georgia blushed which wasn't lost on Julie. "I'm sorry. I'm prying."

"Uh ... it seems I have a little problem with commitment. Sean wanted to move forward and I pushed him away." *Was she really saying this to Julie of all people?*

This time Julie blushed. "Of which I'm fifty percent responsible for this cause and effect." A silence fell between them.

"Yes, you are. Sorry, I know that sounded a little harsher than I intended. But how I deal with it is my responsibility not yours."

"I'm amazed you've tolerated me as much as you have. Along with your broken heart and an assholian stalker, you let me dump my problems on you and move into your life."

Julie rose and started to pace the room. "It's all so complicated, we're so complicated. Do you think you and I could ever be at ease with each other?"

Georgia knew the moment had arrived. Julie needed to hear her decision about Shelby.

"Sit down, I need to say something." The other woman looked like cold water had been thrown in her face. She sat.

"Perhaps if we eliminate some of the complications, things will improve between us. I've made my decision about Shelby."

Julie froze. "So soon? We still have until next week."

She's afraid of my answer, Georgia thought. "Actually, we don't. I had a call from the school today. They're having an open house tomorrow. They asked me to bring Kaela to school to meet with her kindergarten teacher. They want the kids to meet her in advance so they feel a little more at ease on the first day of school."

"Makes sense." Julie whispered, brreathlessly.

"They asked that Kaela be there at 1:00 p.m. I took the liberty of talking to the principal and explained our situation. We have to be there half an hour earlier to register Shelby before the kids meet their teacher."

Julie stared at her. "Dear God … I'd hoped, wished, told our Lawyer I'd make it happen … but deep down I wasn't sure at all." She tried to say more but choked on the words.

The nurturing side of Georgia took over. In a most natural way, she stood and reached out to Julie, holding her in a silent embrace. When they separated Georgia handed her the Kleenex box off the end table.

"I'll make us some tea."

A few minutes later, they settled once again in the living room with steaming cups.

"How did you ever decide with all that's been happening?" Julie asked.

"If it depended on me, I couldn't possibly have come to a decision. I think it was the girls that did it. Shelby's a wonderful child. The past twelve days they've been so close and so happy. They may look alike, but they have different personalities which seems to bring the best out in each of them. It's like they found a part of themselves in each other." Georgia paused, searching for the right words. "They don't see things as just black or white, the grey area comes naturally to them. They see life at face value."

"A great weight has been lifted off my shoulders." Julie closed her eyes and breathed deeply. "You told me we needed to live together so that I could be sure you're the right choice for my daughter's welfare. That's a definite yes."

"Thank you. All that I've done the past two weeks has been done spontaneously. I decided that I had to go with my gut feeling and run with it. However, we've eliminated one complication but added another. My family. I have no idea how they'll react to this turn of events."

Julie laughed nervously. "I see your point. I'm hopeful you'll bring them around."

"Me too."

Sipping her hot tea, Georgia remembered Julie's trip to the city. "Thinking of my family in Vancouver, a change of subject here. I never asked you how your doctor appointments went."

"With the effects of the chemo worn off, I'm feeling a lot better. However, things have progressed and the Doctors tell me to be prepared for the progression of new symptoms soon. I have had some additional symptoms which aren't obvious to anyone else yet. I need to decide my next step. Obviously, I will stay on the Coast, but arrangements need to be made. That's a whole other conversation but not for tonight. I want to savour the moment of knowing my child will be safe and well cared for."

"Fair enough. So what are your thoughts on how and what we tell the kids tomorrow when we take them to school?"

"Gosh, I never allowed myself to think that far ahead."

"I suggest we tell them you're staying indefinitely so I can help you take care of Shelby and that the girls will be going to school together. Again, let's take it a day at a time, one step at a time."

"Okay. Once the kids start school next week, you and I can discuss what's next."

"Sounds good."

That night Georgia experienced a recall of her recent dream about Kaela. This time Kaela was in the water being sucked into a vortex, while the other Kaela sat on the beach crying. She awoke with a start and realized she had cried out in her sleep. It became clear to her that it wasn't two Kaela's but Kaela and Shelby, only she couldn't tell who was who. *What did this mean?*

Chapter 16

People walking the aisles on the ferry swayed with the roll of the boat. It was now mid- September and the winds were early for this time of year. Several crossings were cancelled from Vancouver Mainland to Vancouver Island across the Georgia Straight waterway. However, the Sunshine Coast where Georgia lived was a peninsula cut off from the Mainland by the Coastal Mountains. Georgia was grateful for the protected waters between Gibsons and North Vancouver. The trip across this open stretch of water took only fifteen minutes of the forty minute voyage.

Georgia sat by the window of the ferry watching the huge waves and white water churn. She glanced up the channel towards Squamish where the gale force winds originated. They'd left the protected waters between Gambier and Bowen Islands. She wouldn't dare move until they passed through the open waterway of Howe Sound and into the relatively calm waters of Horseshoe Bay.

Her emotions were as turbulent as the sea. She was on her way to her parents' home to tell them of her decision to become Shelby's guardian. Their support was paramount. Her parents would have concerns for sure, but it was her visiting grandparents from Arizona that left her feeling unsettled. Especially, her grandfather. An old-schooled man whose army career had led him to the rank of General. A pussycat most of the time, but when challenged he played hardball and was very opinionated. The side of her grandfather who was used to controlling situations and men, while demanding their loyalty even if they didn't agree with his beliefs or decisions, was the man Georgia knew she'd be dealing with today.

A man balancing his way past her lurched close to where she was sitting and Georgia shifted to avoid contact with his body. He checked himself to keep from knocking her and spilled coffee on his jacket. "Dammit ..." he mumbled. He glanced at her in embarrassment, dropped his coffee into a trash can and continued his swayed walk towards the men's washroom.

An elderly woman sitting opposite her chuckled. "Serves him right. As if balancing a full cup of coffee wasn't hard enough in this squall, he couldn't stop staring at you. That's why he lost his balance you know. He wasn't paying attention."

Georgia stiffened. "Really? I hadn't noticed." Since she had found out about her stalker, every man that looked her way was suspect. *Better be more alert.*

Twenty minutes later, she followed the walk-on crowd to the passenger disembarkment area. She left the boat, exited the terminal, and made her way to the bus zone. She found a seat on a bus heading to Vancouver and sat by the window.

Scanning the crowd standing outside the bus, she locked eyes with the man from the ferry who'd spilled his coffee. A pretty, blonde girl a lot younger than him, had her arm linked through his. A young baby about ten months old satin a stroller in front of them. Georgia moved her gaze on to other people.

A young Eurasian woman hurried up the street. She went straight to the couple and the baby. The body language of the blonde girl changed. She stiffened, leaned down and kissed the baby on the cheek and backed away. The dark-haired woman said a couple of things to the man and coddled the baby, but ignored his companion. Georgia took another look at the baby; it was Eurasian as well. *The dark-haired woman is the mother of the baby.*

The mother's face contorted with anger. She leaned down and pulled a ribbon out of the baby's hair and stuffed it in her pocket. Georgia glanced at the blonde and saw the look of hurt on her face. The young girl crossed her arms across her chest and tears sprang to her eyes. The man seemed oblivious to the drama and tension between the women. He was too busy trying to grab the baby's attention with baby talk.

The mother said a couple of things to the man and turned towards Georgia's bus. Meanwhile, throughout this scene of hostility, the baby cooed with her father, innocent of the adult game being playing out between the two woman. The Eurasian woman entered the bus and two women stood to let her sit with the stroller beside her. She took a brush out of her purse and brushed the baby's hair. *An unconscious act that seals ownership of her child.*

Georgia turned her attention back to the couple outside the bus. The man gave one last wave to the baby and turned to walk away with his companion. He reached out for her hand, but the girl avoided contact and stuffed her hands in her pockets. He gave her a puzzled side glance but said nothing.

The whole thing bothered her. It reinforced the idea that children are innocent. They don't ask to be brought into this world only to be used as pawns between warring parents. *How long will it be before this child is affected by the emotions and insecurities of her parents?*

She felt saddened and thought of her own situation. *At least there will be no issues of clashing parents. Only an indignant and possessive grandmother. And what about Sean?* She knew he loved Kaela, but what about Shelby? Georgia gave her head a shake. *Why am I thinking about Sean? He's not even in the picture.*

"What? Are you crazy?"

Georgia watched the vein in her grandfather's forehead bulge and turn purple. Something she'd seen many times over the years. "No, Granddad. I'm quite sane."

"Why would you even consider such a thing? Life as a single-mother of one must be difficult enough. Now you want to add another?"

She glanced at her mother who sat quietly with her Nan. Her paternal grandparents were visiting from Arizona. They'd be heading home soon to meet up with Georgia's widowed maternal grandmother who was still in New Zealand. Her grandfather hated the fact that she was raising a child alone. She'd already been through the explanations with her father a short time ago but he was easier to mold to her way of thinking.

"My decision hasn't come lightly. A lot of thought went into this."

"Have you thought about Kaela and how she might feel?" her grandfather asked.

This question angered her. "Of course I have. She was my first consideration. It could be a good thing for both girls. They're sisters."

"Sisters!" He spat the word out. "It's not ... normal."

Georgia smiled. "Oh Granddad, what does that mean?"

"They weren't raised in the same house. They don't know each other as sisters ... do they?"

"Yes they do, and I admit these aren't normal circumstances."

He turned to her grandmother. "Do you agree this whole idea is preposterous?"

Before her Nan could answer, Georgia interjected. "That's not what I said."

Her granddad pursed his lips and stared hard at her. "I don't understand it. This woman is a tramp. She stole your husband. Let the Charles family take care of her kid."

"Alice Charles isn't capable of coping with Shelby's needs any more than pigs can fly. I won't see that poor child sent off to boarding school like her father and aunt were. Even Frank agrees with me on this."

Granddad sighed. "And what about Sean?"

There it was. She knew Sean would be brought into the conversation and she wasn't going to explain the complications in their relationship with him or anyone else. "This has nothing to with Sean. It's my decision."

"You're being selfish," Granddad barked. "The man loves you and Kaela. A love that happened over time naturally and Kaela's a part of you. But this ... how can you expect him to accept another one of Colin's kids?"

Georgia cringed. She knew her grandfather would be difficult, but she was growing tired of his opposition. "I'm not asking anything of him. We took some time apart awhile back. I'm not sure we have a future, but if we do, it's his choice. If he wants me, the girls come with me."

Granddad jumped up in a fit of temper. "From what I hear you pushed him away. Now you're widening the gap."

Georgia glanced at her mother in time to see her jaw set. Sandra Carr, stood and snapped at her father. "Dad, you're overstepping your bounds."

He ignored her. "You should have been grateful the man accepted another man's kid, but to expect he'll accept Colin's second child is naive."

Georgia bolted from her chair and stormed across the room until they were face to face. Her breath came in quick spurts and she shook with anger. "Shelby is an innocent here. She didn't choose the circumstances of her birth. And if Sean thinks like you, I wouldn't want him in my life as a mate or a father to my kids."

Her mother quickly stood between them. "I think you both need to calm down."

"Sandra, she's throwing her life away on a bastard child."

"I'm going to pretend I didn't hear that come out of the mouth of my father-in-law."

Granddad took pause and calmed himself. "I thought my granddaughter had more sense.

Where do you and Robert stand in this?"

"We've expressed our concerns, but it's Georgia's decision and we'll support her."

He ran his hands through his hair, and muttered to himself.

"You're determined to go ahead with this folly?"

Georgia raised her chin and straightened her shoulders. "I am."

"Then hear me now and I'll not mention it again." He spoke each word slowly with conviction. "I don't like it. I don't understand it and I'll have nothing to do with the child."

Her mother cried out softly. "Oh, Dad." Her Nan stared at the floor in distress.

Tears stung at Georgia's eyes. She stood and swallowed hard to control her urge to cry.

"In that case, it saddens me to find out what a judgemental, narrow-minded old fool you've become … or maybe you always were," Georgia said and left the room with her head held high. In the guest room, she sat on the edge of the bed and stared at the floor. She'd never talked like that to anyone in her family, but his words had hurt her. Her chest tightened. Her relationship with her grandfather would never be the same.

A few minutes later her mother came in and sat on the bed. "Are you alright?"

"I'm sorry, Mom. I knew he'd be difficult. I shouldn't have lost my temper."

Her mother laughed. "Guess who you inherited your temper from?"

Georgia gave her mother a weak smile, but she didn't feel jovial. "How could he say such mean things?"

"I'm disappointed in my father-in-law at the moment. You're Dad will be too. Please don't take it to heart."

"How can I not? I've had my own doubts about whether this is the right thing to do and I've made my decision to adopt Shelby. As of right now, we're a family. He needs to forget his stupid rules and see what this means to me."

"Give him some space and time, dear."

"What if he never accepts her?"

Her mother placed a hand under her chin and turned her face towards hers. "We can't always make people see things the way we want them to and that includes family members. If he doesn't come to accept Shelby, it will be his loss."

She gave her mother a hug. "It hurts that he thinks I'm being stupid." *All kids, even adult ones, want the approval of their parents and grandparents.*

"Try to remember that what other people think of you isn't your business. You learned that lesson from some of the publicity that surfaced from your ordeal five years ago."

"Okay, but it hurts when it's in your own family."

"True, but I bet Granddad is feeling bad about this right now, except he's too stubborn to admit it. I don't agree with his position on this, maybe it came from his fear of you and Kaela being hurt more than you already have been."

"You may be right."

The time had come for Georgia to tell her mother about the other reason for her visit. "We need to discuss something else that's going on in my life." Her mother listened as she told her about her stalker and the ongoing police investigation. She answered all of her questions as best she could.

"Now this worries me. You can't be alone."

"At the moment I'm not. Julie and Shelby are staying with us. Although we haven't worked out all the details about that. We plan to discuss it when I return home."

"That's something I guess. If it were only the two of you, I'd insist you move back home for the time being."

"Mom, I have to put roots down somewhere and I chose Gibsons. Kaela has started school and she needs some stability. Now Shelby is a part of all of this and most definitely, she's going to need the same. Moving back here isn't an option. As I've said before, we have no idea how long this stalker thing will drag on. I need to move forward with my life."

Her mother wrung her hands together. "This is going to upset your father. Let me know what you work out with Julie. If you find yourself alone, I don't care if it's only for the day, call me. I'll come over and stay with you. Promise me now."

"I promise. How about you and I go shopping. We need some retail therapy." She tried humour to try and lift the veil of negativity that prevailed.

Her mother smiled. "And you know we both enjoy that."

They stood and embraced for a long moment before heading towards the hallway, seeking out her grandmother to say goodbye while avoiding her grandfather.

Before returning to Gibsons, she decided to visit Trent at the office. She wanted to fill him in on her decision to adopt Shelby. She entered his assistant's office as he opened the door and stepped out with another man.

"Georgia, what a surprise." Trent said. They hugged and he introduced her to his companion. "This is Jim Draper. Jim … Georgia Charles."

Georgia found herself shaking hands with a tall, boyishly handsome man.

"My pleasure, Ms. Charles. Trent and I were talking about you. I'm so pleased to meet you."

"Jim is a freelancer. He's writing a story on the changing world of publishing and the future role of literary agents in the new world of digital technology."

"A timely and controversial subject," Georgia added.

"I, also, want to obtain the viewpoint of some of Trent's client's, including you, Ms. Charles. But, Trent informs me that you aren't giving interviews at the moment."

"That's right. I'm on hiatus from my celebrity at the moment, Mr. Draper. Perhaps another time," she said.

"Well, I'm disappointed to say the least, but I understand. Trent, I'll wait for your call regarding the interviews with some of your other authors." He turned to Georgia. "Goodbye, Ms. Charles."

Georgia nodded. He was a charmer with piercing blue eyes, but she dismissed him from her mind. What with her confusion over Sean, her grandfather's recent behaviour, and her unknown stalker, men were the least of things she wanted to deal with in her life at the moment. She entered Trent's office and waited while he walked his visitor to the elevator.

Chapter 17

"I want you to consider what it will mean to the household as my symptoms progress." Julie said. She and Georgia had gone for a walk and were now sitting in the park across from the house. The girls were still in school. "You need to understand the changes you're seeing in me. For those reasons, perhaps I should move into hospice."

The relationship between the two women had grown closer since Georgia announced her intention to adopt Shelby. Their past history had no meaning now and the awkwardness had all but disappeared. All Georgia could see was a woman and a mother who was struggling with the inevitability of her demise. Their past seemed so petty when faced with the reality of life and death. It was a lesson she'd learned when faced with her own struggle to survive five years ago, and now she was seeing Julie face the same battle. Except they both knew the outcome was ordained and nothing would change the eventuality of Julie's demise.

Georgia also began to understand Julie's concerns. Her balance issues were apparent and she'd progressed to walking with a cane. Her headaches increased despite Julie's taking steroids to keep her brain from swelling. "I know you'll need specialized care. I think you should stay here with me and the girls. We can have a care aide come in to help and a nurse."

Julie shook her head. "Oh, Georgia, it was never my intention for you to be my caregiver. This was all about Shelby's future welfare."

"Isn't keeping you and Shelby together as long as possible part of her well-being?" Georgia stared at Julie with expectation. "Besides, you haven't anywhere else to stay. Frank's place is too far away from amenities.

"True, but before you commit yourself, would you come to my next round of appointments? I want the specialists to explain to you what to expect. Then you can decide."

"Absolutely. It's in both our best interests for me to know all I can. I wouldn't be of any use to you otherwise." Georgia stared across at the house, visualizing its accessibility as a care home and what medical equipment they might need to bring in.

"When I was diagnosed terminal, my doctor team brought in a social worker and a Palliative Care Co-ordinator from Vancouver Hospice. Vancouver and the Sunshine Coast are both under Coastal Health Authority. Since I've decided to stay on here, they transferred my file to Sechelt Coast Hospice. A new co-ordinator and social worker will be calling to arrange a house visit."

"I've heard a lot of good things about our local hospice. You'll have a strong support group around you."

"It's so important to me to keep things as normal as possible for Shelby. But, you must promise me that once I become bedridden, and it's only a matter of time, you'll move me to hospice care."

Georgia stood and paced in front of Julie. "You don't need to go into hospice when you have a caregiver and lots of outside support coming in. Wouldn't you rather be in the comfort of your own bedroom with all of us around you?"

Julie stiffened. "No ... not at the end. And I don't want Shelby anywhere near me when the end comes. Promise me you'll keep her away."

Georgia was shocked. "But ... "

"Promise me or I'll leave your house today," she said, firmly so there was no room to argue the point.

Intuitively Georgia knew this sudden behavior change was due to her illness, but she was shocked at how it had come on so quickly. Julie stood and headed across the street to the house. Once they were inside, she disappeared into her bedroom until dinnertime. Georgia left to pick up the girls from school and told them Julie was napping. The three of them stayed in the kitchen baking cookies.

At dinner, Kaela and Shelby kept them amused with stories from school, alleviating the need for the two women to interact. Later that night Julie approached her as she was making the kids lunches for school. "I'm sorry I snapped at you. It was unfair of me."

"That's okay. I'm sorry if I upset you." Georgia wrapped the sandwiches and packed up fruit, juice and a couple of the freshly baked cookies, placing each lunch in the refrigerator for the morning.

Julie sat at the counter. "I want Shelby to remember me as I was before my illness. I don't want her last memories of me to be of a dying woman. And the reason I want to go to hospice at the end is because I want her to have good memories in this house. Each time she walks past that bedroom, I don't want her to think her mother died in there."

"I understand. If you want to go to hospice at a certain point, I'll see that it's done. But she already knows you're sick. Soon she'll notice the symptoms and we'll have to tell her the eventual outcome. That memory will always be there. If you shut her out at the end, she'll feel abandoned and she won't understand why she can't be with you."

Julie looked crushed and started to chew on her nails. Georgia took a deep breath and continued. "The truth is Shelby will want to be there for you. It's all she has to offer you." She sat down and took Julie's hand away from her mouth and squeezed it hard. "Don't take that away from your daughter."

"I'll think on it. Time for me to turn in for the night."

Georgia watched Julie balance on her cane as she walked across the floor. "Julie? When it's over, I need to be able to tell Shelby that she was of great comfort to her mother at the end."

The other woman stopped, but didn't turn. Her head dropped and came back up again. She continued towards the hallway but before she left the kitchen she said over her shoulder, "You really are the best caregiver. Good night."

The next week, the Palliative Care Co-ordinator from the Coast Hospice paid them a visit. Cara Timmons was a soft-spoken, mild-mannered woman in her fifties. In a matter of minutes, Georgia felt at ease with her. As they settled into the living room, Cara's cell phone rang. The woman stared at the call display.

"I'm sorry but I must take this call." She clicked on the phone and said hello. She stood and mouthed the word "sorry" and walked into the hallway, talking softly into the phone. Georgia turned to Julie who sat beside her on the couch. Julie was staring at a pamphlet in her hands about the Hospice and Georgia followed her stare. She read the inscription centered in a rectangular box on the paper.

The mission of the Hospice Society, a community-based, non-profit organization, is to provide support and advocacy and respect the dignity of those in our Coast community who are coping with grief, bereavement and their end-of-life.

Georgia reached out and took Julie's hand in hers. "Are you okay?"

Julie squeezed her hand and gave her thin smile. "Fine."

Cara Timmons returned and sat down. "I'm so sorry. There won't be any more interruptions." She looked from one woman to the other with her eyes settling on Julie. First, I have a few questions if you don't mind answering them."

Julie gave her a smile. "Not at all. Ask away."

"Your Vancouver doctors and the Hospice you were dealing with have forwarded your paperwork to us. On your paperwork, you state that you're a widow and have no family here except your daughter and father-in-law. However, you've listed Georgia as your caregiver and your first contact, currently and after you reside in Hospice. Can I ask what the relationship is between you?"

"Georgia has become my best friend ... and I consider her family." Julie grabbed Georgia's hand and squeezed it.

"We are related in a way. Our daughters are half-sisters," Georgia said.

Georgia watched as Cara digested this information. One eyebrow rose slightly; the only indication of the woman's curiosity.

Julie freed her hand from Georgia's and leaned forward. "Same father ..." she pointed at Georgia and then at herself, "... different mothers."

It was as though a light bulb came on over Cara's head. She leaned forward "You're the woman who spent the winter lost up north and gave birth alone in a cabin." She stared at Georgia in awe.

"Yes, that's me."

Cara turned back to Julie. "And I'm the other woman...at that time. After Georgia's divorce, Colin and I married."

Cara looked a little embarrassed. "I'm sorry. It's really none of my business. However, if Georgia is going to be your caregiver and support you, we need to know how much she understands you, not only your needs, but your wants as you near your end of life."

Julie sat back in her chair and folded her hands in her lap. "Please, don't be uncomfortable. I sought her out because of our daughters. After my husband passed suddenly four months ago, Shelby's grandparents on her father's side divorced and neither of them are able to deal with what's happening to me or are in a position to take on my daughter. Seeing how Georgia's daughter, Kaela, is my daughter's only other relative, I believed it was only right the girls should be together."

Georgia took over the conversation. "Given the circumstances, we've had to fast track our relationship. Once we saw that the girls want to be together, we knew we had to be completely honest with each other about all things past, current, and future for their sake."

Julie interjected. "Georgia has legal custody of Shelby and after..." Julie hesitated as her voice caught, "... later on she will start the adoption process.

Cara sat quiet, listening to the women tell their story and as she did so, Georgia wondered what was going through her mind. "Shelby is a beautiful child and I'm very fond of her. All of this has happened so fast but Julie and I know what we're doing is right and our daughters will both benefit from this."

The woman opposite them smiled. "I can see your commitment, Georgia, and that you genuinely care about Julie and Shelby. That's all I need to know. A social worker will be paying you a visit as well. I know she has a copy of the custody papers and she'll work with you and your lawyer over Shelby's adoption and see that the transition is an easy one for Shelby and for you."

"Next question?" Julie asked, giving Cara a big smile.

"I need to know your preferences when you are coming close to end of life. At what point do you wish to enter Hospice or would you prefer to stay in the comfort of Georgia's home with a support team of home care nurses and care aides?"

"I've recently moved into Georgia's home. It's been good for the girls and Georgia has been wonderful. But, her place is the future home for my daughter. Shelby is comfortable here and she's building memories of the good times the four of us have shared. I don't want her to remember my passing in this house. We don't know how much time I have left. The symptoms are coming on faster now. When I reach the point of being bedridden and drugged for pain, I want to go into Hospice. Does that make sense?"

"Absolutely."

Cara explained how the home care visits would work and the role Georgia would play in Julie's care. Georgia gave Cara a tour of the house for assessment and was given a list of medical equipment that would be necessary for home care and a referral form to obtain the necessary items.

"Would it be possible for me to have a tour of the rooms at Hospice?" Julie asked.

"It's very possible. Tomorrow would be a good time as the rooms are empty at the moment."

They walked Cara to the door. "How about ten o'clock?" she asked.

Julie looked at Georgia for confirmation. "Perfect," Georgia replied.

The next morning, they arrived at the Hospice housed at the Shorncliffe Care Facility in Sechelt. Julie had progressed from a cane to a walker. Georgia and Cara trailed along behind Julie and an assistant, Linda. There were two private rooms, each with a private bathroom. One half of each bedroom housed a small sitting room with a couch and television. A hospital bed and a reclining chair with a bedside table took up the opposite end. The two bedrooms shared a common living room set between them for family and friends, affording them some quiet time. The common room and the bedrooms had sliding glass doors that opened onto a private courtyard surrounded with lush trees and flowering shrubs.

"The setting outside the rooms is beautiful and so peaceful," Georgia said.

Cara put a hand on Georgia's arm, holding her back as Julie and Linda stepped out into the courtyard. When they were out of hearing she faced Georgia.

"I have the utmost respect for what you're doing for Julie but not everyone is cut out to be a caregiver. If you haven't been through something like this before there's nothing to prepare you when the end comes."

"You know, when I was lost at the cabin, I was forced to face my mortality and that of my daughter's. I found the strength to do what I had to do and I know I can be strong for Julie. The only difference is we know she's going to die. There's no battle to fight here, only to accept." Georgia said.

"I don't doubt your strength but you must be prepared for the changes you'll see in her and you must pace yourself or you'll get burned out."

"I met her doctors in Vancouver a couple of days ago. They prepared me for what's to come. Her symptoms are increasing daily. And I'm sure that you and your staff can help educate me as we move through the various stages."

"Absolutely. I want you know that I think you are a brave woman."

"No, Julie's the brave one."

Cara smiled. "Let's join them in the garden, shall we?" She opened the sliding door.

A cool October breeze caused a swift intake of breath and sent a chill through Georgia.

Chapter 18

Alice Brownlee-Charles sat up straight in her chair and thrust out her chin. "What do you mean you can't represent me? You've represented the Brownlee family affairs for three generations."

Derek Connors took in a deep breath and let it out slowly before he replied. "Yes, I have. Before Colin passed away and you and Frank were still together, I represented the family as a whole. However, when Colin made me executor of his estate and trustee of his daughters' trust funds, my obligations changed. The family dynamics have changed."

"Frank has nothing to do with this. He's not a Brownlee. I don't understand this. Explain!" Alice frowned and tapped her fingernails on the arms of the chair.

"Indirectly he does. I don't represent Frank any longer as you know. But I do represent Colin's widow, Julie. She commissioned me to draw up her final will and testament. As Shelby's trustee, she felt I should also represent her daughter's guardianship and eventual adoption."

"Adoption?" Alice shouted. She jumped up and leaned across the desk. "What does that mean?"

Derek stared back at the irate woman before him, her eyes blazing and her face reddened with anger. He maintained his manner and spoke in a quiet but firm voice. "Sit down, Alice, or this conversation is over." He watched her stare back at him, her nostrils flaring, and her brow furrowed. As quickly as she'd exploded, her control came back. Her facial expression relaxed and the taut muscles smoothed out. She sat back down and looked into her lap, smoothing out the folds in her suit skirt. When she looked up at him, her eyes were expressionless. "Now ... where were we?" she asked in a voice as smooth as silk. "Aw, yes—the *adoption.*"

"The conditions of the papers state that Georgia has guardianship of Shelby during Julie's illness ..."

"I'm well aware of that."

"Let me continue. It is her wish that after her death, Georgia apply to the court for adoption and full custody of Shelby."

"That is the most ridiculous thing I've ever heard. Whoever heard of an ex-mistress giving her child to the ex-wife.? And why would Georgia agree?"

"As lawyer for the mother and the child, I'm not in a position to debate this with you. I'm sorry. This places me in an awkward position and I suggest you find another firm to represent your interests."

He watched Alice's body stiffen again. She pursed her lips and stared hard at him. "Well Julie can't be of sound mind. Georgia isn't even family." Alice rose and put on her coat. "And what does Frank have to do with all of this?"

Derek rose from his chair, standing tall. It put him in a power position. "Should you decide to fight this in court, Frank will be one of many who will stand as a character witness for Georgia and as a supporter of Julie's last wishes."

As she fumbled with the buttons on her coat, Alice's eyes narrowed and she spoke in slow, deliberate phrases. "I *will* fight this. I'll also tell all my friends how your firm betrayed my family name."

"This isn't personal Alice. It's not about you or me but a little girl and what's best for her. The truth is I have represented all members of the family for years. It's not my fault the family has split apart. I must meet my obligations to Colin's estate and his daughter's trust funds first and foremost. I'm sorry."

"Do believe that I have friends in high places. Your firm may not be so proud of you and your principles when I'm done." Alice gave him a haughty smile.

"You obviously haven't been reading the papers. I am the firm, Alice."

Alice stared long and hard and without a word turned her back on him.

Derek watched her move across the room, her holier than thou attitude enhanced by the straightness of her shoulders, the toss of her head, down to the exaggerated sway of her bottom and hips. As she approached the door and opened it, his eyes watched that sway, envisioning his foot making contact with her buttocks at the right moment and kicking her out the door into the outer office, to the surprise of his legal assistant.

Alice moved through the doorway, throwing a last look over her shoulder. As she disappeared from sight, he caught a slight look of confusion, caused no doubt by the amused smile on his face. She was the last of the Brownlee family and he wouldn't miss representing her.

Chapter 19

The girls skipped down the street, giggling and shoving each other, as Georgia followed them from the school to home. Her heart hung heavy. Halloween had passed and the girls had dressed in identical princess costumes. They insisted on identical haircuts, and loved confusing the kids at school. She knew when they reached the house, the fun times would end. Today had been a bad day for Julie. There had been more than a few the past week. Neurological symptoms appeared. Julie developed double vision and her eyelids drooped. This morning she'd been unable to keep her balance even with the walker which meant she needed a wheel chair now. Georgia managed to help her into the bathroom but Julie chose to stay in bed the rest of the day, lapsing into a depression. Soon she'd be confined to the bed. It was time to tell the girls the truth about Julie's illness.

The girls reached the front door as she headed to the stoop. "Mommy, someone sent flowers." Kaela chirped. Georgia came out of her private thoughts and stared at the basket of flowers leaning against the door. Then she noticed the pink letter stuck in the side. "Uh . . . " She gasped and her hands flew to her chest. She unlocked the door and shooed the girls inside. "Who sent them, Mommy?"

"I ordered them for Julie, sweetheart."

It took her less than ten minutes to walk to the school, meet the girls, and walk home. The flowers weren't here when she'd left to pick up the kids. She took a Kleenex out of her pocket and picked the basket up. She glanced up and down the street and over at the park. There were no strangers about, only parents and their kids walking by or playing in the park.

Georgia rushed into the house, slammed the door and locked the bolt. Anger and fear filled her to the core. She hurried down the hallway. The girls were in their room setting up a board game. Continuing past their door and into her bedroom, Georgia placed the basket on her dresser. She sat in the window seat and stared blankly into the garden. *He found me. How? And how dare he? Not today of all days.*

Twenty minutes later she remembered Julie. She should have called the police right away but Georgia chose to wait. There was a more important issue at hand to deal with.

She joined Julie in her room with two cups of tea. She helped her sit up and they sat together in silence sipping the hot liquid.

"It's been two and half months since the doctors told me I had three to four months. We must be realistic. The symptoms are coming on faster now. I don't think I'll make four months." Julie hesitated. "It's time to contact the hospice."

Georgia put her tea down. "I talked to them after lunch. Tomorrow the nurse will come and do an evaluation, and the care aides will start as well. I also slipped out while you were sleeping and picked up the wheelchair and portable toilet."

"Thank you." Julie played with the end of the blanket.

Georgia looked at Julie apprehensively, then cleared her throat before speaking. "I think it's time to tell the girls."

Julie sucked in air. "No," she shouted.

Georgia braced herself. "Yesterday, Kaela asked me if you were becoming sicker. The girls have noticed you're weaker and are sleeping more."

"I'm sorry for nipping at you. I panicked. Oh God . . . I've been dreading this."

Georgia reached out and took Julie's hand. "I know. But now that they're starting to ask questions we can't lie to them. Besides, your physical symptoms are too apparent now."

Julie put her other hand to her forehead. "I think you're right. Would you bring them in? Will you stay with me? Maybe I'm a coward, but I don't think I could do it without you here."

"It's not cowardly to ask for support. We can handle their questions together."

It was the hardest thing Georgia had ever watched. Watching Julie's pain and struggle to find the right words to tell Shelby she was dying, and knowing there was nothing she could do to change it. It tore her apart. She felt so helpless as she sat in the armchair by the bed with Kaela on her lap. All she could do at that moment was stroke Kaela's hair and be ready to comfort both girls when the moment came.

Shelby sat on the bed facing her mother. Julie held her hand and explained her illness. She told her about the symptoms and what caused them. Shelby's eyes never left her mother's face and she never uttered a word. She sat frozen to the spot holding her mother's hand.

"Honey, I'm not going to get well. I'm becoming bedridden and as the tumour grows and causes more pressure … well … I … " Julie stopped and looked at Georgia. Her eyes pleaded with her for help. A lump formed in Georgia's throat and tears filled her eyes. With a deep breath, she kept control and forced herself to smile. She nodded to Julie and spoke in a whisper. "It's okay. Go on."

Julie turned back to Shelby. "I'm going to die, Shelby." Mother and daughter stared at each other in silence, eyes locked once more. Georgia could see Shelby was trying to grasp the words and understand them. "What does that mean, Mommy?"

"It means my soul will leave my body and go to the other side. I'll be with my Mom and Dad, my Auntie who raised me, and with your Daddy."

Tears formed and fell onto the child's cheeks. "But that means I won't see you anymore. Don't die, Mommy. I don't want you to go." Julie reached out and Shelby fell into her arms sobbing.

Kaela started to shake and looked up at Georgia. "I don't want Auntie J to die, Mommy." Georgia folded her into her arms and rocked her back and forth as the child collapsed into tears.

"Why can't I go with you?" Shelby asked her mother.

Georgia looked up to see Julie push Shelby's head back and look at her. She used her fingers to brush her daughter's hair away from her eyes. "Because you're young and healthy and have your whole life ahead of you to live. My body is sick and I have to leave it behind." The tears poured from all four of them and continued until they had no more to give.

Shelby sat up beside her mother. "But what will happen to me? Where will I live?"

"You're going to stay right here with Auntie G and your sister."

Shelby laid down beside her mother and put an arm across her. Julie closed her eyes and held her daughter tight. Georgia nudged Kaela and whispered in her ear. "Come on, sweetheart. Let's give them some time together." The two of them left the room and Georgia closed the door. That night Kaela slept with her mother and Shelby cuddled in the twin bed with Julie.

The next morning, Georgia asked Frank if he would take the girls for the day. It was better for them to stay in routine, at least until Julie went into hospice, but tomorrow would be soon enough for them to return to school. Georgia assured Shelby that her mother wasn't going to leave her this soon.

Frank and the girls left moments before the nurse arrived with one of the caregivers. They spent an hour with her and Julie explaining the care they would provide and co-ordinating their times so Georgia could leave to deliver and pick-up the kids, grocery shop, and have some down time.

It was almost lunch time when Georgia finally called the police regarding the flowers left by her stalker. Her skin crawled as she went to the dresser and retrieved Constable Denning's business card. Inside of twenty minutes, Constable Denning sat in her living room. She'd turned the flowers and card over to him.

He examined the card on the flower basket and the pink letter. He looked at her with a serious look and when he spoke, his tone was firm. "Why didn't you call us right away when you found these on your doorstep?"

"Something important needed to be taken care of at the time."

"More important than your safety?"

I deserve that. I need to fill him in on my state of affairs. "The last time you were here, I explained that my ex-husband's second wife and daughter were visiting. What you don't know is that Julie is terminally ill. She's mostly confined to her bed down the hall. Yesterday we had to tell our daughters that Julie has an inoperable brain tumour and that shortly she will go into hospice. The stalker was only one of the major things on my mind. I intended on calling you after we told them, but dealing with two hysterical five-year-olds took priority."

Constable Denning's demeanor softened. "I'm so sorry. Discussing death with a child is never easy. Where are the girls now?"

"With their grandfather for the day. I didn't want them here when you arrived and didn't have the heart to make them go to school today."

"Understandable."

"I have legal custody of Shelby and intend to adopt her per Julie's wishes."

"Impressive, given the history," he noted.

"Death has a way of putting things into perspective, especially the past."

"I respect your integrity, Georgia. Still, had we known yesterday your stalker was in the area, we could have done a sweep right away. But what's done is done. Since we do know he's been in the area, we'll step up our patrols along your street, especially at night. We'll also talk to the other residents on this block to see if they saw anyone delivering flowers. Trent informed us that you installed hidden cameras to cover the walkways. I'd like to retrieve the memory cards for both."

Georgia blushed. "I'd forgotten all about the cameras. Of course." She showed him where the cameras were and gave him new cards to install.

"We'll move on this right away. By the way, we didn't lift any prints off the last two letters. Maybe we'll have more luck with this card since it hasn't been through the mail system."

"Constable ..." Georgia hesitated a moment, then continued. "Will you tell me what the letter says, please?"

The constable looked uncomfortable but read it to her.

My Dearest Georgia Peach,

I cannot believe I've found you at last. Although, it was not as hard as I first anticipated. In fact, you practically fell into my lap. Prepare yourself my love, our time together will come soon.

All my love,

Your ever closer Admirer.

p.s. You are even more beautiful in the flesh than in your pictures.

Georgia's skin crawled. "Bastard." *That cryptic P.S. is meant to freak me out and it's worked.*

"Take extra precautions with doors and windows and be aware of those around you."

"Thank you for coming so quickly and next time I'll call right away." She saw him out the door and made sure the bolt was locked. She vowed to be careful now she knew the creep was in town, but she had far more important things to worry about. She headed down the hall to check on Julie.

The days wore on and Julie spent most days sleeping. She was having trouble swallowing now and Georgia spoon fed her soft foods. The nurse came in every second day. Julie was on a catheter now. The caregivers were in daily, and helped by giving Julie a bath. Georgia had no problem doing it but left it to them, allowing Julie to retain some dignity.

"Aren't you the lucky one today, chicken broth and chocolate pudding. I love anything chocolate." Georgia gave her the last of the pudding and wiped her mouth with a flair.

Julie smiled. She talked slower, in clipped short sentences and slurred words. "Me too. Ish nurse coming today?"

"Yes, in about an hour. How would you like me to wash your hair and blow it dry for you?"

"Love it. Never know who you might meet in bed these days." The two women laughed. Julie still had her sense of humour.

Georgia had devised a method of dry shampoo. She mixed baby powder with cornstarch, put it into Julie's hair and brushed it out. Then she dampened her hair and blew it dry. It eliminated the stringy, greasy look , while the blow dry gave it back some body, and her hair smelled good to boot.

"Thanks. Ish nurse coming today?" Julie slurred.

"Yup, should be here any minute." Georgia noted that Julie had been experiencing memory loss. Forgetting that she'd already asked about the nurse coming was another example and marked the progression of her illness.

Shortly after that, the nurse arrived. She examined Julie and joined Georgia in the living room. "How's she eating?"

"Not a lot, her swallowing is worse. I've noticed a slight rasp in her breathing."

"Any coughing or trying to clear her throat?"

"Not yet. The Dilantin seems to have the seizures under control but her memory loss has increased."

"How's her pain level?"

"Unchanged."

"Good. I want you to watch her breathing. If it worsens, call me. Soon, she'll refuse to eat. When that happens you need to have her moved to hospice okay? I believe we're only looking at a couple of days until then."

Suddenly, Georgia felt exhausted. She sat down and felt tears building in her eyes. The nurse sat with her while Georgia shook her head, determined to not give in to the stress. She gave the nurse a limp smile. "Sorry, having a weak moment. I need to be strong for Julie and the girls. No matter how much I thought I was prepared for this, nothing can really … I guess you have to live it."

"You've done a wonderful job with Julie and the girls but you're only human. You're going to have your moments when you feel overwhelmed. You're on an emotional roller coaster. Releasing your emotions is a good thing."

"Thank you."

"How are the girls holding up?" the nurse asked.

"Kaela has been so gentle with Shelby. And I know Shelby needs her right now. As for Shelby … since that initial release, she's internalized it all. She goes to school, and reads to her mother each day when she comes home. She insists on feeding her dinner. So on the surface, she appears to be handling it all. But it's like she's going through the motions robotically."

"That's a very normal way for kids her age to handle something they can't totally comprehend. I wouldn't worry about her at this point."

Georgia sighed with relief. "That's good to hear."

"Time for me to go. Remember to take care of yourself too. You need a break from all of this. When's the caregiver's next full day?"

"Tomorrow. My mother's coming over and we're going out for the day. She'll be staying with us from now on. I suspected Julie would move to hospice soon and I need her here to help with the girls. I want them to stay in school as close to Julie's passing as possible. We can determine that once Julie's in hospice. I promised Shelby she could be with her mother there."

"Good girl. See you soon."

Two days later, Julie worsened. She refused to accept food and the coughing started. The nurse arrived and examined her. She pulled Georgia aside.

"Julie's having a hard time clearing fluid from her lungs. It's time for her to go into Hospice." An ambulance was called and Julie was moved to the Hospice residence in Sechelt.

The staff were wonderful. In no time, Julie was settled in. Georgia had barely settled in the arm chair when the nurse came to set up an intravenous catheter. Julie was barely awake.

"We're setting up a butterfly needle subcutaneously, Julie. You'll feel a little pinch."

Georgia watched the nurse insert a winged needle under the skin. Julie paid no attention.

The nurse turned to Georgia. "We've increased Julie's Hydromorphone and it's on a timer. We'll be in and out regularly but I'm going to show you how to administer it. If she needs it, you can give it to her."

Georgia never left the hospice, opting to sleep in the common living room.

Her mother brought the girls up after school the day Julie entered the hospice, and from that point the two sisters never went back to school. She knew it was only a matter of time, so the girls stayed at the hospice with her. Julie slept almost the whole time. When she did wake up, it was only for a few moments. Shelby sat in the armchair for hours reading, and waiting for those moments when Julie would open her eyes and smile at her. She'd smile back at her mother and whisper, "Love you, Mommy."

It became routine that each morning, Sandra Carr would scoop the girls up and take them back to Gibsons to change clothes and have some relief time from the hospice.

On the third day, Georgia and her mom were sitting in the common living room. Kaela was asleep in an armchair and Shelby was sleeping beside Julie's bed.

"You know I don't agree with the kids being here," her mother began, "I don't think it's healthy."

"Mom, we've been through this. Julie and I discussed it at length. Shelby needs to feel she's helping. You've seen how she beams whenever Julie wakes up and looks at her. If I kept her away, she'd never understand why."

"Fine, but what about Kaela? There's no need for her to experience this first hand."

"Kaela and Shelby have been inseparable for months now. I can't separate them and send Kaela away. Kaela is really good for her sister right now."

"Well, in my day, it wouldn't be allowed. Children didn't even go to funerals never mind sit by death beds." Her mother pursed her lips.

Georgia looked sternly at her mother. It was rare that they disagreed and this was one time Georgia wouldn't have it. "Mom, I know you mean well, but these days they believe it's part of the healing process for children to be included. Otherwise, they could have emotional issues that could affect them long after. Children have a way of blaming themselves, of thinking something was their fault, when they're too young to understand the why of it. The girls stay, and Julie and I agreed. And I won't break my promise to Shelby."

Her mother sighed. "Alright, I'll say no more."

"I'm going to sit with Julie for awhile. Why don't you try sleeping?"

Chapter 20

Julie opened her eyes. She braced herself for the pain that enveloped her body each time she woke up. She stared straight across the room, afraid to move her head for fear that her raging headache would once again render her helpless. The past few days ravaged and exhausted her. The morphine helped of course, but the soothing effects of the drug lessened daily, prompting another dosage increase, which knocked her out right away. The numbing morphine would wear off, forcing her awake to face the all-encompassing pain once more. Julie hated the fact that she wasn't in control and hated that those around her were forced to watch as she slowly ebbed away.

Hang on ... this was different ... no pain.

All was quiet in the room and Julie let her eyes shift from side to side, still afraid to move her head. Her eyes rested on Georgia asleep in the lazy boy beside the bed. One of the girls lay curled up in her lap, her face buried in Georgia's chest. Since Shelby and Kaela insisted on having matching haircuts, it was hard to tell who was who unless staring them directly at them. Without thinking, she shifted her body slightly and turned her head to obtain a better view of the sleeping child.

But there was no discomfort. Nothing. Julie relaxed, perplexed at this new change of events and let her gaze follow the length of the child's outstretched arm to a tiny hand and then delicate fingers. *There it is. The birth ring I gave Shelby for her last birthday.* A smile tugged at her mouth. Georgia had both arms protectively wrapped around the child. In that instant Julie knew she'd made the right choice for her daughter. The scene before her told Julie that whatever Shelby had to face once she lost her mother, Georgia would be there to help. For the first time in a long time, she felt at peace.

It was then she sensed a change in the room and looked around. At the bottom of the bed a figure emerged.

Julie's smile broadened. "Mom?"

"Yes, dear. It's me. It's time for you to join us."

Her mother looked as she remembered her before her parents died in that fateful car crash so many years ago. She pushed the covers back and sat up. "I'm coming."

She couldn't believe the ease with which she stood. She caught a glimpse of her image in the dresser mirror. What she saw pleased her. She looked healthy with glowing skin and shiny hair. She glanced back at the bed and observed her emaciated body, happy to leave it behind.

Pausing by the chair, Julie pushed the hair back from Shelby's face, tucking it behind her ear. She turned to her mother. "This is my daughter, Shelby ... your granddaughter."

The figure moved beside her. "She's beautiful. She doesn't look like you though."

"No. She looks like her father. You should see her half-sister. They could be twins."

The woman took Julie's hand and the two women stared into each other's eyes. There was no need for words or actions; their eyes spoke volumes. A look of love and communion passed from mother to daughter. "It's time for us to go, sweetheart."

Julie turned for one last look at Shelby. She bent down and kissed the sleeping child on the forehead. Then she lifted her hand and touched the birthstone ring on Shelby's finger.

"I love you, Shelby. Be good and have a great life." As she stood, she looked at Georgia and found her eyes were open and staring right at her.

Julie smiled and spoke softly. "My mother's here. She came for me." She watched Georgia blink rapidly and open her mouth to speak, but nothing came out. "Shelby is yours now. I know she's in safe hands and she'll come to love you as I have. Goodbye, Georgia."

Julie let her mother lead her across the room. All definition of the room disappeared before her and she followed her mother through a blinding whiteness to the threshold beyond.

Chapter 21

Georgia couldn't move. The spot where Julie had stood was now dark and empty. A beautiful Julie … the woman who had turned heads and the one Georgia envied all those years ago. Unable to talk or feel her body, she felt frozen in that moment of time.

A tingling sensation cursed through her body. It started at her feet and moved slowly up her body and through her limbs. Sensation returned. Georgia turned her head towards the bed. The woman before her showed the ravages of her illness, but something was different. Whenever Julie passed out on the morphine, her face still mirrored her pain with a furrowed forehead and her body twitched with discomfort.

This face was serene with a smile at the corners of her mouth. Her eyes were closed and her forehead smooth. Georgia knew she'd gone and believed the verity of her vision.

She glanced down at the child curled in slumber on her lap. Her world had changed forever. She inched forward slowly in the armchair, lifting Shelby up when she stood. She placed her gently down in the chair, trying not to disturb her. *Sleep a little longer, sweet one.*

She felt for Julie's pulse and listened to her heart. Nothing. She took a brush from the side table and gently combed her hair into some semblance of style.

"You look so at peace," she whispered. "I'm so grateful I saw you before you left." Her shoulders began to shake and Georgia felt tears run down her cheeks. Julie had become one of her family and now she was gone. The woman had inched her way into her life. "I came to love you too," she said, softly.

She ran a finger down Julie's cheek and gave in to the sobs that followed … a much-needed release. All the weeks of watching Julie suffer and being strong for Shelby had taken its toll. She curled up in a ball on the bed beside Julie and let it out as quietly as she could muster, aware Shelby still slept beside them.

A short time later, she pulled herself together. She went to the adjoining bathroom and washed her face. Georgia had made a promise to Shelby that she would wake her if anything changed. Now was the time and she needed to be strong for her. First she called in the nursing staff to confirm what she already knew. They removed the morphine drip and left her alone to be with Shelby. Georgia placed Julie's hands together on her chest and pulled the sheet up to her chin. She stood by the bed looking down on the woman who had changed a lot of lives in a matter of weeks. Several minutes passed and Georgia pulled herself back to the present and the task at hand.

Shelby was still sleeping when Georgia approached. She picked her up and talked to her softly as she settled back down in the chair. Her hand gently brushed the hair back from her eyes. One day she would tell the child about her vision, but not now. Rocking slowly in the chair, Georgia spoke in barely a whisper. "Shelby, honey. Wake up."

It was a quiet memorial service that November 16th. Three months had passed since Julie had walked into her life in mid-August. Julie had no family on her side to attend so the service was held in Gibsons. Georgia's friend and Agent, Trent came along with Colin's sister and husband, Mary and Steve, also came. Mary was even civil to Georgia this time around. Of course Frank was there and his friend Bill. But not Alice—no surprise there.

Georgia's father had come to stay the day Julie passed to lend his support. After the service they all went back to Georgia's house. She was in the kitchen making coffee when the phone rang. Her paternal grandparents were back in Arizona and Grammy, her maternal grandmother who owned the Gibsons house was still in New Zealand.

Her mother placed a hand on her arm as she moved toward the telephone. "I'll get it. You finish making the coffee."

Mary carried plates of sandwiches and veggie trays into the dining room. When she returned she leaned against the counter and watched Georgia. "How's Shelby holding up?"

Georgia checked the coffee pot and fussed with the napkins. "She's holding her own. I'm a little concerned as she seems a little too much in control."

"She's not ready to deal with it yet. When she is, she'll let go."

"It's been a lot for her to handle in a short period of time." Georgia handed Mary a tray of cups and spoons. "I guess I didn't expect a five-year-old to internalize. It's heart wrenching to watch."

Mary put the tray back down on the counter. "Listen, when I first heard that you were Shelby's guardian, it really hurt. I thought that Julie would have turned to me and Steve. But I don't feel bad about it anymore. Steve and I have created a lifestyle for ourselves that didn't include children. Julie knew that. My point is; you're the right person for Shelby. You and her sister, Kaela. You'll do a great job with her and eventually Shelby will settle into a life with you and her sister."

Georgia was moved by Mary's words. She decided to push the envelope a little. "You're mother won't like it."

Mary shrugged and smiled. "Mom never likes anything if she can't control it. She'll get over it."

Georgia chuckled. She was impressed with this new side to Mary. "I'm sorry we didn't know each other better when Colin and I were married."

"We were kids. All that was a lifetime ago. I want you to know that Steve and I will help in any way that we can. Shelby is our niece ... and so is Kaela." Mary picked up the tray. "You know I've seen changes in my mother recently. Oh I know there's some things about her that will never change and she can be so annoying, but she's been through a lot this year too. She lost her son, her husband, Julie, and she thinks she's lost her granddaughter."

"It was never anyone's intention to take either of her grandkids away. That was her own doing," Georgia stopped herself. "I'm sorry, this isn't the time or place to rehash old hurts. I didn't mean to sound so harsh."

"Don't apologize. Her problem is, she doesn't know how to admit it when she's wrong." Mary turned and carried the tray out to the dining room.

Georgia stood dumbfounded over her conversation with Mary when her mother came back into the kitchen.

"Honey, Shelby needs you." Her mother looked upset. "That was Alice on the phone. I have no idea what she said to that poor child, but she's near hysterics. She won't talk to me."

"Where is she?"

"She's in your bedroom with Kaela."

Georgia flew down the hall to her room. When she entered, Shelby was curled up in a ball in the middle of the queen-sized bed sobbing. Kaela sat beside her looking distressed, her small hand patting her on the back.

"Kaela, why don't you go help Nana set the lunch table?" Her daughter looked grateful to be able to leave. She stopped, leaned up, and whispered, "Is Shelby going to be okay?"

Georgia gave her an affirmative nod and mouthed a yes and walked her to the door, closing it quietly behind her.

Settling herself on the bed beside Shelby, she let her cry while slowly stroking her hair. After a time, Georgia talked to her softly. "Would you like to tell me what happened?"

"Grammy Alice told me God took Mommy because he needed her more than I did."

Georgia seethed inside. *What a stupid thing to say to a five-year-old.*

"I told her I was only a little kid and God was an adult, so why would he need her more than me."

"What did she say?"

"That he had a plan. So I asked her what kind of a plan and she didn't know. She said we had to believe that he had a good reason."

The tears started again and Georgia's heart went out to the child. She let her cry while thinking of a response. *A child couldn't possibly understand Alice's words.*

Shelby wiped her face with her hand and Georgia handed her a Kleenex from the box on the bedside table.

She looked up at Georgia with such an intense distress. "If ... if ... he had a good reason to take Mommy away from me ..." Shelby faltered. "... then he must have had a good reason to take Daddy too." Her face screwed up and her big eyes searched Georgia's. "Was I bad? Is that why God took them ... because I didn't deserve them?"

Georgia's heart jumped into her throat and tears filled her eyes. *What was she hearing?* Her hands cupped Shelby's face, her thumbs stroked her wet cheeks. "My poor, poor child. I don't believe anyone's God would take parents away from their child deliberately. And no ... you weren't bad."

"Then what did Grammy Alice mean?"

With a deep sigh and all the confidence she could muster, Georgia spoke with a quiet deliverance. "Sometimes, people don't know what to say when someone loses a loved one. They don't have an answer so they turn to their faith and say it's part of their God's plan."

"Do you believe in Grammy Alice's God?"

"I believe in a higher power. But I'd never believe in a God that was vengeful or hurtful. The important thing is that Grammy Alice didn't mean to upset you. The truth is we can't control some of the bad things that happen to us. Your Mommy and Daddy both became sick and nothing could help them. I'm so sorry this happened to you. But Shelby, it had nothing to do with you or anyone else. It happened."

Shelby slipped her arms around Georgia and she held her tight for several moments in silence.

"Would you like to join us for some lunch?"

"I'm not hungry."

"You don't have to eat if you don't want to. But I know the family would like to spend some time with you. Is that all right?"

Shelby sat up and gave her a small semblance of a smile. "Okay."

Georgia stood up and held out her hand. "Let's go wash your face and brush your hair."

A couple of hours later, the doorbell rang. Georgia looked out the front window and saw a taxi pulling away from the curb. She opened the door to find Alice Charles standing on the stoop with Peter Martin, Frank's ex-law partner. Speechless, she could only stare and she felt her body stiffen. A feeling she was only too familiar with whenever she and Alice were in the same room together.

"May we come in?" she asked.

"Of course." Georgia stood aside and they walked past her into the hallway. All conversation in the living room stopped.

Frank saved the day. He was the first to stand and approach them. His hand went out to his old colleague. "Hello, Peter. How are you?" he nodded to his ex-wife. "Alice."

She tensed, nodded at Frank, and half turned towards Peter.

Georgia found her voice. "May I take your coats." By this time, Mary joined them. She gave her mm a practiced hug and said, "Come in and join us."

Alice's eyes searched out the people in the living room. "First, I need a word with my granddaughter."

"Which one?" Sandra Carr asked.

Georgia stared her mother down. This was no time to be defiant. Sandra and Alice hadn't seen each in five years but it was obvious there was no love lost between them. Her mother ignored her and turned and yelled down the hallway. "Girls? Your Grammy Alice is here."

The two girls came down the hallway hand in hand. Both looked reluctant when they stopped in front of Alice. With similar expressions on their faces and matching haircuts, Georgia knew Alice would have a problem deciding who was who.

Alice was obviously taken back by their similarities. "Oh my … look at you two. It's like looking at your father when he was your age."

To Georgia's surprise, tears sprang to Alice eyes. Maybe it was the sombre mood of the day with emotions rising high or too many losses lately, but for the first time in years, Georgia felt empathy for the woman and decided to take the lead. "Shelby, why don't you take Grammy Alice and show her your room. And Kaela, come and help me make fresh coffee and put out some more goodies."

A short time later, Shelby brought Alice into the kitchen. The child was smiling and seemed a little more at ease. As she helped Kaela add cookies to a tray, one slipped off and onto the floor. Shelby scooped it up and brushed it off with a napkin, broke it in half and handed a piece to Kaela. The girls popped them into their mouths and giggled as Kaela carried the tray out of the room with Shelby following on her heels.

Alice watched the whole scene play out. "They seem to like each other."

"They've been inseparable." Georgia said.

"Thank you for letting me come in. She was crying on the phone and I tried to help. I only made matters worse."

"I know you didn't mean to upset her. And whatever you said to her now, seems to have worked."

"Shelby told me what you said. Thank you for not making me sound like an ogre."

Georgia faced her . "You're her grandmother. I would never try to turn her against you."

Alice blushed. "It's been a tough year for us all hasn't it? Peter has been a good friend. He's helped me put a lot of things in perspective."

Georgia felt puzzled. What was she eluding to here? "He's a good man. I remember him from the old days. Coffee?"

"Please. Yes, he is." She accepted the cup Georgia handed to her and walked over to the counter for some cream and sugar. "I want you to know that I'm not going to fight you on adopting Shelby. She belongs here with you and her sister. I know I've been a bitch about it. I was afraid you'd cut me out of her life. Please don't."

"And what about Kaela?" Might as well be blunt about it. She deserved an answer.

Alice squirmed and had trouble looking her in the eye. "Well ... Kaela is my granddaughter too. If you allow it ... I'd ... I'd like to have her in my life as well."

Georgia knew this was as close to an apology she would ever receive from Alice. Now was not the time for egos. "You have grandmother rights. But I won't tolerate interference. You must accept my decisions where the girls are involved. And I won't allow you to play the girls against each other. If you can accept that, you can be in their lives."

"My dear, Peter and I intend on doing a lot of travelling together. Something Frank never enjoyed. I plan to make up for lost time which means I only have time to be a grandmother. My motherhood days are over."

"Then let's join the others and you can tell us all about your travel plans."

The two women moved into the living room. Georgia sat down beside Alice. As Georgia glanced around the room, she winced at her mother's pursed lips, realizing she would have to act as a buffer between her mother and Alice.

Nana Alice would be held at arm's length and require monitoring, her grandfather needed to be won over to her side, and Georgia needed to ensure the happiness of her daughters. *Family dynamics would always play a part in our social gatherings.* She sighed. *A perfect family would be a boring family.*

PART 2

The bond that links your true family is not one of blood, but of respect and joy in each other's life.

Richard Bach

Chapter 22

Georgia stepped out of the shower and heard the doorbell ring. She froze. *Who could that be?* She reached for her housecoat and ran to the bedroom and peaked out the window. She gasped at the sight of the man standing on her stoop.

She descended the stairs of the split level home, took a deep breath to steady her sudden onslaught of nerves, and opened the door. "Sean?"

He looked her up and down and pushed past her into the house. "Do you always answer the door dripping wet in your bathrobe?"

Stunned at seeing him and confused by his arrogant attitude, Georgia shut the door and turned to him. "Uh ... hello, would you like to come in?"

He ignored her attempt at sarcasm. "Why didn't you tell me what you've been dealing with here?"

"What do you mean?"

"You know exactly what I mean. Julie, Shelby, a stalker. I could have been here to help you."

"We broke up remember? I couldn't dump this on you."

Sean opened his mouth to respond, looked her up and down for a second time and shut his mouth.

"You're dripping all over the floor. Go upstairs and put some clothes on?" he demanded.

Her brow rose. She'd never experienced this attitude he was laying on her but decided to ignore it. Grateful for some time alone to compose herself, she started back up the stairs. "I'll be right back."

She threw on a pair of jeans and a sweatshirt, combed back her wet hair, and applied some eye shadow, blush and tinted lip gloss. Her heart pounded as she joined him in the living room, but she was back in control. She noted how handsome he still was and how tanned for November. *Probably down south somewhere with his 'schoolgirl'.*

"Would you like some coffee?" she asked, needing a distraction.

"No thanks." Sean turned and they stared at each other in silence.

"Please, have a seat." Georgia motioned to the loveseat and sat on the arm of the chair closest to her. She didn't trust her knees to carry her too far. He stared at her with anger in his eyes.

"You're still angry with me." she said.

"Of course I am. Did you forget your stalker? You opened the door without any clothes on and without checking to see who it was. What if I was him?"

Georgia thrust out her chin. "That's not true. I checked out the bedroom window before I came to the door. I knew it was you."

They stared at each other defiantly. Sean spoke first. "So why didn't you call me?"

She assumed he meant about Julie, not about them. "How did you find out about all of this?"

"Trent told me."

"Trent?" Her face blanched. *He'd broken her trust.*

"Yes, Trent. He was my agent and friend before he became yours. He's worried about you being alone here. But I would have liked to hear it from you."

"Like I said, we broke up ..." Georgia slid off the arm of the chair onto the cushion, her fingers tapping nervously on the arms.

"Doesn't mean I don't care about you or your safety."

Georgia's heart skipped a beat. "Of course, but it's hard to be friends with this ... thing between us."

Sean stiffened. "And what *thing* is that?"

She didn't know where or how to begin, and so she said nothing.

Sean answered for her. "This thing as I see it is your not wanting to commit. You don't trust me ... or maybe you didn't love me as much as I thought you did."

The thought that he'd think she didn't love him tore her apart. Now was her moment. *Talk to him girl ... now.* "I loved you ... love you. I was stupid to send you away, fearing I'd be hurt again. You're right, I didn't trust you, but more than that I didn't trust my instincts." She stopped as suddenly as she started. Her face clouded over. "But now it's too late."

Sean leaned forward in his chair. "Why is it too late?"

She looked at him confused. So much emotion in the past few months, she felt drained. "Because ..."

"Because why?" Sean pushed.

Georgia threw her arms up in the air, exasperated. "You have someone else and so do I."

Sean's face became a thundercloud. "You've met someone else?"

Georgia stood and paced in front of Sean. "No, not me, you."

"Me?"

"Yes, little Miss Hotness."

Sean looked startled. "Miss who?"

Frustrated, Georgia stopped in front of him and shouted into his face. "Your sweet smelling, gorgeous, younger than anybody, Jasmine, from the night of the movie premiere."

Sean fell back into the chair and laughed taking her completely by surprise. She placed her hands on her hips. "I finally open up to you and you laugh?"

"You're jealous of Serena and I couldn't be happier."

"I'm not and you're really making me mad."

"You are so. Serena is the daughter of the Tahltan Chief. She's an actress and a friend of the family."

"But you went to L.A. with her didn't you?"

"Yes. She was starting a movie down there and her father asked me to escort her down and help her settle in. I knew my way around L.A. and she didn't. It was her first time away from home for any length of time and he was concerned."

"That's it? No ... girl-boy stuff."

"No hanky-panky. Strictly paternal. Now cough up. What do you mean you haven't found someone new, you said we both did?"

Georgia frowned and felt a headache coming on. "There's no one."

"What about Trent?"

All she could do was stare at Sean. "What about him?"

"The movie premiere...you and Trent running out on us all holding hands, with you the sexiest looking woman there...and a no show at the after party. How do you think that made me feel?"

Georgia cocked her head. *So he had noticed her efforts to look sexy that night.* "You were jealous of Trent?" She couldn't help but smile.

"Damn right I was, and angry as hell too."

"Trent insisted I go to the premier and we went as friends. That's it."

Sean's face softened. "Then who is it you have in your life?"

"Oh right, I was talking about Shelby."

She turned to go back to the arm chair, but Trent caught her arm and pulled her down into his lap. "And how would that change anything between me and you—if there is a me and you?"

It was unnerving sitting on Sean's lap but Georgia was afraid to move, her limbs felt like jelly.

"People told me it was natural for you to develop a love for Kaela when you met us, but it was too much to expect you to accept Colin's other daughter, especially since she isn't related to me or you."

Sean sighed. "What people?"

Georgia thought and answered. "Well ... my grandfather for one ... and me."

"So what's wrong with her?"

Georgia struggled to concentrate. Her nostrils filled with that old familiar scent of his aftershave. She pushed away past memories and focused n their conversation at hand. "Um ... what's wrong with whom?"

"Shelby."

"Nothing. She's a beautiful child. Kaela is more of the daredevil, while Shelby's a quiet thinker. The girls adore each other." *Marion's words came to mind. Don't use Shelby as another excuse to push Sean further away.*

"So if you think you can love her then I could too. So what's the problem?"

She stared at him, speechless. Sean continued. "The only drawback I see is if for some inane reason she hates me."

Georgia smiled. "She'd never hate you."

"So when can I meet her?"

"Mom took them to Vancouver for the weekend. It's only been ten days since Julie passed and we thought a change of scenery would be a good thing. I'm hoping to send them back to school on Monday. The sooner Shelby falls into a routine the better it will be for her."

Sean ran his finger down her cheek and along her chin. Georgia melted.

"So what do you say we spend today and tonight figuring out if there is a you and me?"

He leaned forward and kissed the tip of her nose, then lowered his mouth and brushed his lips against hers. Georgia lost herself in the moment. Suddenly, she stopped. "Not so fast." Georgia stood and moved back to the armchair.

"What?" Sean asked.

"Look, I know I made a mistake sending you away. Once I realized your ex-wife wasn't a threat, I panicked when you wanted to take our relationship a step further. I feared losing my newfound independence and falling into old habits. Then, you showed up with a date. Along came Julie and Shelby ... my life became so complicated."

Sean leaned forward. "And here I am thinking I can un-complicate it. I recognize that you've been under a tremendous amount of stress starting back in the spring with Colin's passing. I'm not going to pressure you, but I want you back in my life."

Georgia knew she wanted him back in her life too, but she wasn't ready. There were still some unanswered questions. "Why did you let me send you away? It made me feel that you didn't care enough to fight for me."

"Wow ... I do remember telling you I didn't know what to say to make it right between us and you said you wanted to be alone. You didn't exactly give me any options."

"Okay. I get that you were frustrated with me which made you lose your temper and stomp out." Georgia sighed. "I guess I thought you'd get over it and come back."

"I can't profess to understand a woman's mind. I'd been hurt badly before and when you sent me away, it cut deep. Believe me, I wanted to come back but I was afraid you'd send me packing again."

Georgia digested his words and nodded, as she sorted out her thoughts.

"I wanted to respect your need for independence. I waited for you to call me," Sean added. "Maybe I'd like that coffee now."

"Let's move to the kitchen."

"I do want to know why you're here alone. Trent said after Julie passed, your mom was here. Now I find you all alone, taking no precautions."

"I am taking precautions. I'm just so exasperated by this whole thing. Every time I think about it, I freak."

"Then why are you here alone?"

"I had an appointment yesterday and told Mom I'd take a later ferry. Then, I ran into Frank in lower Gibsons and he invited me up to Halfmoon Bay. So I called Mom and told her I'd be staying at Frank's and would join them today. I stopped here for some things and decided to shower first." She carried two cups of coffee to the counter.

"Trent brought me up-to-date on the details about this creep. Is there anything new I don't know?" Sean asked.

"Nothing. I haven't heard anything more from him or the police."

"Hmm ... call your mother and tell her you're staying here and Sean will take good care of you." He paused and slurped his coffee. Tomorrow, we'll go to town, grab some things of mine, pick up the girls and come home."

Georgia choked on her coffee. "You're staying here?"

Sean pulled out a stool and sat down opposite her. "Yes, I am. Someone has to. Your mother can go back to her life and you and I can start one."

All she could do was stare with her mouth open.

Sean gave her a scathing look. "Don't even think it. You're not pushing me away this time. If you're worried about all this being too quick, I'll sleep in the guest bedroom. I'm your bodyguard."

She laughed at that remark, and promptly snorted. "That won't work."

"And why not? I've missed that cute little snort of yours by the way."

Georgia stuck her tongue out at him. "Because the girls don't know about the stalker."

"Then we have to tell them. We don't want to scare them. We'll say a crazy fan of yours wants to meet you and might try to reach you through them. Something like that. They already know not to talk to strangers don't they? Let's try to keep it light."

Georgia fell silent.

"What?"

"You're right. They have to be told. It's only with everything else they've been dealing with ..." She trailed off, shaking her head.

"Kids are more resilient than we give them credit for. They'll be fine. As for you and me, you want to be independent? Fine by me? I'm going to take care of you just the same until all of this blows over. In case you don't know it, I'm the best you'll ever get when it comes to loving you."

Georgia laughed. "Aren't you the cocky one?"

"And, you are the best thing that ever got lost in mine. I don't want to take over your life, Georgia. I want us to enhance each other's life. We'll take it slow, okay?"

She saw the love in Sean's eyes and recognized the sincerity in his words. "Okay," she said, softly.

They spent the rest of the afternoon walking the beach at Bonniebrook. It was a brisk, bright fall day and they returned home with rosy cheeks and red noses. They settled on the couch in the living room with a hot toddy and Georgia filled him in on her time with Julie.

"Our friendship was a short one but I came to love and appreciate her. She taught me that nothing stays the same. Life is never constant, so never take the people in your life for granted."

Georgia snapped her fingers, "They could be gone just like that."

She and Sean stared at each other. He reached out and ran his finger down her cheek. Georgia felt the electricity of his touch and shuddered. When his finger reached her mouth, she kissed it.

He leaned forward and showered her lips with light kisses. She pressed her mouth on his and hungrily demanded more. His hands slipped under her sweatshirt and cupped her breasts. Georgia groaned and slipped her hands under his shirt. His muscles were taut. Their passion grew and they groped each other with abandon, their kisses finding the old familiar places.

Sean's voice came in a whisper and quite husky. "I've missed you so much."

Without hesitation, Georgia stood and led him to her room. There were no romantic gestures, slow teasing, or murmurs of love. They pulled off each other's clothes and collapsed onto the bed with such an intense frenzy, ten minutes later it was over. Clothes, sheets, and blankets lay on the floor in disarray. The couple lay naked on the bottom sheet wrapped in each other's arms, hot, sweaty, and spent.

"Wow, maybe we should separate more often," Sean said.

Georgia threw a leg over his as if to take possession. "So much for taking it slow."

Sean laughed. "We're both so irresistible."

"Our love making has always been great. I'm never sending you away again."

Sean ran his hand up and down her leg. "I'm so sorry I caused you to mistrust me."

"I'm sorry I didn't trust myself."

Sean leaned on one arm and stared straight into her eyes. "Please believe that since the first time we met at the cabin, I have never cheated on you. Nor will I ever."

"I believe you and I've never cheated on you either."

He leaned forward and kissed her on the nose. "What say we shower and then I'll make us some dinner?"

She gave him a big smile. "Sounds great to me. For some reason I'm really hungry."

The shower took a little longer than planned. Once in, they soaped each other, which led to another burst of passion. This time they took it slow and easy, exploring each other as if it was their first time. Sean took her against the shower wall, her legs wrapped tight around his waist. With each thrust, they moaned and cried sweet words of love.

Georgia sat at the island in her kitchen watching him cook.

"What are you smiling at?" he asked.

"I never thought when I awoke this morning; I'd be having three showers today."

"The day's not over. Hmm … squeaky clean." He leaned across the island and gave her a kiss. "Maybe we should go back upstairs."

She gave him a playful shove. "Not before we eat. Back to the stove before you burn my dinner."

That night they slept together in Georgia's room, wrapped in each other's arms. The next morning as they drove to the ferry that would take them to Vancouver, Georgia broached the subject of Sean staying with her and the girls.

"Even though we've made the decision to be together again, I still want to move forward slowly," she said, hesitantly.

Sean glanced at her quickly and returned his eyes to the road. "Meaning?"

"The past five years, Kaela never saw us sleeping together. I'd like to keep it that way for awhile. We all have a lot of adjustments to make and my relationship with Shelby is too new. I don't want to overwhelm her with a man suddenly sharing my bedroom."

"I can understand that."

"So you don't mind staying in the guest bedroom?"

Sean reached over and squeezed her hand. "Of course not. I don't want to become a complication. I told you yesterday, no pressure. Slow and easy. Okay?"

They went straight to Sean's condo in Vancouver and picked up his clothes and personal items. Their next stop was her parents' home to pick up the kids. Her mother gave Sean a tight hug. Georgia could see she was thrilled that Sean was back in her life. "The others are on the back deck."

The girls had their backs to them as they stepped outside. "Which one is Kaela?" Sean whispered to her mother.

"The one in the red sweatshirt."

"He snuck up behind Kaela and tickled her under the arms."Hi, pipsqueak. Got a hug for me?"

Kaela turned and squealed with delight. She jumped up into Sean's arms and planted kisses all over his face."Sean, I missed you so much."

Holding her in his arms, he turned to Shelby.

His face registered surprise. "Wow, you're like a mirror image of your sister." He put one hand out to her. "Pleased to meet you, Shelby. I'm Sean, a friend of Kaela's mother."

Shelby shyly shook his hand. "Hello.

They all sat for awhile and chatted while the girls jumped around in the leaves Grampa had piled up in one corner of the yard.

"I must say, I feel so much better knowing you'll be around to protect Georgia from this stalker fellow," her Dad said. "And to have my wife back home." Sandra gave her husband a glare. "Oops, I guess that sounded rather selfish but you know what I mean."

"Don't either of you worry. Sooner or later they'll catch that guy." Sean said.

That evening, they made the return trip on the ferry to Gibsons. A card was stuck in the door asking Georgia to call Constable Denning. She left him a message and put the girls to bed as the officer arrived at their door.

Introductions were made.

"Mr. Dixon, it's a pleasure to meet you."

Georgia knew the constable recognized Sean and the was pleased to know he was planning to stay on in the house.

"Please sit down, Constable." Georgia led them into the living room.

"Thank you. We were able to lift a partial finger print from the envelope. Can you come into the office in the morning? We'd like to obtain your prints, Georgia. We can at least eliminate you."

"Certainly. What time?

"Ten o'clock?"

"Alright," she said.

"We also have a picture of a man coming up your walkway carrying the flowers. We obtained it from the hidden camera here in the living room window. I'd like you to look at it and tell me if you recognize him." He pulled it out of his briefcase and handed her the picture.

Georgia stared at the face in the picture. It was a bit grainy, but defined enough for her to see. "I know this man ... I mean I don't know him ... but there's something familiar about him."

"Take your time. Don't force it. Look away and think on it and then take another look." Constable Denning coached. She did what he said and looked back down at the photo.

"No." She shook her head. "He's familiar but I can't remember from where."

Sean leaned over her shoulder and looked at the man. "What?" He took the photo from her hands and gave it a good look. He looked at Georgia. "I don't know why he's familiar to you, hon." His eyes shifted to the officer. "But I know him. His name's Jim Draper."

Georgia frowned. "That name's familiar, too."

"How do you know this man, Mr. Dixon?" Constable Denning asked.

"Please, call me Sean. My agent, Trent Matheson, set up an interview between him and me. Jim Draper is a freelancer doing an article for a magazine. Apparently, he'd interviewed Trent and asked to interview some of his clients."

Georgia interjected. "That's right. I remember now. I met him in September in Trent's office. I'd popped in to see Trent when I was in town and they were coming out of a meeting. We were introduced and the man mentioned he wanted to interview me. I declined."

Sean shuddered. "The bastard. I hate that he was that close to you."

The constable asked Sean to tell him about the interview.

"He asked the usual questions, nothing out of the ordinary." Sean filled him in on the rest of the conversation between them.

"Did he ask about Georgia?"

Sean scratched his head. 'Umm ... yeah, towards the end. He touched on our personal relationship, which of course is common knowledge if you've followed our lives. I told him that was off limits. Neither of us ever talked about our personal lives with reporters."

"How did he react to that?"

"Okay." Sean shrugged. "He didn't pursue it."

Constable Denning stood. "We'll contact Trent and see what he can tell us about Mr. Draper or his whereabouts and get this picture to Border Integrity. That's all for tonight. We'll see you in the morning Georgia. Nice to meet you, Sean."

After he'd left, Sean took Georgia into his arms. "They now have a face, although the name is probably phoney. They'll catch him, sweetheart."

"Thank God you were here to identify him." She turned her face up to his. "I love you, Sean Dixon."

Chapter 23

Anger filled every fibre of his body. His head pounded so hard, his eyes blurred. "Damn," he snarled. For months her house had been like Grand Central Station. She was never alone. At first, he wondered who that other woman and kid were. *Some sort of relation 'cause the kids look alike.* Suddenly, they're all gone for days. Then she's home and all the world's visiting her. The obits in the newspaper finally cleared up the identity of the mystery woman. *At least she's out of the way. Now that bastard writer's here. He doesn't deserve her. He'll soon learn that Georgia belongs to me. The kids, too, definitely not part of my plan.*

And there's the cops. He watched the police car stop in front of the house and moved further into the bushes. *She'd obviously involved the police. They always did.* The same cop that had been to the house before, exited the car and went into the house. He'd have to be more careful now. He felt sure they didn't know who he was but he decided to slow things down a little. He'd waited a long time to be with Georgia and he knew he could wait a little longer.

He swallowed hard and concentrated on staying calm. There were other people in the park and he didn't want to draw notice to himself. He needed to work out a plan. This hadn't been as easy as he thought it would be. A lot of people were waiting for his next move. *I should never have sent the letters. Big mistake.* But it had started out as a psychological game that no longer satisfied him. *I've been a fool.* The difference between Georgia and the others was that he'd always planned more carefully. It was all part of the game of control. Not one of them meant anything to him. They were strangers who served a need and a purpose. When that need was satisfied and he became bored, he disposed of them. *Just like Rose.* However, this woman claimed him body and soul. He loved her and this was a new emotion for him. It garnered her some control in the game and that didn't suit him at all because it gave her a degree of control over him. He'd been thinking with the wrong head. He'd let his obsession with her throw him off his game. He knew what he had to do.

Let them wait, wait, and wait some more ... and become bored. He'd do nothing. The cops would move on to other cases and Georgia would let her guard down. When he returned, it would be to put a new plan into action. He'd have the element of surprise on his side. He'd go home for awhile and live on his fantasies. There were loose ends that needed to be dealt with anyway.

The man moved through the bushes to the next street and walked the couple of blocks to his car. A sinister smile spread across his face. *Maybe I'll pick up a juicy tidbit on the drive home to hone my skills and feed my appetite. And when it ended, I'll be sure to let her know that she gave her life to the greater cause.*

As he drove to the ferry docks, he made a promise. "I'm not done with you yet, my sweet Georgia peach."

He stayed in his car on the ferry, looking at the blue file. He sat two photographs side-by-side. Both were brunettes, both had hazel eyes. They could have been the same woman, except the contrast between them was blatantly apparent. One face was full of sweetness, yet an innocent sensuality; the other showed the ravages of alcohol abuse. His sweet Georgia peach held his heart now. He knew that's what made her different from the others. She looked like his mother, but she represented everything his mother wasn't. That's why he loved her and why he had to have her. Seeing her in the flesh brought up mixed emotions. Georgia had taken him out of his comfort zone and that scared him. He needed time to sort out his thoughts.

The line-up through the border was an easy twenty minute wait and he headed south along I-5. By the time he reached Seattle, it was late. He found a motel and grabbed some take-out food for dinner. He was up and gone at dawn, heading towards Portland. Here he left the I-5 and headed southeast on a secondary highway.

It was outside of Redmond, Oregon that he saw her. A young woman, probably early twenties, with short, spiked blond hair and too much make-up stood at the side of the road. As he approached, her thumb went out. He glanced in his mirrors and up ahead. This secondary highway was empty. Normally, she wouldn't be his first choice. He needed to satisfy his sadistic needs and she was convenient. Too much anger and self-reproach about his mishandling of the Georgia situation left him confused and feeling inadequate. Nothing like a cold, unemotional fix with a stranger to satiate his appetite and put him back in control. He pulled over and watched her in the side mirror run up to the truck door. On closer look, she had a hard-edged look to her, but a killer body. His lip curled. That's all that counted.

She opened the door on the passenger side, and gave him a huge smile. "How far ya going?"

"Nevada. Where you headed?"

"Cool. I'm going to Klamath Falls." She threw her backpack over the seat and climbed in. "I'm Sammy."

"Carson." He lied and smiled. *Of course, Jim Draper isn't my real name either.*

The woman talked non-stop which suited him. The more she talked about herself, the less he had to lie about himself. The more he listened to her; he wondered if anything she said was true. Something about her bothered him.

"I have a job waiting for me at Klamath Falls for the winter. What do you do?" she asked.

"I'm a salesman."

"You got a wife at home?"

"Nope."

They drove through the city of Bend, Oregon and headed towards the National Park. Sammy was scanning the main street as they drove through. "Pretty quiet here, not many people about."

He ignored her comment. *Who cares?*

"Not much of a talker, are you?" she asked.

"Nope." *Honey, you wouldn't like what I'd have to say.*

He'd travelled this stretch of road often. Once through the National Park they'd hit Klamath Marsh. A smile crossed his face. He knew it well. *That would be the spot.*

They weren't far out of Bend when the conversation took on a different slant. Sammy finally shut up and he could sense she was staring at him.

"You know, I bet I could make you give me your wallet right now," she said.

Jim gave her a quick glance and frowned. "What are you talking about?"

"Well, you see, I've done it before. Many times." She spoke with an arrogance but her attitude came across as a tease.

So she likes playing games. He was amused. "And how are you planning to make me give you my wallet."

"I have two methods. You would have seen the first one in Bend, had I seen a cop. See I ask you for your wallet while I open my window. If you say no, I threaten to yell rape and try to jump out of the vehicle right in front of the cop... The trick is to not give you any time to think it through. Most guys worry 'bout their wives being pissed that they picked up a female hitchhiker. A lot of 'em would have made a pass at me eventually, so they feel guilty. They worry about the publicity and their jobs if the cops believe me. Most men hand it over pretty quick."

He was on his guard now. "I don't see any cops around here. So that's not going to work is it?"

"Nope, so here's how we're going to do this." Sammy pulled a small revolver out of her pocket and pointed it at him. "You're going to pull over to the side of the road right now."

Jim hit the brakes really hard and at the same time extended his right arm out. He jerked it up under her hand holding the gun. Sammy flew forward with the sudden stop and when Jim knocked her gun hand up, she dropped it by her feet. He reached down with his right hand and grabbed the gun. On the way up, his elbow jerked back hard against her nose. She let out a scream and slumped back in the seat. He left the vehicle right there in the road, grabbed the keys and jumped out. Sammy tried to open the door but Jim was too fast for her. He pulled her out of the vehicle and onto the ground, tucked the gun into the front of his jeans, and kicked her good and hard in the ribs. "You god damn whore, nobody gets the better of me."

Sammy brought her foot up and tried to kick him between the legs. "You sick son-of-a-bitch," she yelled.

He jumped clear of her and then straddled her, pummelling her face with his fists.

A voice bellowed behind him. "Stop or I'll shoot."

Jim froze. Time stood still as he thought through his next move. In one swift movement he dove sideways onto his back, pulled the gun from his belt and fired at the officer standing a short distance away. The bullet burst into the man's chest with a thud, knocking him to the ground.

"Shit, shit, shit ... where'd you come from?" He ranted, as he got up. He staggered over and picked up the lawman's gun, wondering how he hadn't heard him drive up. Looking up and down the road, he saw they were alone then heard someone calling the cop on his radio. Reaching inside the vehicle, he ripped the receiver off of the unit.

A moment later, he paced back and forth between the cop and the girl who lay on the ground. The cop was still and quiet. Checking his pulse, he knew the man was dead. That made him a cop killer. Sammy laid moaning and rolling on the ground. He wanted to kill her right then and there but it seemed sloppy. He didn't like loose ends.

He walked over to Sammy and gave her another good kick. "Bitch. This is all your fault." Staring at the gun in his hand, he got an idea and talked it out as he thought it through. "Okay ... the cop stopped and saw you were armed, pulled his gun, standoff, he shoots, and you fall and shoot back. You both die."

Jim kicked Sammy onto her back, raised the cop's gun, aimed, and shot her in the chest. He wiped the gun clean with his t-shirt, walked over to the Sheriff and placed it into his right hand. Sammy's gun was cleaned as well, pressed into her hand for fingerprints and dropped in the dirt beside her. He surveyed the scene. It was the best he could do.

Better get the hell out of here. He returned to his vehicle and turned it around. No sense travelling towards Klamath Falls. He needed to leave Highway 97. He headed back to Bend, turned east onto Highway 20 until reaching Highway 78. Totally out of his way, but a safer bet.

He was pissed off. How had this happened? His whole world had spun out of control. The past fifteen years he'd always managed to stay off the police radar. No arrests, accusations, or even a speeding ticket. His record was clean. His fists pounded the steering wheel. Even his name, Jim Draper, was an alias. No one knew what his real name was.

Obsession! That's what did it. Georgia. If this was what love was, he didn't like it. Oh, he'd have his way with her eventually, but only on his terms.

He crossed into Nevada on the Idaho-Oregon-Nevada Highway and followed it through Orovada, continuing on to Reno. Exhausted, he reached Carson City and home after driving for twelve hours straight.

Jim showered, packed more clothes, and fell into bed for a few hours sleep. He woke up four hours later. Gut instinct told him to travel as far away from Carson City as possible. The car was repacked and back in the study, he walked straight to the bookcase, hit a release button and watched it open. A spin of the dial opened a built-in safe hidden in the interior wall. He smiled and ran his hand over the smooth leather of the journals within. The books, along with an expandable file containing maps and photographs were placed into his brief-case. A stop at the post office to pick up his mail and a trip to the bank completed his chore list. He stopped at an open field with a lake. Removing the sim card and battery from his cell phone, Jim threw them into the lake. He smashed his cell phone and threw it into the bushes.

Four days later, having driven east through eight states, he reached the Adirondack Mountains in upstate New York. He'd enjoyed the quiet of the drive east. At this time of year the secondary roads were pretty much traffic free and once he hit the mountainous area of the state, even less so. He preferred the desert of his home state of Nevada, but the dense anonymity of the mountains and forests of this North Country held a certain appeal. The mountainous roads were all but empty and he enjoyed the lonely stretch of road. This vast area could swallow him up and offer a sanctuary for the ensuing winter months and allow him time to regroup.

The Town of Malone loomed up ahead as he drove out of the mountains into the foothills. A typical small-town America with approximately six thousand people, it was the perfect hide-a-way he needed. Jim stopped to pick up supplies and used the pay phone to call Dan Barton, an old friend from his childhood days. Dan gave him instructions to find his cabin.

Fifteen minutes later he reached Lamica Lake and his safe house.

Chapter 24

It was a beautiful Saturday afternoon in mid-December. Georgia and Sean were having lunch at Molly's Reach in lower Gibsons. The girls were at a birthday party for the afternoon.

"Let's take the kids up to the cabin for Christmas." Georgia said.

"Really? I thought we were all going to your parents for Christmas dinner?"

"There's going to be a lot of people there and it may be a bit overwhelming for Shelby. It's only been a month since Julie passed."

"True." Sean said. "But don't you think the more the merrier would help to take her mind off of it?"

"She hasn't shown much enthusiasm for Christmas. Even Kaela's excitement hasn't brought her around. She hasn't met a lot of the people that will be there and I'm afraid she'll feel like she doesn't belong."

"So what are you thinking?" he asked.

"We could fly to Terrace and rent a vehicle. Drive to Dease Lake. I wouldn't want to drive the road in to the cabin at this time of year. Maybe Tom could fly us into the cabin. We can take decorations and a turkey with all the trimmings. And think of the fun we'll have with the girls, cutting down a tree. Shelby may actually enjoy it."

"I can see you're up for it." Sean smiled. "I know you worry about Shelby being introverted. She hasn't really released her grief yet and she won't talk about it. A change of scenery might be the thing."

Georgia sighed. "You realize I haven't been back to the cabin in the winter since my ordeal. I'd love to spend time there with you and the girls."

"I suspect too you aren't entirely comfortable with Christmas at your parents this year either. Am I right?"

"What do you mean?" Georgia tried to act surprised at his question, but Sean knew her too well.

He gave her a look. "Come on give it up."

"Okay. I 'm a little wary of seeing my grandfather. But not for myself. I haven't talked to him since we had our big fight in September about Shelby. If Shelby feels uncomfortable at all, I don't want his attitude to make it worse for her."

"He wouldn't be obvious about it though, would he?"

Georgia pulled a face. "I would hope not, but he said he didn't want anything to do with her. He might ignore her and she's sensitive enough that she'd pick up on it."

"What about your mother? I know she's looking forward to having all the family together."

She hesitated. "She'll be disappointed. I think she's hoping the reunion will bring Granddad around. But, she'd understand if I left that part out and voiced my concerns about Shelby being overwhelmed by a family she hasn't met yet."

"Okay, the cabin it is. I'll call the airlines and rent a car. Although you realize the flights will all be booked. We'll have to pay a fortune for a charter. Then, I'll call Tom and see if he's available to chopper us in to the cabin."

Georgia clasped her hands. "Oh, honey, thank you."

When they told the girls that night, Shelby perked up.

"When are we going, Mommy?" Kaela asked.

"We're going to Vancouver next Saturday, to Sean's condo. We'll exchange presents that night with Nana and Grampa, and the next day we're flying north."

"Flying?" Kaela asked. The kids looked at each other and started to squeal. "Yay ..." Kaela clapped her hands and Shelby put her hands over her mouth but her eyes were big and full of excitement.

Georgia and Sean watched and listened as the girls chattered about what clothes to pack. "I'm not sure last year's clothes will still fit. I see a shopping trip this week," Georgia said. The girls giggled and ran off to their room to sort through their old winter clothes.

Sean gave her a squeeze. "I must say, you were right. Shelby seems excited at the idea of going to the cabin."

"Doesn't she? I'm so pleased. She needs to have some fun and laughter, and remember how to be a kid." She curled up beside Sean and put her head on his shoulder. They cuddled in silence listening to Michael Buble's Christmas album.

Sean broke the quiet. "I'm perplexed about one thing. The girls are not even six years old and they're so fashion conscious. When did that happen?"

She laughed. "Welcome to the girls of the millennium. Television, movies, and videos open a whole new world to kids today, even though we restrict their access to a lot of it."

As Georgia surmised, her mother wasn't pleased about them not being around for Christmas, but she understood the why of it and agreed Shelby could benefit from a complete change of environment.

The week passed quickly and Saturday arrived. That evening, they'd finished dinner when the phone rang. It was Georgia's grandparents from Arizona. They all took turns talking to Nan and Granddad. Her mother handed her the phone to talk to her grandfather.

In an instant, Georgia knew this had been instigated by her mother. *If you can't bring Mohammed to the mountain, then bring the mountain to Mohammed.* She took the phone. "Hi Granddad," she said, cautiously.

"Hi, Georgia. So your mother says you are off to the cabin tomorrow for Christmas."

"That's right." She wasn't quite sure how to approach this conversation.

"I hope you're not going out of town to avoid your old grandfather's arrival tomorrow?"

Georgia walked out of the room with the phone, unsure where the call would lead. She didn't want the girls to hear her side of the conversation.

"Not entirely, Granddad. Sean and I feel Shelby would be overwhelmed amongst family she doesn't know. The girls are really excited about going to the cabin and we want to try to give Shelby a Christmas she can handle. It's only been five weeks since Julie died."

"You said 'not entirely', which means I'm part of this equation and that saddens me."

"Granddad you said you wanted no part of Shelby. I don't want her picking up on your disapproval. Not when she's so fragile." There was a silence at the other end. She waited for him to speak first.

"I said a lot of things that day. Things I shouldn't have said. It's not too often I think that I'm wrong or admit it when I am, but I was. I'm sorry I misjudged your intuition and your intentions."

"This would have meant so much more if you had said this to me before Sean came back into my life." She knew she should accept his apology and move on, but she had a point to make.

"Why should that make a difference?"

"Because you only changed your mind when you knew Sean accepted Shelby."

"But what difference does it make what made me change my mind? I was wrong and I apologized for it."

Georgia turned to see her mother standing in the room, watching her. She knew that look. *Make peace with him for the sake of family. Well, she wasn't ready to do that yet.*

"Do you know what that tells me, Granddad? That you trust Sean's judgement, but you don't trust mine."

Her mother rolled her eyes and shook her head.

"You're right. I'm old generation and I was trying to protect you. Even an old fool can learn something new."

Georgia remained silent. It still irked her that it took Sean's coming back into her life to open his eyes. However, some things about her grandfather would never change. He lived in a man's world and saw things from that perspective.

"So, am I forgiven?" he asked.

Georgia sighed. It was time to leave the past behind them. "Yes, you are. And I'm sorry for some of the things I said to you."

"Thank you, sweet pea. It's a generational thing. Let's leave it at that. Have a Merry Christmas and remember I love you."

"Merry Christmas to you, too. Love you. Bye." Georgia hung up and embraced her mother. There was no need for words. Holding each other was enough.

The next day the four of them flew to Terrace and picked up an SUV rental. They arrived in Dease Lake at dinner time. They stayed at Tom's for the night and flew out by helicopter Monday morning to the cabin. It was December 23rd. With arrangements made for Tom to pick them up January 2nd, they set about making the cabin warm and cosy.

Shelby was like a different child. She and Kaela were already outside making a snowman in the four feet of snow in the front meadow, while Sean made a fire and turned on the generator. Georgia unpacked their bags of food, clothes, and presents.

That evening they all sat in the living room sipping cocoa and eating popcorn.

"Tell us about your Christmas here, Mommy." Kaela said.

"Oh yes, Auntie G, tell us." Shelby added.

"Okay," Georgia said. "Of course the cabin wasn't like it is now. It was only this living room. Sean added the loft and the bedrooms and bathroom later on. There was no electricity, an outhouse for a toilet, and no running water ..."

"Ewww ... must of froze your butt off." Kaela interjected. They all laughed.

"That I did. Anyway, I cut down a little tree and brought it inside and found enough pine cones, pieces of wood, paper, and crayons to make ornaments for the tree. Then I used a doily to make an angel for the top, and tried to cook popcorn on the stove to make a garland. The cabin smelled of burnt popcorn for days."

The girls giggled.

A frown crossed Georgia's brow. "I haven't thought about those ornaments for years. I meant to save them."

Sean got up and left the room.

"What did you eat for Christmas dinner, Auntie G?" Shelby asked.

"I opened a tin of cooked chicken, heated it in the oven, and cooked some rice in the chicken juice. I remember making some raison and cinnamon bannock. Last of all I soaked a jar of beets in some vinegar ..." Georgia stopped talking, lost in thought about that day.

"What's bannock, Auntie G?"

"It's Indian bread, very heavy. In the old days, they made it up and wrapped the dough around a stick and placed it over the fire to cook. Nowadays, it's fried in a fry pan."

"Yum ... I love bannock," Kaela said.

"Oh ... I'll bet you were lonely and scared ..." Shelby's voice trailed off as she lowered her eyes and played with a button on her sweater.

Georgia gave her a smile. "I wasn't alone you know. There was my native spirit, Nonnock. Her white man name is Kaela, and I named you know who after her. I use her Tahltan name to avoid confusion. She came to me whenever she felt I needed her." She glanced at Kaela. "Kaela was with me too."

"But I wasn't born yet." Kaela said.

"Not at Christmas, but being eight months pregnant, I was out to here." Georgia formed a huge circle with her arms in front of her stomach, puffed out her cheeks and the girls laughed. "You were kicking pretty good by then and I'd rub my tummy and talk to you. I called you Sweet Pea."

Kaela giggled and Shelby said, "Aw, that's cute."

"And then there was Feathers," Georgia added.

"Feathers?" Shelby asked.

Kaela picked up the conversation. "He was a black raven. He sat on the railing outside and flew around the meadow with Mommy."

Shelby smiled.

Sean came back into the room with a box and placed it on the couch beside Georgia. She looked up at him in surprise.

"Open it." he said.

Georgia took the lid off of the box. Inside were all her hand-made ornaments. "Oh, Sean, you kept them for me?" A lump formed in her throat and her eyes glistened. The girls came close to see what the box held.

"I'd forgotten all about this box until you mentioned them. When we did the renos I put them away," he said.

Tears stung her eyes. She was speechless.

"Could we decorate a tree with them tomorrow, Auntie G?"

"Yeah ... could we?" Kaela parroted.

"Really? We brought prettier ones from home. I'm afraid these are rather crude."

"No, Mommy. We want yours, can we, can we?"

She looked up at Sean who wore a huge grin. "Yeah, Mommy, can we?" he pleaded.

"Of course."

The girls clapped their hands and yelled "Yay!"

The next day, Sean cut a tree and the girls decorated it with Georgia's ornaments.

They all stood back and admired the little tree.

"All that's missing is the burnt popcorn smell," Georgia said.

Later, they added some red ribbons Georgia had brought for wrapping presents and the tree was done. They cut pine boughs and put them around the cabin. The resinous smell was heavenly.

That night, after the girls fell asleep, Georgia placed the presents around the tree, and when she was done, cuddled with Sean on the couch under a blanket and watched the fire in the woodstove.

"Listen? Hear that?" Georgia asked.

"What am I supposed to be hearing?"

"The log walls cracking from the cold. I remember lying in bed the winter I was alone wondering what was causing the noise. I figured it out eventually, but when the trees cracked, it freaked me out because it sounded like a rifle shot."

Sean held her tighter. "Funny how little unknown things like that can scare a person."

"And the creaking of the ice heaves on the stream when they rub together. Thinking about it all now though, it's so familiar and comforting. I feel like I'm home."

"Knowing we're in contact with the outside and have a helicopter picking us up helps," Sean teased.

Georgia looked into Sean's face and stroked his cheek with her fingers. "And having a family to share it all with." She leaned over and brushed his lips with hers. They wiggled under the blanket until they faced each other.

"Are you trying to seduce me, Miss Georgia?"

"You better believe it. I'm visualizing a memory of the day you found me here and it's made me all warm and fuzzy."

Sean laughed. "A crazy mud-caked man breaks through the door, demands to know who you are and why you're living in his cabin—and that makes you frisky?"

Georgia giggled. "It isn't that part I'm thinking of. It's the part where the mud-caked man needs to take a bath. I sat with my back to you in the rocking chair pretending to read a book while you stood in a metal tub behind me." She planted kisses on his cheeks and the tip of his nose.

"And?" Sean asked.

"Well … I wasn't reading." She said, coyly.

With a husky voice, he asked, "So what *were* you doing?"

"Visualizing a handsome and totally naked man splashing soap and water all over his body, like this." She ran her hands all over his body until she felt his response.

"You little vixen, and I thought you were the sweetest, most innocent thing I'd ever seen."

"You were totally deceived." Georgia placed her parted lips on his and teased him with her tongue.

Sean pushed her away and sat up. "I think we need to retreat to the loft." He stood and put his hands out to pull her up on her feet. Arm in arm, they climbed the stairs to the loft, stopping to steal kisses on each step, until they finally collapsed on the bed, arms and legs entangled in a frenzied state of passion. Later, as they whispered quietly to each other, Sean reminded Georgia she'd better head to the other bedroom before they both fell asleep. This prompted her to move closer to him and pull the cover up higher.

"Don't you think it's time we stop the charade with the girls? They obviously love you to pieces. Maybe it's time for us to move into one bedroom."

"Seriously? Are you saying what I think you're saying? Sean whispered.

"I am. Merry Christmas, my love."

Sean reached out and drew her close to his chest. His arms tightened around her and she could feel his breath on her cheek. "Merry Christmas, sweetheart."

Christmas morning, Georgia came down the steps of the loft to find the girls on the couch wrapped in a blanket. Sean was stoking up the wood stove. Shelby and Kaela took one look at her, glanced at each other and giggled.

"Merry Christmas, Mommy," Kaela said.

"Merry Christmas, Auntie G," Shelby chimed in.

The girls broke into another fit of giggles.

"Merry Christmas, girls." Georgia knew they were too young to totally understand the intimacy of her relationship with Sean, but they knew enough to know that last night something had changed and they seemed okay with it.

Christmas day was filled with family love and warmth. A beautiful sunny day, they all went out tobogganing across the creek in the parallel meadow that had a hill at one end. That afternoon, the girls laid on the floor playing a game while Sean and Georgia prepped their Christmas dinner. Outside a distinct "Kraa, Kraa" could be heard. They all stopped and listened. The girls ran to the front window.

"It's Feathers," Kaela yelled.

They stood by the window and watched as a raven sitting on the porch railing cackled at them. "Kraa, Kraa, toc, toc, toc."

"I don't know if it's Feathers after five years." Georgia said.

The raven appeared to be staring right at Georgia. A low guttural rattle emanated from his throat. Georgia's mouth dropped open and her hand went to her chest. "The only time I heard Feathers use that kind of talk was the day I gave birth to Kaela."

Sean placed a hand on her shoulder. "I've read that ravens can live up to forty years."

She ran for her coat and boots. "Then let's see if he is Feathers."

She opened the door to the cabin and while the others stayed in the window and watched, Georgia flew down the stairs and started to run through the meadow. The bird watched for a moment and then flew after her. She ran all around the outside edge of the meadow and the raven flew low over her head, turning summersaults then soaring high up and diving back down to swirl in circles above her. Georgia ran back up the stairs and stopped by the wooden railing. The raven landed in front of her on his favorite perch. She reached out and stroked his head while he gave her a repeat of the guttural roll from his throat. "You are my Feathers." she said, softly. Tears rolled down her cheeks. Kaela came out of the cabin to join her.

"Mommy, you're crying." Kaela said in distress.

"Happy tears, Sweet Pea." She drew Kaela in front of her. "Remember Kaela, Feathers? She's that little baby you watched over when the spring came and we sat right here in the sun."

Feathers moved his head from side to side, looking first at Kaela, then at Georgia. One more guttural roll escaped his throat and he turned and flew off into the trees.

Back in the cabin, the girls asked questions about the black bird.

"The first time I noticed him, was in mid-December. I'd walk the perimeter of the meadow out front for exercise and he'd fly above me and follow me in a circle. I wondered why he was still here in winter and why he was alone. He'd sit on the railing and watch me through the window." She checked the turkey in the oven, basted it and closed the oven door.

"He came to visit on Christmas Day, as I was feeling alone and missing family. That's when I decided he must be my protector and I gave him the name, Feathers. We became great companions after that. I talked to him about my pending childbirth and he was a great listener." Georgia imitated his stance, cocking her head from side to side, until the girls doubled over in laughter.

"Tell Shelby about the day I was born, Mommy."

Georgia smiled. "Yes, Valentine's Day, a day for love. I spent the day prepping for your birth, counting the minutes between contractions. There was a howling wind and blizzard raging outside. I went to the window to close the shutters and saw Feathers hunched over on the railing. It surprised me because it would have been difficult for him to fly in that wind and he was unprotected sitting in the open ..." She lost herself in thought.

"Auntie G?" Shelby asked.

"Sorry, where was I? Feathers! That was the first time I heard that low guttural rattle emanating from his throat. I truly believed he knew it was my day to give birth and he was there offering support."

"Tell us about your native spirit coming to help." Kaela prodded.

"Well, the birth started and Nonnock hadn't shown up like she said she would." Georgia tweaked her daughter's nose. "You had a mind of your own and weren't waiting for anyone." The girls looked at each other and giggled. "When I started to panic she was here. Not really here. I never saw her, only heard her voice speaking in my mind. She reminded me of my exercises and kept me focused. Then your head popped out and there you were. This tiny, perfect baby and red all over from screaming."

"Why do babies scream when they're born, Auntie G?"

"It's a normal and necessary part of birth because it opens their lungs so they can breathe through their mouth and nose on their own."

Shelby frowned. "But you said, Kaela's head popped out and she was born. Where did it pop out from?"

Sean was sitting behind the girls, who were on the floor in front of Georgia. They locked eyes. He raised his eyebrows and gave her a horrified look. Before she could answer, Kaela saved the day.

"Us girls have a spot near our private parts. It's small, but when we have babies, it becomes really big and opens up and the baby pops out. Simple," Kaela said.

"Ohh ..." Shelby fell silent, her face registering a number of emotions.

Georgia stood. "That's enough lore for the moment. Why don't you girls wash your hands and set the table for dinner?"

The two girls headed to the bathroom to wash up. Sean and Georgia stifled a laugh.

"Nice save, Mommy," he said.

Chapter 25

As the days passed, Shelby became more relaxed. She and Kaela played hard and it was obvious to Georgia and Sean that Shelby had found her childhood again. Sean knocked himself out, especially with Shelby, teasing and making them laugh. One afternoon, the girls came in soaking wet from making angels in the snow. Georgia asked them to strip down in front of the wood stove and was busy hanging the wet items on a clothes line above the fire box to dry. Shelby had already redressed, while Kaela was taking her time removing her wet clothes. Sean headed out the back door for more firewood.

"Can I come and help?" Shelby asked. She grabbed one of Sean's jackets and put it on. It hung to the ground.

He laughed, tugging the hood down over her face. "I guess it works for the short time we'll out there. Grab your boots."

"Me too." Kaela searched for something to put on over her wet clothes.

Georgia stopped her. "Oh no you don't. You still have wet clothes on. Don't want you to catch a chill."

"But …"

"No. Take those wet things off and put on some dry clothes please."

"Awww …" Kaela's mouth formed into a pout and she stamped her foot. Georgia gave her a look and Kaela did as she was told.

Georgia could hear Sean and Shelby laughing outside. Once in a while, Shelby would squeal with delight. It warmed her heart to see Shelby in such a space for once. It also made her love Sean all the more for his extra efforts to ensure the child's place in their family.

The sound of a helicopter could be heard overhead. Georgia looked out the window and watched Tom land the red bird.

A few minutes later, they all stood in the living room, Sean said, "We didn't expect you back until after New Year's."

"I know. I was out testing my Christmas present and thought I'd come and show it to you." Tom was beaming like a little kid. "But you have to come out to the chopper."

The two men left the cabin to check out some new electronic gizmo Tom's wife had bought him for navigation. The girls retreated to their bedroom to play a game while Georgia pulled out leftovers to heat for dinner. Barely ten minutes passed when she heard a commotion from the back of the house. The girls were yelling at each other and she heard Shelby crying. "Good grief." She hurried down the hall. Shelby was sitting on the floor sobbing and Kaela was sitting on the bed with tears running down her face."

"What's going on in here?" Neither one spoke. She walked over to Shelby. "Are you hurt?" Shelby shook her head but continued to sob, so Georgia turned to Kaela. "What happened?" she said, firmly.

Kaela's face took on a guilty look and she dropped her eyes to the floor. Georgia knew her daughter had started whatever transpired. She turned back to Shelby who by now was crying softly. "Shelby, tell me what happened, please."

Shelby gulped in some air to steady her breathing. "Kaela pushed me onto the floor."

Georgia looked at Kaela in shock. "Why?"

Kaela started to cry. "I don't know."

Georgia was upset with her daughter. She didn't quite know how to handle this. Kaela had never done such a mean-spirited thing. Feeling puzzled, the one thing she did know was she couldn't punish Kaela until she understood what had brought on such bad behavior. Instead, she calmed herself, leaned down and took Shelby's hand. "Stand up, sweetheart and come with me. Kaela, you can stay right here until you're ready to explain yourself. I'll talk to you later." Kaela threw herself onto the bed and sobbed, while the other two left the bedroom.

Shelby sat quietly on the couch, staring ahead.

Georgia talked, softly. "Why did Kaela push you onto the floor? Please tell me."

"She was mad at me."

"And why was she mad at you, honey?"

A confused look passed over the little girl's face. "I'm not really sure. I know she was mad 'cause I could help Sean with the firewood and she couldn't." The picture became clear to Georgia. *Sibling rivalry, but that didn't condone violence.*

"So she pushed you on the floor because you helped Sean with the wood, is that it?"

"Well, that was some of it. She yelled at me and said that she knew Sean first and he was her friend more than mine." *That little snot.* The tears started to flow again. Shelby looked at her hands in her lap and started to play with her fingers. "She told me I stole our Daddy away from her and I couldn't have Sean too."

Georgia was stunned. So that was it. This went deeper than sibling rivalry. Kaela was jealous. She lifted the child onto her lap and put her arms around her. "Kaela was mean to you because she was jealous. Your Daddy never spent a lot of time with her, but Sean did. Now, Sean's back in our lives, she's afraid he'll spend more time with you than with her. He has a big heart and enough love for all of us. Can you understand that?"

"Yeah ... but I didn't spend a lot of time with Daddy either. He was always at work."

"You and I know that, but I guess Kaela doesn't. When I talk with her I'll explain it. But none of this gives her the right to push you over and Kaela will have to be punished for her bad behavior."

Shelby looked into Georgia's face with eyes big and wide. "What will you do to her?"

Georgia pursed her lips. "Making her stay alone in her room might be enough."

When she checked on Kaela, she'd fallen asleep on her bed, so Georgia closed the door and left her. Tom left and Sean came back into the house and asked why he'd heard crying outside. Georgia told him she'd explain later. She went back before dinner and found her daughter on her back staring at the ceiling. Georgia sat down on the bed beside her.

Before she could say anything, Kaela turned to her. "I'm sorry, Mommy. I know I was bad. I didn't mean to push her but I was mad at her."

"Would you like to tell me why?"

Kaela frowned. "I was unhappy 'cause she was having fun with Sean."

"Shelby has had a lot to deal with, you know that. Don't you want her to be happy and having fun?"

"Yeah, but..."

Georgia knew Kaela was having trouble finding the words to express her feelings. She decided to help her out a little. "Shelby said you told her Sean was your friend, not hers and that she stole your Daddy away from you. Is that true?"

"I guess. That was really bad wasn't it?"

"Yes, it was. As for your Daddy, Auntie Julie told me once that he was such a workaholic, he didn't spend a lot of time with her either. That's who he was, honey. He didn't favour one of you over the other. Do you understand that?"

"Yes."

"And you know Sean loves you. You lost your Dad, but you've always had both Sean's and my love. Shelby lost both her parents and she needs to know she's loved by Sean and me.

Kaela started to cry. "Well … you and Sean broke up. I didn't think he loved me anymore and since he's been back, he pays more attention to Shelby than me."

The light went on and Georgia's heart went out to her daughter. "Come here, sweetheart." She held her in her arms, as she had Shelby. "I'm so sorry I didn't realize what you were feeling. I was so caught up in Shelby's loss, I assumed you were okay. Sean's trying to help her feel as though she's a part of our family. Of course, he still loves you and he has enough love for all of us. Our breaking up was an adult thing and had nothing to do with Sean's love for you. That never changed. She took her daughter's face in her hands and kissed the tip of her nose."Does any of this make sense to you?"

Kaela gave her a smile. "Yes. I feel better now. And I'm sorry I was mean to Shelby."

"I think Shelby would like to hear that. Why don't I send her in? Then you both can wash up and join us for dinner."

"Okay."

Five minutes later the girls came to the table their old selves, laughing and giggling.

That night in bed with Sean, Georgia filled him in on the whole episode. "I hope this isn't something that will keep happening between them," she said.

"I don't think so. You saw them at dinner. What happened has been building since Colin died. Now it's out in the open, I expect things will be better between the two of them."

"I doubt myself, sometimes," Georgia said.

"In what way?"

"As a mother. I was so worried about Shelby; I didn't see Kaela's pain."

Sean turned and looked into her face. "Parenthood doesn't come with a handbook. We learn as we go along. We don't have psych degrees when we become parents."

Georgia laughed. "Maybe it should be a requirement."

He brushed a kiss across her lips. "You're a wonderful mother. I didn't realize I was favouring Shelby either. I'll give the girls equal treatment from now on. And, we were both amiss when we broke up. We were so caught up with our own feelings; we didn't realize that Kaela suffered too."

Chapter 26

January 8th – Gibsons, B.C.

Georgia and Sean had been called to the RCMP Detachment and sat with the Constable and his superior, Corporal Gordon Teaves.

Constable Denning opened a file on his desk and searched for a paper. "Here we are," he said. "Georgia, we have the identity of your stalker. His real name is Jim Pearson. Jim Draper's an alias. His last known address is Carson City, Nevada. We know he crossed into Canada at the Pacific Border Crossing in September in a rental vehicle and towards the end of November, he passed back to the U.S. in the same rental."

Georgia looked perplexed. "That makes no sense. He comes all the way up here in September, delivers flowers, and then leaves in November? It's now January and I haven't heard from him since. I don't understand it. And why me?"

The two officers looked at each other and Corporal Teaves picked up the conversation.

"We did a background check on Mr. Pearson. He had a bad upbringing. Alcoholic parents, taken into foster care at the age of ten. One year later, his mother, clean and sober, got him back. She'd separated from his father. They had two years together, when Daddy talked his way back into the house. Six months later, the parents died in a murder-suicide." The Corporal sifted through some photographs, picked one up and handed it to Georgia.

She took in a sharp intake of breathe and her head jerked backwards. She looked up in surprise.

"His mother," Corporal Teaves said.

She handed the picture to Sean. He stiffened. "So you think because they look alike, he's targeted Georgia?"

"It's a good guess and one our Profiler backs up. Mr. Pearson has been a busy boy. Now I don't know why he left here, unless he knew we were watching for him. Maybe, he needed to go home. Whatever the reason, he did go home. He picked up a female hitchhiker in Oregon, probably with bad plans in store for the lady. But we believe she tried to turn the tables on him. She had a history of forcing drivers to turn over their wallets or she'd call rape. Our man was beating the hell out of her when a County Sheriff drove up. He killed him and then the girl. He tried to make it look like they shot and killed each other, but the camera on the dash of the Sheriff's vehicle showed the whole thing. Pearson didn't realize he'd been filmed."

Georgia's stomach lurched. "Dear God ..."

"There's more. Meanwhile, we've been working with cross border agencies. They identified him through the Nevada Motor Licensing Branch and obtained a search warrant for his house. His neighbours said law enforcement only missed him by a couple of days. The bookcase in his study had a hidden safe that was open and empty when the officers went in. He may have gone home to retrieve whatever was in there. He told his neighbours in August that his wife had left him and gone out of state to her family. The FBI is involved and they're trying to track them down. However, we believe she probably met with foul play at the hands of her husband."

"Why did you come to that conclusion?" Sean asked.

"Because her clothes, purse, and personal effects were all still at the house." Corporal Teaves paused before continuing. "They found traces of Mrs. Drayton's blood in the study."

Sean reached out and took Georgia's hand. "Do you think he'll come back here?"

"Something sent him racing home. Intuition to protect himself? I don't know. But he's exhibited an obsession with Georgia. Our profiler says in all probability he'll be back."

"So I continue to live with this hanging over my head, looking over my shoulder," Georgia said with resignation. "What's worse, my stalker is also a murderer."

"And you have no clue where he is?" Sean said.

"No, but he's tagged in BOLF ... that's Be on the Lookout For. There's a nation-wide warrant out for his arrest, here and in the states, and Border Integrity have his identity. Hopefully, if he crosses into Canada again, a diligent border guard will pick up on it. We'll keep you informed if we receive any more information. If he makes any contact with you whatsoever, please call us right away."

Georgia was silent as they drove home. Sean tried to draw her out but she ignored him.

The weeks in January passed slowly, with Georgia falling into a depression. Phone calls and noises in the neighbourhood freaked her out but she internalized it.

One morning towards the end of the month, she sat in the love seat staring out at the park. Sean brought her a cup of coffee and sat opposite her in the arm chair.

"Babe, we need to talk about this," he said.

"Talk about what?"

Sean sighed. "Don't play dumb. You know what. Ever since we found out who your stalker is, you've shut me and the world out."

Georgia stared at him silently. "I know." She sipped her coffee and lowered her eyes.

"Talk to me. Tell me what you're thinking and feeling. Please."

"It was better when I didn't know anything about him. Even when I had a face, I could handle it. But now, knowing he's not only a stalker but a murderer …" Her voice trailed off.

"You're scared, Babe. Who wouldn't be? I get that, but don't shut out the people who want to be there for you and protect you."

"It wasn't something I consciously thought about doing. It happened as the whole thing became more real."

Georgia moved over and sat beside Sean. She reached out and took his hand.

Sean squeezed her hand, "I know you're the one who's being threatened here, but I need to share this with you. I'm frustrated too. There are so many unknowns. Will he show up again, and when will he show up? Can the police protect you, and can I? I feel so helpless, but as long as we talk to each other and stay aware of what we're each feeling, we can stay strong."

"You're right. We can't let him take control of our lives. My depression took me away from you and I'm so sorry." Georgia leaned over and put her head on Sean's shoulder.

The next week pulled her out of the state she'd slipped into, as the girls sixth birthdays loomed. Georgia wrapped herself up in party plans and preparations.

Shelby's day was on February 1st and Kaela's on February the 14th. Georgia wanted the girls to maintain their individuality and planned a family dinner with her parents on both dates to celebrate. The girls decided a combined party with their friends on the weekend in-between would be fun. February came and went in a festive mood.

Days and then weeks passed with no contact from Jim Pearson, or updates from the RCMP. As time wore on, Georgia tried to put it all behind her. The whole affair definitely made an impact on her awareness of her surroundings. Whenever she went out with family or friends her guard was down but as soon as she found herself alone some place, her radar picked up on the activities of those around her. Sean started writing a new series and set up a computer station in the guest bedroom. He saw to it that Georgia was rarely alone.

Some weekends they went to town and stayed in Sean's condo, visiting family, and taking the girls to events in the city while Sean did research at the library for his book.

Although Shelby settled into her new life living with her Auntie G, Sean, and her sister Kaela, she was still introverted with her grief and refused to talk about her mother. One Saturday afternoon, the girls and Georgia were baking muffins for a party at school.

"Look at you two. I think you have more flour on yourselves than in the batter." Georgia said, with a smile. The girls took a good look at each other and giggled.

"So, what kind of icing do you want, girls?"

"Umm ... cream cheese?" Shelby asked.

"Ya, cream cheese. Can we decorate the tops with faces, like the pumpkin ones we made with Auntie J at Halloween?" Kaela asked.

"Sure we can." Georgia answered, glancing at Shelby. *Uh-oh.* The child stiffened and said nothing more for the rest of the bake.

Georgia knew Shelby took a picture of Julie to bed with her at night. But she did participate with the other kids at school and outgoing Kaela drew her out of her shell. Still, Georgia waited for the day Shelby would open up to her.

Sibling rivalry popped its ugly head once in a while but Georgia knew that it was normal. Kaela showed compassion with her sister and there were no more fits of jealousy where Sean was concerned.

Chapter 27

April 21ˢᵗ - Lamica Lake, New York

Dan hid Jim Pearson's car in an outbuilding behind the cabin and tarped it. The two men climbed into his Range Rover and set off towards Hogansburg.

It was April and the snow was all but gone. Jim glanced at his friend. Dan had lived a quiet life there for fifteen years. He kept to himself and that's why Jim trusted him. Since Dan's discharge from the army, he supported himself on a disability pension. No one knew his real source of money came from smuggling ... not liquor, drugs or cigarettes, but human trafficking.

An hour and a half later they arrived at their destination, a house in Hogansburg. Although, it was currently empty, Dan used it frequently to hide customers who paid hefty amounts to immigrate illegally into Canada. They waited there until darkness came and then set out for the bordering town of St. Regis, on the St. Regis Mohawk Reservation. It sat adjacent to the reservations across the border in Ontario and Quebec. The Mohawks had the right to cross the Canada-US border freely from one reservation to another and considered it a sovereign nation. Smuggling was a lucrative venture for Dan and the Mohawk who chose to be a part of his business. The reservation encompassed fifty-four kilometers of land, including five kilometers of water. A series of islands in the St. Lawrence River maintained access by the frozen river in winter, which allowed unobserved crossings from the US to Canada or in reverse. April was the last freeze and the last time this season that Dan would use the frozen river to smuggle customers across.

The process was not without danger. The Mohawk had their own police force that regularly patrolled the reserve lands, and the RCMP monitored the highways on the Canadian side, pulling over any suspicious vehicles. At this time of year, the river could thaw and refreeze, which caused unstable ice fissures.

Dan pulled up to the front of a house not far from the river. He told Jim to stay in the car while he disappeared into the house. A few minutes later, he emerged with a first nation's man who approached the car. The man stared at him and told him to exit the vehicle. Jim stood by the open car door and said nothing as Dan had coached him. The man looked him up and down and then nodded to Dan, who pulled an envelope of money out of his jacket pocket and passed it to the man.

"This is goodbye my friend." Dan said to Jim.

The two men shook hands and Jim patted him on the shoulder. "Thanks for the hospitality."

He followed his new smuggler to another vehicle and climbed in. The man never said a word as they drove onto the river and began their crossing. This suited Jim. A few times, the ice creaked and he could see water seep over the ice. He glanced at the driver but he didn't seem too concerned. They crossed the river without incident and the man continued on into the closest city on the Canadian side of the border, Cornwall, Ontario. He dropped him at a motel. Jim offered his hand. "Thank you," he said.

The driver ignored the gesture, leaving his hands firmly planted on the steering wheel. He nodded and waited for him to exit the car.

The next morning, Jim searched the phone book in the room for a car rental. He walked to the location, rented a four wheel drive SUV, and purchased a highway map. Finding Highway 40, he began his journey west to British Columbia.

The closer he got, the more excited he became. He stared at the picture of Georgia on his sun visor and smiled. Jim fantasized about the two of them together. His sweet peach would make him complete. His plan was to kidnap her and eventually, she'd see his love for her and know they were meant to be together. Staring at her face always aroused him. A vision of his mother's face spoiled his mood.

He thought of the time he and his mother had lived alone together. It was the happiest he'd ever been. It wasn't long before she began drinking again. He'd reached puberty, a fact that hadn't missed his drunken mother's eye. The seduction began and she allowed him to drink with her. At first, he'd been repulsed, but eventually, their abnormal relationship pleased him. It was their dirty little secret, until one day his father returned. Once he'd wormed his way back into his mother's bed, she stopped her trysts with her son.

Anger seethed inside him, boiling over to the point that Jim began to pound the steering wheel. His tantrum was over as quick as it had begun. A slow warmth spread through his body and a dark grin spread across his face. "But I showed you, didn't I? And, I fooled everyone."

The night his parents died they were both drunk and the fighting started. Jim snuck out of the house to get away from the yelling. When he returned, he'd hoped to find them passed out. Instead, he laid in his bed listening to their loud sighs and grunts of lust. He placed the pillow over his ears to shut them out. Eventually, he heard his father's loud snoring and knew they were asleep. He hated his father for disrupting the quiet life he'd been living with his mother. And he hated his mother for abandoning him yet again.

Jim got out of bed and stripped naked, retrieved the rubber gloves under the sink in the bathroom, put them on and tip toed into their bedroom. He retrieved the pistol from his father's bedside table. He rolled his father onto his left side, placed the gun in his right hand, aimed his father's hand at the back of his mother's head and pushed his finger on the trigger. His father awoke with a start but in his drunken stupor, was no match for Jim. Jim turned the gun towards his father's temple and forced his finger over the trigger before the man could pull himself together and react.

Jim washed himself down, put on his pajamas and called 911. No one questioned his story that he awoke to the sound of gunshots and found his parents dead in their bed. Their history of domestic violence spoke for them. He was a victim.

He drove on into the dark night. If anyone had seen him, it would have been a strange site to watch this man driving all alone, laughing hysterically.

Chapter 28

Georgia sifted through the soil, removing debris with her fingers. She let the dirt fall freely between her fingers. She loved the soft, damp feel of it. Planting May flowers was a comforting hobby that brought back childhood memories of helping Grams in this garden so many years ago. She leaned back from her knees to rest on the backs of her heels and lifted her face to the sun. Her skin soaked up the heat offered to her on this beautiful warm day.

She inspected the garden beds and felt satisfied with her work. Of course, she was doing this not for herself, but for her grandmother who would be returning home sometime over the summer. Now that Georgia had added two people to her life, they'd found another place to live. They couldn't possibly impose on her Grams when she returned. They intended to keep the condo in Vancouver as it served them well when in the city on business or pleasure and the cabin at Dease Lake was their escape.

Georgia stood and stretched her sore muscles from sitting on the ground for so long. Sean and her had spotted a house for sale at the end of the street by the school. It bordered the far end of the park. The lovely two story home with four bedrooms, one en suite, plus two full bathrooms was perfect. The girls still wanted to share a bedroom, but the extra room was there when they were ready for their own rooms. For now it would serve as an office, and the fourth room as a guest bedroom. They would take possession August1st.

Feeling thirsty, she turned and headed into the back of the house. There, she poured herself a glass of lemonade and wandered into the living room, the doorbell rang. She went to open it, but stopped. She was home alone. The girls were still in school and Sean had gone to the book store on the Landing in lower Gibsons to pick up a book he'd ordered, expecting to be gone only fifteen minutes.

For her own safety, she walked over to the window and looked to the stoop in front of the door. "Omigod ... it's him." She jumped back but not before she was seen.

Jim Pearson aka Jim Draper walked over the grass and stared in the window at her. He raised his hand and gave her a big wave and a huge smile.

The thought occurred to her that he may not know that she knew his real name, believing him to be Jim Draper, the writer. Georgia forced a smile and waved back. She signalled she was heading to the door. Once there, she pressed the panic button beside the alarm box, ran upstairs and locked herself in the master bedroom. She picked up the telephone on the bedside table and called 911.

A voice came through the line immediately. "911. What's your emergency?"

Georgia heard the back door open and realized she'd forgotten to lock it. "Oh shit, shit, there's a stalker in my house."

"Where are you in the house?"

"I've locked myself upstairs in the master bedroom," she whispered. She backed up against the wall by the window. Her heart jack-hammered as her breath was stolen away. She swallowed hard.

The calm voice of the dispatcher settled her a little. "What's your name?"

"Georgia Charles. Constable Denning has a file on Jim Pearson. He's my stalker."

A voice called out to her. "Georgia? Are you up there?"

"Uh ... he's calling my name. I hear him on the stairs."

"Stay calm, Georgia. We have a unit on the way. Don't answer him."

She watched the door handle wiggle and a soft pounding on the door. "I know you're in there. Open the door. There's no reason to fear me."

"I can hear him talking to you, Georgia. Is there somewhere you can hide in the bedroom?"

"The en suite," she said in barely a whisper.

"Go in there and lock the door, okay?"

Georgia scurried across the floor and into the bathroom, locking the door. She heard the man force the door open to the bedroom. Her eyes frantically searched the bathroom for a weapon.

The dispatcher called out to her. "Georgia. Are you there? Stay with me, okay? Are you in the bathroom?"

"Yes," she whispered.

"Is the door locked?" the dispatcher asked.

"Yes."

He shook the lock on the bathroom door. Terrified, Georgia grabbed Sean's straight razor. *Thank God for men who like to shave the old fashioned way.*

"Come on my sweet Georgia peach, be a good girl and open the door."

She put the phone down but left it open. There was nothing the dispatcher could say to help her now. The door pushed out, not in. When he forced it open and pulled it towards him, she would be right out with it, ready to do damage where ever she could on his body. The element of surprise was all she had in her favour. In a split second, she reasoned it out. Her left arm would go out at him first. His instinct would be to grab that arm. Meanwhile, the right arm with the razor would come in hard and fast cutting whatever she made contact with.

She could hear the dispatcher calling out to her, but she ignored her, forcing all of her concentration on that door, readying her body for that important charge.

He was fumbling with the door lock but it wouldn't budge. Pulling a door outwards didn't have the same power as forcing it in with his body weight. She realized he had given up on the lock and was using a tool of some kind to remove the pins from the door hinge. Georgia shifted her weight and stance accordingly to the opposite side of the door and waited.

He pulled the door back and Georgia screamed as loud as she could muster and charged out the door. She raised her left arm as if to strike him and he grabbed her left arm with both hands. Her right arm came at him a little lower and she thrashed out, slicing him in the abdomen through his t-shirt. He fell backwards with a yell and looked down at his left side. Blood was already soaking his shirt. He placed his left hand over the wound and looked up at her with disbelief. "Bitch!"

Georgia lunged at him again and he jumped back. She had barely enough room to side-step him and run across the bedroom and out into the hallway. The sound of sirens echoed in her panic-stricken mind as she scurried down the stairs. Half-way down, she slipped on the hardwood steps and bounced the rest of the way to the bottom. Her right hand still gripped the straight razor and when her elbow hit the wall, the force knocked her hand down and into her upper right thigh. She screamed in pain as the razor sliced through her jeans and over her skin.

An RCMP officer ran into the lower foyer with his gun drawn. He looked at Georgia, who through her pain and tears pointed upstairs . He pointed his gun up the stairs and scanned the upper foyer. Seeing no one, he reached over to the front door and unlocked it. Two more officers entered the foyer. Two of them proceeded up the stairs with guns drawn and pointed. The other stayed with her and called for an ambulance.

Sean came home as Constable Denning arrived. Three police cars, an ambulance and a fire truck were parked on the street. A large crowd of people were being held at bay across the street in the park. Georgia heard him yell her name and saw him run through the door. When he saw the amount of blood on her clothes and on the floor, he leaned down beside the paramedic who was applying a pressure bandage to her thigh. "I'm so sorry. I should never have left you alone."

Fresh tears fell down her cheeks. She was never so happy to see him.

Sean looked up at Constable Denning. "Did you catch him?"

The Constable shook his head. "I'm afraid not. In spite of the injury Georgia inflicted on him with that straight razor, he managed to climb out of the bedroom window and make his way onto the branches of the willow tree and escape through the forest out back."

Sean was beside himself with anger, guilt, and fear. "That bastard. Look what he did to you."

Georgia tried to refute his statement, but she was in too much pain and felt too weak to try.

"No, sir," said the officer, who'd called the ambulance. "After she injured the intruder, she ran out of the room and down the stairs. She lost her balance and injured herself."

The paramedic finished with her leg and stood. "Let's move you to the hospital." He and the other paramedics lifted her onto the stretcher.

Sean looked puzzled. "What about the injury to her abdomen?"

The paramedic gave him a broad smile. "That's not her blood, sir. That's the other guys."

An hour later, Georgia went into surgery in St. Mary's Hospital in Sechelt. The damage to her thigh was minimal and would heal without any permanent damage.

However, she had lost a lot of blood and an intravenous blood transfusion was set up. The doctors decided to keep her in overnight and release her the next day. Sean arranged for Frank to pick up the girls after school and take them to Halfmoon Bay.

Constable Denning stationed an officer at her hospital room door and that evening he paid her a visit.

"We've set road blocks up and down the highway from Langdale to Pender Harbour. Powell River RCMP searched all vehicles leaving the Saltery Bay ferry from the peninsula, and the West Van RCMP did the same thing at the Horseshoe Bay Terminal. We're monitoring marinas and all float planes flying out. Sooner or later, we'll catch him."

"I hope so," Georgia said, with a sigh.

"You did great today, Georgia. You didn't panic and you used your head."

"I couldn't have stayed calm without the help of that dispatcher. She was so calm and she talked me down."

Sean stayed with her until she fell asleep. The next day, he arrived to take her home. When Frank brought the girls home, they told them she'd fallen and cut her leg and spent the night at the hospital. Georgia didn't want them to know about her stalker's visit to the house. Sean had seen to it that the doors were fixed and the blood cleaned up before they came home.

"But why didn't you tell us Mommy was in the hospital?" Kaela asked Grampa Frank when they were all seated in the living room with Georgia propped up on the couch.

"I asked him not to, sweetheart. I was afraid you both would think it was worse than it was and have a bad night. Did you have fun with Grampa Frank?"

Both girls giggled. "Yeah," Shelby said. "He let us stay up late and we had popcorn with lots of butter."

That night Georgia cuddled up to Sean in bed.

"How's the pain? If you're uncomfortable, I can sleep in the guest room."

"It's okay right now. And no, I want you here with me." She stared at the moonlight filtering in through the window slats and could see the shadows of the tree limbs against the backlit blinds.

As if he could read her mind, Sean cut into her thoughts. "I'm going to call a tree trimmer in the morning and have those branches against the house cut off."

"Sounds like a good plan. I hope they catch him soon. How much longer can we live like this? Always in fear."

The pain killers kicked in and before Sean could answer, she fell into a deep sleep.

Chapter 29

One morning in early June, Sean sat Georgia down. "Let's take the girls out of school early and go to the cabin for the summer. It's only kindergarten and all they're doing is field trips and such. It would do you good to leave here for awhile. My research is done and the tranquility at the cabin is what I need to pull my book together."

Georgia smiled. "Like the old days before we came into your life. You always spent the summers doing the final manuscripts. With the road all the way in to the cabin, we can take some trips out, so the girls don't become too bored."

"You bet. I'd like to take about ten days and go to the Yukon. The girls will love it."

Georgia laughed. "We won't be able to step foot in the Yukon without visiting Marion."

"Of course we will."

By the end of that week, the suitcases were packed, mail was redirected, and the four of them left at dawn to start the drive north. They had moved all their personal things out of her Grams house into storage and prepared the house for her return. When they came back in August, their new house down the street would be theirs. Her parents were away, which meant they didn't have to stop in North Vancouver to say their good-byes. They decided to head north from Horseshoe Bay through Whistler and over Duffy Lake to Lillooet. They took their time, staying in Clinton, the entrance to the Cariboo. The next morning they visited Clinton's historic museum and it's pioneer cemetery. Quesnel was their next stop for the night, visiting the restored gold rush town of Barkerville.

They walked the streets of Barkerville exploring the old buildings. There were private retail shops in some of the old buildings and all the people working in the town dressed in late 1800's costumes.

Sean and Georgia watched the girls pan for gold at the General Store. They dipped their gold pans into the sluice boxes, swirling the sand and water, peppered with real gold colour, the way the proprietor had shown them.

Shelby squealed with delight. "Kaela, look at my gold." A few minutes later, it was Kaela's turn to find a tiny nugget in her pan.

Georgia pulled them away from their reverie. "Come on, girls. The show at the Royal Theatre starts in a few minutes."

As they drove back to their motel for the night, the girls chatted excitedly in the back seat about their day. "I *loved* the canned dancers," Kaela added.

Sean laughed. "Can Can Dancers, sweetheart."

"Oh…well, whatever. Weren't they pretty?" Kaela said.

"I liked the stagecoach ride the best. That was really cool," Shelby added.

Sean and Georgia exchanged looks. "We have a lot to be thankful for," Sean said. Georgia reached for his hand and smiled.

They travelled through to Dease Lake on the third day, visiting with Tom and his family once again and on the fourth day they arrived at the cabin.

The meadow was alive with multi-coloured wild flowers and birds sang their songs in the warmth of the sun. The stream running beside the cabin gurgled over rocks, all of this splendor now displayed in sharp contrast to the stillness of frozen ice and the four feet of snow at Christmas. A different kind of beauty than winter's landscape.

They all settled in to the peacefulness. The girls helped Georgia dig a garden and plant vegetables, small plants they'd brought in from one of their shopping trips out, while Sean wrote. When he needed relaxation time, he took them to his favorite fishing holes along the stream and to hidden lakes to swim. He filled their heads with stories of his childhood at the old cabin with his grandfather, a true Tahltan. They loved his stories about his grandfather's days of trapping before he became a guide for the gold seekers heading north. Sean taught the girls how to respect nature and also know her perils. Kaela loved being out in the forest and soaked it all up. Shelby, true to her nature, was a little more timid, always aware of the noises. Georgia noticed that Shelby was always cognizant of Sean's whereabouts when they were in the forest and kept him in sight.

One day in mid-July they decided to drive into Dease Lake for some supplies and to visit with the town people. Georgia left the girls with Sean at the gas station while she headed to the gift store. When she reached the store, it was closed. Not the usual case for this time of year. She decided to walk around the back because she knew the owners lived behind the shop. The window blinds were closed and no one appeared to be home. As she mused about their whereabouts, she didn't notice someone come up behind her.

"Hello, Georgia."

She spun around to find a man wearing sunglasses and a ball cap coming towards her. It only took a moment for her to realize who it was. She gasped. "Mr. Pearson!"

He smiled. "I thought I saw you out front of the store. And I see you know who I am. I'd guessed as much in May by your reaction when I showed up at the house in Gibsons. You can call me Jim."

A dozen thoughts raced through her mind at once. *Stay calm.* She glanced all around noting that they were all alone. She needed to buy some time while she decided what to do next. "How did you find me?"

"Not so hard. When I realized you weren't in Gibsons, I managed to con one of the neighbour's kids into telling me your whereabouts. I had no idea where your infamous cabin was and expected it would take me a little longer to figure that one out. So imagine my surprise at arriving in this shit hole barely an hour ago, and here you are."

Georgia stiffened. "Poor timing on my part. So you found me. Now, what do you want?"

A huge smile spread across his face, and his eyes lit up like a child's. "Now, now, you aren't that naive, my dear. You know what I want is you."

His condescending tone and syrupy voice sickened her. "You've wasted your time finding me. I must go back to my family." She tried to side-step him, but he moved over to block her path. She stepped back and he stepped forward. She was afraid, but she sure as hell wasn't going to let him know it.

"You're not going anywhere. I've waited far too long to claim you." He kept his voice quiet and controlled and pulled a gun from his pocket and pointed it at her. "Now be a good girl and walk slowly ahead of me around to the front of the store. My vehicle is there and we're going on a little trip." He turned sideways for her to walk forward and past him.

Chills ran up her spine. There was still about ten feet between them. "I've been down this road before and let me tell you, I have no intention of climbing into a vehicle with you," which brought about a laugh from Jim. Continuing on, she added, "So if you intend to use that gun, now's the time."

She turned away from him with the intention of screaming as loud as she could muster and running as fast as she could around the opposite side of the store and back towards the gas station. If she could reach the main road, others would be there to help her. If he chose to shoot her right then and now, it would come sooner than later. Georgia knew, without a doubt, that if she entered his vehicle, this demented man would never let her walk away alive.

A voice in distress shouted out behind her. "Mommy?" She stopped in her tracks and spun around. The man had a hold of Kaela by her jacket, the gun pointed to her head. The girls must have rounded the corner to the back of the store as she'd turned away. Shelby stood frozen behind them staring on.

Georgia yelled. "Shelby, run."

Jim looked at the girl and his face turned to stone. "You move and your sister's dead." He turned back to Georgia. "Now, let's all of us move together around the building to my vehicle. No more heroics, my sweet peach, or the kids will suffer the consequences."

Georgia felt helpless. The girls were in grave danger. For now, she had no choice but to do as he said.

They reached the vehicle and he put the three of them in the back seat and hit the childproof lock button on the driver's door, so they couldn't escape. He slid into the driver's seat, pulled his cap down low. "All of you lean over in your seats, real low." He drove towards the airport and onto the Telegraph Creek Road.

Déjà vu! Georgia could not believe that six years after she'd been kidnapped by the bank robbers in Whitehorse and brought to Dease Lake that she found herself in the same situation, heading in the same direction. Only this time, her daughters were a part of the equation. She reached over and tried the locks, knowing it was futile. He controlled them up front.

Quiet from obvious shock, the two girls now began to cry and whimper. "Shut them up," Jim hissed.

She held the two girls close to her sides and whispered to them. "Shhh ... we'll be fine. It's going to be okay." She knew he had no choice but to take the back road. As soon as Sean realized they were missing, he'd have the Dease Lake

Detachment out looking for them. With hundreds of miles of nothing in either direction, the highway couldn't hide them from road blocks and helicopters. He could disappear with them in the wilderness, but that offered no way out. He really did chose a dumb place to kidnap her and she needed to figure out a way to turn it into her advantage.

He zigzagged from one logging road to the next. Finally, he took a track which was nothing more than tire tracks into deeper forestation. It brought them to an abandoned cabin.

"I guess this is home sweet home, ladies. Out." Jim said and kicked open the cabin door. As it fell on its hinges, he motioned them inside.

The interior was a shambles of dirty furniture; leaves and dirt had blown in from shattered windows, and broken planks in the wood walls exposed the cabin to the outside elements. Georgia wondered who would bother locking the front door to such a place.

He checked out the second room to the cabin and ushered them in. It had been used as a bedroom, no window, only a dresser and an old double bed on springs, covered with a dirty, stained wool blanket. Her kidnapper looked the three of them up and down. Georgia saw a look of doubt cross his face as he stared at the two girls. "Stay in here," he barked. He left the room and closed the door.

Chapter 30

Kaela and Shelby ran to Georgia and she wrapped them in her arms. They began to cry. "What does he want with us, Mommy?" Kaela asked.

"He's not interested in you girls, only me. We're going to be fine." Georgia didn't feel the conviction she used to reassure them. She remembered the look Pearson gave them. He only grabbed them as pawns to force her to come with him. He was unpredictable and now that he had her, had no more use of them. She shuddered at the prospect that came to mind.

She glanced around the room. With no window and the door closed, it was considerably darker now. Her eyes caught a ray of light shining across the floor on the other side of the dresser. "Hang on, girls." She let go of them and scurried over to the corner and looked between the dresser and the side wall. A hole in the clapboard wall let light into the interior. If she could quietly break off the cracked board above the hole it could be big enough for the kids to crawl through. She gestured to the girls to come over and placed her forefinger over her lips. "Shhh ... " she whispered. She pointed out the hole to them.

The dresser was empty and lightweight. She lifted it up easily and moved it over a couple of feet closer to the door. Down on her hands and knees, she worked the broken board until it snapped off. The noise sounded thunderous to her. She waited for a moment and listened for their captor's footsteps. But there was only silence.

She pulled the girls close and whispered to them. "Both of you can fit through this hole. I want you to go now and run."

"But what about you?" Kaela asked.

"I can't fit through, but once you two are safely away, I'll keep working it and I'll follow."

"No ... I won't leave you," Kaela whimpered.

Shelby's crying rose a pitch. Georgia placed a hand over her mouth and talked quietly but firmly to her. "Stop crying, now." She held the two girls close to her sides. "Listen to me and believe what I'm telling you. That man only brought you here to force me to do what he says. If I say no, he will hurt both of you. He doesn't want to hurt me. I can deal with him on my own terms if you two are gone and safe. Do you understand?"

Kaela nodded as tears ran down her cheeks. Shelby wasn't convinced. "But Auntie G, we'll be lost and it's scary out there."

"Honey, you can hide in the forest. It will protect you. If you stay here, that man will kill you," She said, hating to add to the child's fear. But if she was going to get the two girls to leave it was imperative she stress the danger they were in. "Kaela, I need you to lead Shelby to safety. Remember what Sean has taught you about the forest. Once you're out of the cabin, run straight ahead into the trees. Then circle through the trees to the track that brought us to here. Follow it back to the forestry road. Can you do that for me?"

"Yes," Kaela croaked, through her tears.

"And honey, don't go onto the roads, follow as best you can through the trees."

"But why?" Shelby asked. "Wouldn't it be easier and faster on the road?"

"Yes, sweetheart, it would be. But if the bad man in the other room tries to find you, you're safer in the trees. If you hear his car coming, you can hide in the brush. On the road, he'll see you. Okay?"

They both nodded.

Georgia gave each girl a hug."Believe me, girls, we're all safer with you away from here. I'll join you soon." She helped Shelby through the hole first. Once she was through, she squeezed her hand, forced a smile and a wink. "Love you." As Kaela started for the hole, Georgia held her back for a moment. "If you hear a plane or helicopter, run out into the open. Jump up and down and move your arms so they can see you. And if you see a vehicle different than the one we came in, flag it down."

"Okay, Mommy."

"And honey, promise me you'll be strong for your sister." Kaela nodded and Georgia said, "I love you."

She held her breath and watched Kaela climb through and join Shelby. As the girls ran into the forest, she hung there looking on until she was sure they weren't coming back. The fact that she couldn't see them any longer was good. *If I can't see them, neither will he.*

Satisfied they were as safe as she could make them, she collapsed back against the wall and dropped her head into her hands. *What did I do?* She felt relief that the girls were safe from the demented man in the next room, but sending two little kids out into the wilderness alone? *'Stay strong for your sister, Kaela.' Did I really say that to a six-year-old? Dear God ... forgive me and please keep them safe.*

The minutes passed and her resolve returned. For the moment, she knew she'd done the right thing. Time to turn her thoughts to her own survival. Georgia examined the boards around the rim of the hole and found they were solid. She knew she could work them but at what cost? The noise would bring her kidnapper running. She moved the dresser back to cover the hole and then snickered. He might not see the hole, but he would notice the girls were gone. She sat on the edge of the bed and waited. The longer the girls were gone, the further away they would be from her captor.

While Georgia was scared, it wasn't the same as it was six years ago with the bank robber s. She didn't doubt her ability to survive this time like before. Instead, she was determined to fight her captor tooth and nail to stay alive. The girls needed her. Losing wasn't acceptable!"

Thirty minutes later, Pearson came into the room, gun in hand. He glanced around the room. "Where are they?" he demanded.

Georgia said nothing. He marched over to the bed and backhanded her across the face. Grimacing, she fell across the bed. He pulled her up into sitting position . "I said, where are they?"

"They're gone, you bastard." She steeled herself and waited for another blow as she stared him down.

He stalked around the room looking for the means of escape the girls had used. Toppling the dresser over onto the floor, he found the hole.

"They're gone, away from you, you sadistic creep," she spat. Enraged, he raced back to the bed and grabbed her by the throat. Defiant and struggling to breathe, she looked into his eyes as he ran the gun barrel over her throbbing cheek. He ran the gun barrel over her swelling, bruised cheek bone. Once he saw her resilience, he snarled and let her fall back onto the bed.

"Don't you dare move," he said, in a slow deliberate tone. He turned and ran out of the room, slamming the door shut behind him.

Georgia sat up again and listened. If he thought the girls were running down the road, he might take the car and take up the chase. If so, she'd be out of there and into the forest. But she didn't hear the motor and knew he was checking out the perimeter of the cabin instead.

He came back five minutes later as calm and charming as the day last fall when they'd met in Trent's office. "You're right, my sweet peach, they're gone. Actually, you did me a favour. Let the forest finish them off. It's a lot cleaner than a bullet. I like that," he said as he sat beside her on the bed. "I can see that you and I are a lot alike."

She looked at him puzzled. "What do you mean?"

He smiled at her and reached out and pushed her hair behind her ear. "Getting rid of them like that. You knew they'd only be in our way, so you took matters into your own hands."

Georgia cringed inside at his touch but stayed perfectly still. *He wasn't only demented, he was deranged.*

"They're of no threat to us. Two kids lost in the wilderness? They'll never find their way out," he said.

Hard as she tried to stop them, the tears came and poured down her face. A look of surprise crossed his face. "What? The little mother cares? Come on. You should have thought of that before you sent them out there."

"You bastard." Georgia spat in his face and instantly knew she'd made a mistake. Jim stood and dragged her to her feet. Lifting the butt of his gun, he pistol-whipped her across the cheek. She fell to the floor, crying out in pain. This time she could feel the blood gushing down her face and tasted it in her mouth. He kicked her, his foot striking her ribs. With the wind knocked out of her, she gasped for air as he straddled her and grabbed her hair with his fist. He lifted her head and banged it hard against the wooden floor.

As she drifted into unconsciousness, she heard his booming voice echoing in her ears. "You can stay in here until you learn some respect."

Chapter 31

Kaela grabbed Shelby's hand and ran into the forest. They hid in the brush. She could barely make out the roof of the cabin from their hiding spot.

"I don't want to leave Auntie G," Shelby said.

"Me neither, but Mommy says we must go or he'll kill us." Kaela shuddered at the thought of leaving her mom with that nasty man. The two girls clung to each other. Kaela could feel her sister shaking. They remained that way for several minutes, unable to leave.

Kaela strained to hear something, hoping her mother would find her own way out and join them. She was confused and scared. Eventually she realized her mother wasn't coming, and seeing how she'd promised to be strong and lead Shelby to safety, she said. "Come on. Maybe we can find Sean and save Mommy. She told us to circle behind the cabin to the track." Once they reached the rutted grooves in the grass, she led the two of them through the trees. She never looked back because she was afraid of what she might see. It wasn't long before they found the dirt road.

"Which direction did we come from?" Shelby asked.

"That way." The two girls made their way through the brush and trees, making sure to follow the road as they'd been told to do. Eventually, they merged into another dirt road and this time, Kaela didn't know which way they should go. She sat down for a rest and stared up and down the road, afraid to make a wrong choice.

A sudden noise in the bush behind startled them both. Shelby screamed and ran down to the roadway. "Shelby, wait." Kaela yelled. But Shelby crossed the road and ran down a path on the other side and disappeared into the forest. Kaela was up like a shot, chasing after her sister. She ran down the path crying Shelby's name. When she reached an intersection of several pathways, she stopped and yelled for her sister. A tiny voice echoed to her right and Kaela ran in that direction. She found Shelby waiting for her to catch up and the two girls fell into each other's arms and cried. "You shouldn't have run away, Shelby. I was so scared."

"I'm sorry. I thought it was him," Shelby said, clinging to her sister.

"It was a small animal of some kind. But we need to stay together. Please don't run away again," Kaela pleaded.

"I won't."

The two girls turned and started back to the road holding hands as they walked. But after a little while, Kaela realized they were lost. The path they were on led deeper and deeper into the forest until it reached a stream. Tired and anxious, the girls stopped for a drink.

Shelby stared down into the water. "We're lost because of me, aren't we?"

Kaela glanced at her sister to see her bottom lip quivering. She took her sisters hand in hers. "We were already lost when we stopped to rest."

Shelby looked up at her. "I thought when I ran away into the forest I got us lost."

Her sister shook her head. "No. I didn't know which way to go when we got to that second road." The two girls clung to each other.

They soaked their feet in the cool water, each lost to their own thoughts. The sun had disappeared behind the trees and Kaela knew it would be dark soon. They had escaped that horrid man. She hoped her mother was okay and would find them soon."Let's stay here tonight. We can get some pine branches to sleep on over there between those logs."

Shelby cringed. "It's scary out here at night."

"I know, but it's scarier walking in the dark. At least here we can hide if we have to."

They set about making their bed and decided to strip down and swim in a shallow part of the stream. For a short time, they became kids and lost themselves in the moment, splashing each other and giggling. Clean and cooled down, they put their clothes back on and huddled together in the next of pine boughs.

"Maybe we should wait here for Sean to find us," Shelby said. "He always told us to stay put if we were lost."

Kaela thought about that. "Sean said you can survive if you have water." Kaela felt too confused and tired to make a decision. Initially, every noise in the looming darkness made the girls start, and so sleep did not come easily. Eventually, sheer emotional and physical exhaustion took over and the two girls dozed off.

Sometime during the night Kaela awoke. For some time, she lay listening to the strange noises of the night as the light from the full moon created scary shadows. Her eyes darted from left to right, her imagination piqued by the unfamiliar sights and sounds. From time to time, she glanced at Shelby, who was curled up beside her in a fetal position, lost to a deep sleep. She envied her sister: wishing she could sleep again.

Startled by a noise she bolted up upright. A dark shadow on the path moved towards them. Kaela froze, unable to see what it was. The shadow turned a pale gray and started to change shape. She drew in her breath. "Uh ..." *Was it him?* She began to shake. *Or maybe her mother?*

In mere seconds, the silhouette of a man, surrounded by a white mist appeared before her. Kaela inched closer to Shelby unable to speak.

"Don't fear me, little one. I'm here to help you and your sister."

Kaela relaxed a little. "Are you here to rescue us? Where are the others?" She looked all around but saw and heard no one.

"I'm alone." The man squatted on his haunches so his face was level with hers.

Long gray braids hung down his chest over a tanned leather vest. His face was weathered. Kaela decided he must be an elder of the Tahltan band, but she hadn't seen him before.

Her eyes wide, she asked, in a tiny voice, "Who are you?"

"I'm an ancestor. We are soon to be blood and I'm here to protect you both."

Her forehead creased. *What was he talking about?* Whatever it meant, she only cared about going home where it was warm and safe. Her face filled with hope. "Will you take us home?"

He smiled. "I can only tell you where you must go. You'll be found there."

"But...but why can't you take us?"

The elder ignored her question and stood. He pointed down the trail. "My time here is short, so listen to me carefully. Follow this pathway and always keep to the right, even when you reach a smaller track than this one. Stay to the right and the path will take you to a great waterfall."

"But Sean told us we should always stay put. Shelby reminded me and I ..."

"That's good advice, little one, but you will not be safe here. Go to the waterfall. Stay there and they'll find you."

Kaela listened as the elder gave her more instructions. She still didn't understand why they couldn't go with him, but whenever she tried to talk to him about it, he cut her off.

"Sleep now. You'll be safe until morning." He started to walk down the trail.

She jumped up and yelled. "Wait, don't leave us." She watched the man's shape dissipate and once more she saw the white cloud. She started to cry. *Why was he leaving?* "Please come back." She couldn't move, nor could she take her eyes off of the light mist before her that became smaller and smaller. She didn't understand what she saw. *Maybe I'm dreaming.* The small white mist changed shape and grew darker until it became black. She watched in awe as it turned into a raven and flew up to a nearby tree.

Her heart pounded in her chest as a low guttural sound came from the Raven's throat as he watched her. The blackbird flew up to her and swooped before her in an array of aerial acrobats, lit up by the moonbeams of the full moon. *No, it can't be.* "Feathers?" He disappeared down the path with one final outburst. "Kraa Kraa."

She ran down the path a short distance. "Feathers, don't go," she cried. "Don't leave ... please, stay. Feathers come back." The distraught child returned to Shelby and sat down. *How did he turn into a bird?* She rocked back and forth unable to understand it all until exhaustion and cold overtook her. She cuddled into the small of Shelby's back and fell asleep.

Dawn broke through the tops of the trees and all was still in the forest, the next time Kaela opened her eyes. Birds were singing their wake-up songs, and the streaming sunlight filtering down through the branches gave promise to a hot day ahead. Drawing her knees up to her chest, she wrapped her arms around her legs. She tried to sort through the vivid memories of her vision. The images had seemed so real she'd been surprised to wake up and find them alone. Looking down beside her, she saw Shelby stirring in her sleep.

"Wake up," she said, shaking her sister's shoulder.

"Huh...wh...what?"

"Wake up. We have to go," Kaela ordered, standing up to stretch.

"Go?"

"Yes...to the river."

Kaela walked to some bushes and squatted to relieve herself. When she returned, she found Shelby staring back and forth along the trail.

"I thought we were waiting here for Sean?"

"They won't find us here: we need to go to the river. Come on, we have to go." Kaela urged her sister to follow.

"How do you know?" Shelby demanded.

"Well, ummm ... I do."

"But we don't know where the river is."

"Uh ... I know how to reach the river." Kaela held back not quite sure how to explain her vision.

Shelby looked unsure. "Then why didn't you take us there yesterday?"

Kaela sighed. "I dreamed of the river last night. There was this beautiful waterfall, and water to drink, and lots of wild berries to eat."

"A dream? Dreams aren't for real." Shelby stared at her sister in disbelief.

Kaela shifted from one foot to the other, finally she blurted it out. "This one was real. It ... it wasn't really a dream."

"What's that mean anyways? A dream is a dream."

"This one was a vision. He said to go to the river to be safe." Kaela didn't tell her everything he said about once they reached the waterfall. Shelly was having a hard enough time believing her vision.

"Who said?"

"The native ancestor. He told me how to find the river and said we'd be safe there until rescuers come."

Shelby looked shocked. "An Indian told you? Daddy was right. Auntie G is crazy...and so are you!"

"Don't call him an Indian and Daddy wouldn't say that about Mommy."

"Oh yes he did. My Mommy wanted to buy Auntie G's book but Daddy wouldn't let her. He said she'd gone crazy living in the woods and told Mommy not to bring it in the house."

"He did not."

"Did too."

Kaela burst into tears and rushed forward. Shelby took a step backwards, tripped over a log and sat down hard on her bottom. She began to cry.

"Oh, Shelby, I'm sorry." Kaela rushed to her sister. "Are you alright?"

"Yeah."

"Please come with me," Kaela pleaded.

Crossing her arms across her chest, Shelby looked up at her sister with defiance. "I'm not going anywhere with you. I'm staying right here 'til Sean comes."

The two girls stared at each other. "Fine—stay here—I'm going to do what the ancestor told me."

Shelby shouted. "Fine!"

Kaela turned and marched along the path. The promise she'd made to her mother stopped her in her tracks and she turned to see her sister staring at her with a frightened look on her face. She knew she couldn't leave her and she didn't want to be alone either.

Chapter 32

"Ewww...I hate you, Kaela Charles!" Shelby stood up and ran down the trail after her sister. "Wait for me!"

Kaela led them along the pathways for about an hour, staying to the right each time they came across another trail. Finally, they stopped at a crossroads and sat for a rest.

"When will we be there?" Shelby asked.

"Soon."

Shelby didn't think her sister sounded as confident as she had earlier. "I'm hungry and thirsty."

"Me too. Stop whining." Rising, Kaela started off on a narrow trail to the right of the larger path they'd been on.

Shelby hesitated. "Maybe we should stay on the main trail."

Kaela ground to a halt and gave her sister a long stare. She placed one hand on her hip and pointed along the main trail with the other. "You want to go that way? Go! I'm staying to the right like he said."

Shelby pouted and stomped down the path behind Kaela. She wiped her wet brow and tried to ignore her grumbling stomach and her sore feet. *Shoulda listened to Sean and stayed put. But her sister insisted on finding the river.*

They hadn't gone far when Kaela stopped dead in her tracks. Shelby smacked right into the back of her and grabbed a hold of her t-shirt to keep from falling. "Wh...what is it...a bear?" Shelby whispered, looking past her sister in fright.

"No...listen!"

She strained her ears. "I don't hear anything."

"Listen. The water? I hear the waterfall." Kaela grabbed Shelby's hand and began running down the path. Shelby ran behind, trying to keep up without tripping. The trail became wider as it led them towards an open area ahead. They burst out onto the sandy bank of the river. Looking to her left, Shelby saw a magnificent waterfall tumbling over a rock face onto a pile of boulders. The white churning water pounded its way downstream through the rocks at a tremendous speed. The hot air seemed cooler and more energized by the mist hanging above the turbulent water. The girls jumped up and down, gleefully hugging and laughing as they danced in circles.

"It's like my dream—the river, the waterfall—and look at the blackberries," Kaela gushed, heading to the bushes.

Shelby followed her sister's lead and they stuffed their mouths with berries until their faces, hands and t-shirts were stained purple. The sisters looked each other up and down and giggled. She wasn't sure why she was so excited. *We're still lost, but Kaela found the waterfall just like in her dream.*

She watched Kaela strip to her underwear and wade waist deep into a shallow pond to the left of the waterfall. "Don't go too far," Shelby called out, glancing at the wild water beyond the pool.

"It's okay. I can see the sandy bottom."

Shelby watched her move further out in the pond until the water reached her chest. With a change of direction, she headed towards the boulders beside the waterfall.

A commotion above caught Shelby's attention and she looked up. Two crows dive-bombed an eagle. Their disturbed cries could be heard above the noise of the river. Shelby was mesmerized as the pair continued their attack on the magnificent bird until the eagle gave up its pursuit and flew away.

When her gaze fell back to the pond. Kaela was nowhere to be seen. Shelby stood frozen to the spot, staring at the still water.

"Kaela? Kaela…where are you?" Shelby shouted, running to the water's edge and searching the surface with darting glances. Nothing. Her heart pounded. Fearful, she shielded her eyes from the sun and ran along the river's edge looking for a bobbing head. Again nothing. Panicked, she shook all over. Back and forth she ran. "Kaela … Kaela … *Kae … la*," she yelled, until she was hoarse, her voice overpowered by the enormous resonance of the waterfall.

Collapsing to her knees on the sandy bank, the six-year-old looked all around. She shivered and wrapped her arms around her trembling body.

"Kaela …"she cried, in a small voice that gave way to tears, "I'm scared."

Chapter 33

Georgia opened her eyes. The room was dark save for a greyish light filtering through the clapboard, hinting at predawn. One glance around the room confirmed she'd been left alone, at least for now. Then she realized that she was no longer on the floor, but on the bed with that dirty wool blanket over her. The vision of his arms lifting her up and holding her next to his body made her cringe. Pain in her left side brought back the memory of her predator's attack, and her laboured breath increased her discomfort. Everything hurt; her face, ribs, and her perpetual pounding head.

But a smile played at her lips. *The girls had escaped.* That thought was quickly replaced though with the fear of them out in the wilderness at night. Georgia pushed it from her mind. *They'll be found. It's imperative to concentrate on my own survival.*

All of her contact with her captor, way back to the pink letters, meeting him at Trent's office, and the past twenty-four hours were scrutinized. She examined his behaviors and a realization came. It was all about control—his control . When Georgia stood up to him, he became enraged. When he saw or sensed her fear, he became sweet and charming. *It was all about control ... his control.*

Her smile broadened. "Oww ..." Her hand went up to her face. Her eye, and the whole right side, was swollen. A deep gash ran across her cheek and a silver dollar size lump was on the back of her head. A quiet anger filled her. The man certainly had a sadistic way of professing love. *Okay.* "I get you, Jim Pearson," she muttered.

Physically, she was at a disadvantage, but psychologically, they were on equal terms. Two could play this game and she felt determined to win. Daylight now shone across the floor from the hole in the clapboard. Georgia forced herself up into a sitting position and gasped from the effort. She pushed herself up and walked slowly around to the end of the bed. She sat down and pulled her shirt up to examine her ribs as Pearson opened the door, gun in hand.

He took one look at her bruised rib cage and winced. "Look what you made me do."

Dropping her shirt, she raised her pounding head and hiding the anger seething within her, she gave him a 'puppy- dog' look.

Jim put the gun on the corner of the dresser and sat beside her. "We had a bad start yesterday. But you were a naughty girl. Maybe today we can begin again. I'm sorry I hurt you."

I bet. Georgia cleared her throat and whispered. "I'm sorry I spit in your face, Mr. Pearson."

He took her hand in his. "Call me Jim.

"Okay … Jim. I was so afraid."

"You don't have to fear me. Don't make me mad and we're good." He put his finger to her jaw and tilted her face so he could get a good look. "That day we met in your agent's office, I knew you were attracted to me. I could see it in your eyes."

Georgia felt her face grow hot. Embarrassment overtook her because she thought he was attractive that day and he'd noticed it.

He flashed her a big smile. "See … you're blushing. That's so sweet."

She gave him a dim smile, then dropped her eyes demurely. *Let him have his fantasy. It only helps my cause. Creep.*

"We'll have to hide out for a few days here. That will give you some time to rest up and heal. Are you hungry? I brought some food and water."

"Water please."

He left her alone. This time he left the door open but he did take the gun. Georgia felt light-headed and wanted nothing more than to curl up on the bed and sleep. But she needed to stay alert and focused. She worried that she had a concussion.

He returned with a bottle of water and some cheese and crackers. She devoured the food and instantly felt nauseous. She drank some water and fought to keep it down, knowing she needed the nourishment for strength. Watching her closely, he stood by the dresser, the gun tucked into his waistband.

"I need to relieve myself," Georgia said. She stood on wobbly legs and felt dizzy.

"No plumbing around here, you'll have to go outside. Jim linked his arm through hers to help her walk through the cabin to the outdoors. She hated his touch but gritted her teeth and accepted his support. Pain resonated from the waist up to the top of her head. Leading her to the side of the cabin, he let go of her and backed away as Georgia undid her jeans and pulled them down.

As she held onto the side of the wall for balance, she felt his gaze on her. *Yeah, keep watching, creep. It's the only bit of flesh you'll ever see.* Georgia accepted his arm to walk back to the cabin and her legs felt stronger. The nausea passed. She knew she could manage alone this time, but she held back from letting him know. *Let him think I'm weaker than I am.*

He ushered her into the back room. She hated going in there again but didn't resist. He placed the gun back on the dresser as they passed through the door.

"Perhaps you should go back to bed and rest," he said, softly.

She stood about two feet from the bed and turned to face him, ready to give a performance of a lifetime. "I'll do whatever you say." As tears filled her eyes, she hoped she looked vulnerable.

Jim's face softened and he stepped closer. Georgia cringed and stepped back. "It's okay, my sweet peach. I'm not going to hurt you." She let him step up to her, his legs slightly apart, as he cupped her face with his hands. Leaning forward he closed his eyes and placed a kiss on her forehead.

In an instant, Georgia placed her hands on his arms for stability and brought her right knee up between his legs as hard as she could. His eyes popped open and he yelled out, as his hands dropped to his crotch . He doubled over towards her. She stepped back and balled her right hand into a fist, opening her forefinger and middle finger into a V. With all the strength she could muster, she drew her arm back and thrust her hand into his face. Her two fingers straddled his nose and poked him in both eyes. She grabbed his hair with her left hand to hold his head steady and raked her fingernails down his eyelids, all the way down his cheeks and over his chin, breaking the skin in the process. All of this took mere seconds. Georgia moved away from him and he fell onto the bed in agony, tears and blood flowing freely down his face.

She covered the distance to the dresser and grabbed the gun. Making sure the safety was off, she cocked it and pointed it at her captor. Her adrenalin was flowing and she was shaking so hard that she tightened her grip on the barrel to keep from dropping it.

He writhed in pain for a few minutes. He used the blanket to wipe his eyes
. "Bitch," he yelled. "Don't hurt me. I'll do whatever you say," he mimicked in
a falsetto voice. "You're a liar and you're going to pay."

Georgia let him rant and rave, it gave her a chance to control her emotions
and steady her breathing, although his yells and taunts didn't help her pounding head. She leaned back against the dresser to steady her balance.

Pearson calmed down, his rage spent for the moment. He pushed himself
up on the bed.

Her hands still shook. "Don't move," she yelled.

He gave her a crooked smile. "So now what? We stay like this until someone
finds us?"

So we're back to the head games. Only now I'm in control. "Where are the car
keys?" she demanded.

"In my jeans pocket. Why don't you come and take them?" he laughed, ar-
rogantly.

"And why don't you reach slowly into your pocket, drop them by your foot
and kick them over to me."

"I see. Then you back out of the room, take the car and drive to freedom. Is
that the plan? Well, guess what. You will never be free of me, my sweet Georgia
peach. I'll find you wherever you are. You might win this battle, sweetheart,
but you won't win the war."

"You'll be caught and you'll rot in jail."

He shrugged his shoulders. "Maybe yes and maybe, I'll disappear, only to
reappear in your life again."

"You're so cocky. Maybe I'll take you with me and make sure they lock you
away."

"Okay, new plan. Now we're leaving together. So I drive and you hold the
gun. Do you really think I'll take you back? What's stopping me from running
into a tree or driving off a hair-pin turn on the Telegraph Creek Road to the
Stikine River far below."

Georgia frowned. "Why would you do that? You'd only kill yourself in the
process."Because, my sweet peach, if I can't have you, there's nothing nobler
than our dying together." He stood and took a step forward. His face hardened.
"No one else will have you either."

She stiffened and pointed the gun at his chest. "You make one more move
and I'll shoot. Don't try me.:

A sinister smile broke out on his face. "So, what's it going to be, my sweet. What are we doing? Oh here, I'll try to make it easier for you." Jim pulled the keys out of his pocket, dropped them down beside his feet and kicked them over to her.

She gave a quick glance down at the keys by her feet and looked up at Jim with his arrogant stare and cocky stance. Suddenly, Jim faked a charge at her. Her whole body shook as she stretched out her arms and locked her elbows to steady the gun.

He laughed. "Sweetheart, you're shaking so hard, you'd never hit the side of a barn." Then in one swift move he lunged forward, screaming like a banshee, flailing his arms in all directions.

The gun went off and kept firing as Pearson fell to the floor. As the blood rushed out of his chest and pooled around his body, he looked up at Georgia in disbelief. She staggered back against the dresser, watching his eyes turn to glass.

Her body jerked as the gun hit the floor. She hadn't realized she'd dropped it. Her hands flew to her mouth. "Dear God ..." She'd begun to shake again and couldn't take her eyes off of his lifeless body. *Did I really kill him?* There was no doubt he was dead. Minutes passed before she felt she could control her reactions, physical and emotional. *It's time to leave.* She stooped slowly to retrieve the car keys from the floor.

She turned her back on the gruesome scene, took a deep breath to steady her nerves and walked into the front of the cabin. Hand foods and bottled water sat on the table. Georgia threw them into a bag and went out. By the time, she reached the car, her head pounded. She gripped the door for balance as the dizziness worsened. Lowering herself into the driver's seat hurt like hell. The excruciating pain she felt, almost rendered her unconscious.

Georgia sat in the car staring all around at the forest, afraid to leave. *What if the girls were hiding close by and never ran away?* The gunshots would have freaked them out. She lowered the windows and called their names. "Kaela. Shelby. It's Mommy. It's okay, come out." Then she honked the horn . She did this repeatedly until she knew she had to leave.

When she reached the dirt road, she repeated her cry to the girls and honked. She ripped a piece of her red t-shirt and tied it to a branch to mark the driveway to the cabin. Her movements were mechanical as she drove on. Each time she hit a crossroads, Georgia repeated the process, calling, honking, and tying the red material to a tree or bush. The constant chore of lifting her beaten and bruised body in and out of the car came with a price. Her breathing became more laboured, her voice raspy as she called out to the girls. Finally, she reached the Telegraph Creek Road and made the last turn that would eventually take her back to Dease Lake.

The road was not for the faint of heart, especially in her condition. A twisting, sometimes narrow track, that followed the Stikine River far below it, it was full of hair pin turns that went up and down hills. But the lives of her kids were at stake and she had no choice. Nausea returned and with it double-vision, making it near impossible for her to navigate at any great speed or even to drive in a straight line. The road seemed endless but the thought of her daughters alone in the wilderness kept her going. *How could they ever walk out of here?* She prayed they would be found. "Stay safe, girls ... stay safe."

Twenty minutes later, she began to weave back and forth across the road. Her impaired vision and excruciating pain was taking its toll. She blinked, trying to focus on the road ahead and found herself near a steep drop-off. She jerked the wheel to the left just in time and the car headed across the road towards a ditch.

She passed out before the car left the road and landed in the ditch.

Through the miasma, a waterfall roared. Georgia couldn't believe how loud it was. Her eyes followed the river downstream, it's massive swirl of white water disappearing from view.

She looked back at the waterfall and the pond beside. Kaela and Shelby were floating in the water. *Oh no. They're dead.* She couldn't tear her eyes away from their motionless, half-naked bodies. It tore at her heart.

A voice out of the void spoke to her. Georgia looked around but saw no one. "They're not dead. Send the searchers to the waterfall."

Georgia recognized the voice of her native spirit. "They're alive?"

"Yes, child. They are safe at the waterfall."

She turned back to the pool. Shelby was standing in the water, staring at her sister. "I beat you, Shelby. I could float longer than you." Then the girls disappeared under the water.

Georgia felt confused. "Nonnock are you still here?"

"Yes, I'm here."

"I'm afraid. Where did the girls go?"

"They're safe behind the waterfall. Sean will find them." Nonnock said.

"I killed a man today."

"And you saved three lives today."

Georgia thought about that. "It's been a long time, Nonnock. I've missed you."

"And I've missed talking with you too."

"How can I live with the thought that I killed someone."

"Listen to these words carefully... don't lock your mind into mental slavery, child."

The noise became so much louder. She shut her eyes and held her head. "How could the sound of water be so painful?" she muttered.

"She's awake."

Georgia opened her eyes. A helicopter had landed in the road beside her, the *whap whap* sound of the blades hurt her head. She shifted her eyes and saw a man staring through the car window. "Sean?" she whispered. She tried to focus her eyes.

"Yes, baby, it's me. Stay still. The medics will get you out of here." He turned to someone she couldn't see. "She said something about water, I didn't catch it."

The medics lifted her out of the car and onto a stretcher. Sean leaned over and held her hand before they put her into the chopper. He looked so tired, so scared. "You're going to be okay. Sweetheart, where are the girls?"

"The waterfall ... go to the waterfall, you'll find them there." Georgia closed her eyes and the world disappeared once again.

Chapter 34

"There it is." Sean pointed down to the waterfall. He and Tom reached it before the RCMP helicopter. They circled above and came in as low as they could. "I don't see them."

Tom landed in a meadow close by and hiked back to the falls. When they reached the bank of the river, Sean scanned the area. "Shelby ... Kaela ..." he yelled.

"Sean, over here." Tom called.

He joined Tom and saw two pairs of sandals and two red-stained t-shirts lying on a bush. He grabbed the shirts, stared at them, and sank to his knees. "No ..." he shook his head and tears sprung to his eyes.

Tom leaned down and took a shirt from him. "You're thinking these are blood stains. They're not. Look at the bush they were on."

Sean looked over at the bush. He stood. "Blackberry stains? But where are they?" He turned in circles calling their names. "Kaela ... Shelby." He turned to the water and stared into the calm pool beside the waterfall.

Suddenly, a small head popped up. A few feet away, another one came up. "Beat ya!" Kaela yelled at Shelby.

But Shelby paid no attention to her. She stared at the bank and screamed."Sean!" Kaela turned. The two girls headed to shore screaming his name and Sean ran into the water, meeting them halfway. They jumped into his arms and he held them to his chest while he waded back in, collapsing to his knees on the bank where the three of them hugged and cried.

"I told you he'd find us here," Kaela said, giving her sister a hug. Shelby nodded in agreement.

"You both popped up out of the water. Where were you?" Sean asked.

The two girls started talking at once. "Under the waterfall." Shelby said excitedly,

while Kaela added, "In a cave behind the waterfall."

Sean looked up at Tom in surprise. "I never knew there was cave back there."

"Neither did I." Tom said.

"Are you okay?" Sean looked them both over, seeing nothing wrong with either of them.

"We're okay. 'Cept we're hungry." Kaela said.

"The helicopter is close by. Let's go girls."

The smile left Kaela's face. "Sean? Did you find Mommy?"

He smiled and gave her another hug. "Yes, honey, we'll take you to her."

Shelby started to cry. "I thought that bad man killed Auntie G." Sean picked her up. "Auntie G is in the hospital in Terrace, but she'll be okay. So girls, shall we go see her?"

The two girls nodded. Tom and Sean led them to the chopper and soon they were up in the air. Tom radioed the RCMP with the news that they'd found the girls and were taking them to the Terrace hospital. Sean wanted them to see Georgia as soon as possible. He, also, wanted them checked over by a doctor.

As soon as they arrived, Sean took the girls straight to the Emergency Room. They found Georgia in a corner propped up in bed with an oxygen mask on. The two girls took one look at her bruised face and the intravenous into her hand and burst into tears. Sean cringed. *Damn, I should have prepared them.* Georgia opened her eyes. "My babies," she cried. She put her arms out and the girls flew into them. She winced. "Careful of my left side." She stroked their hair and cried. "I can't believe you're here."

A doctor came in, introduced himself to Sean and reported on her status." She has two broken ribs, a cracked right cheek bone, and a contusion on the back of her head. She's suffering with a concussion. We'd like to keep her in for a few days under observation. There's a possibility that she has a pinhole puncture in her left lung, which we expect will heal on its own. All of her injuries while serious, will heal. The orderly will be here in a few minutes to move her to a room upstairs."

Sean breathed a sigh of relief. "Thank you, Doctor. I'd like the girls to be checked out. They spent two days in the wilderness alone. Also, I know they must be starving. All they've had to eat is blackberries and water."

The doctor looked at the girls and smiled. "And judging by their clothes, lots of them. I'll take them to admissions personally." He looked at his watch. "Dinner is due any minute. I'll make sure they receive some food."

Tom put a hand on Sean's shoulder. "I'll go with the doctor and the girls. Why don't you stay with Georgia?"

"Thanks, Tom. Doc can I talk to you alone for a moment?"

"Certainly." They stepped out of emergency and stood in the hallway. "What is it?"

"Was she … did he …" Sean choked on the words. He looked pleadingly at the doctor.

"No. He beat her pretty bad but he didn't violate her." The doctor smiled and placed his hand on Sean's shoulder and squeezed. "I asked her that first thing and she told me she'd gotten the better of him before he could hurt her further."

Sean heaved a sigh of relief. "Thank you."

A few minutes later, Sean followed the orderly who moved Georgia upstairs to a private room.

The new Staff Sergeant from Dease Lake RCMP Detachment arrived. "I'm Staff Sergeant Bruce Wayans, Ms. Charles. I hope you don't mind if I ask you a couple of questions. We can get a full statement later on, but I'm hoping you can clear a few things up now."

Georgia looked distressed. "I understand, Staff Sergeant."

"Can you tell us where Mr. Pearson took you and the girls?"

"To a cabin off of Telegraph Creek Road."

"Do you know where he is now?"

Georgia swallowed hard. "Yes, he's at the cabin." The words came out in barely a whisper."

"How did you and the girls escape, Ms. Charles?"

"Umm…could I have some water, please?"

Sean placed a cup with a straw up to her mouth. She took a few sips and put her head back on the pillow with her eyes closed.

"Ms. Charles?"

She opened her eyes and continued. "The first day we arrived there, I found a hole in the wall of the room he put us in. The girls were able to squeeze through and I sent them away. It was me he wanted and they were in his way. I was worried he'd hurt them. I told them to follow the road out."

"And how did you escape?"

Her face contorted and she tried to keep her emotions under control but it was a losing battle. Sean felt his gut tighten as he reached out and took Georgia's hand. "Can't we do this later? You can see she's been through hell."

The Staff Sergeant's tone softened. "We're almost done. Ms. Charles, can you tell us the location of the cabin."

Georgia took a deep breath. " I don't know where it is but as I came out, I tied a piece of my red t-shirt onto a bush at the driveway into the cabin and at each road turn I tied a piece beside the direction he turned to."

"Any idea how far into the bush it is?"

"I don't know how long I drove. A couple of hours maybe, 'cause I kept stopping to call the girls names and honk. I tied some material on Telegraph Creek Road when I reached it too. I don't think I travelled that long before I went into the ditch."

"That was smart thinking. So Mr. Pearson has had all day to make his escape on foot. He couldn't have gone far out there."

Georgia shook her head. "No. He's still there."

"You know this, how?" the Sergeant asked.

She swallowed hard once more and looked at the officer. "Because I shot and killed him."

Sean gasped and squeezed her hand tighter.

Constable Wayans showed no reaction. "I see. Are you sure he's dead?"

"I shot him several times. He's dead." She put her head back on the pillow and closed her eyes.

"One more question, Ms. Charles and I'll leave you to rest. What did you do with the gun?"

She spoke so softly, the man had to lean forward to hear. "I dropped it on the floor in the cabin."

After the Staff Sergeant left, Sean picked up her hand and kissed it. Georgia opened her eyes. "I killed him, Sean"

"The man kidnapped you and your kids and he beat you. If the only way for you to escape him was to shoot him, then he deserved to die."

"But I had the gun. I could have fired a warning shot or wounded him when he charged me."

"If you hadn't shot him, he may have overpowered you. Look at yourself, Georgia. You're badly injured. There's no guarantees a warning shot or an injury would have stopped him."

Georgia still looked unsure.

Sean changed his approach. "There was a briefcase on the seat beside you in the car. Do you know what was in it?"

"No, I didn't open it."

"When you went into the ditch it must have fallen on the floor and flipped open. There were pictures of women, Georgia. Lots of women, beaten and dead." Georgia flinched. "Dates, maps marked with X's, including his wife's, to indicate their burial locations. Journals with details of the last twenty years of his life. I read some of it while we waited for the Medi-vac. He was a demented murderer and a serial killer. And...remember the murder suicide of his parents. Not true. He wrote that he killed them. They were his first."

She gasped. "I was so lucky."

Sean leaned forward and stroked her hair. "Georgia, for twenty years that man terrorized, and murdered women and held them under mental and physical slavery. Don't let him hold you under mental slavery after he's dead." Sean watched her face blanche.

"What did you say?"

He started to repeat himself then stopped. "What's wrong?"

"Nothing. It's just when I passed out in the ditch, I had a vision. In it, Nonnock said, 'Don't lock your mind into mental slavery'."

"Then, I guess you needed to hear it again, my love."

Chapter 35

Sunlight filtered through the picture window of the cabin. Georgia, propped up in her king-sized bed in the loft, could see the Cassiar Mountains looming clear and rugged at the far end of the front meadow.

A week had passed since Jim Pearson had kidnapped the girls and her. This was her second day home from the hospital. Kaela and Shelby sat at the end of the bed and Sean in the arm chair beside the bed. Apart from a few scratches and bruises, the girls checked out fine physically.

"Mommy, when Sean found you in the car, you told him we were at the waterfall. How did you know where to find us?" Kaela asked.

"Because I had a dream in the car. In fact, I've been having dreams since last year of the two of you at a waterfall. I didn't understand what they meant. In my final dream, my native spirit, Nonnock told me you were safe and to send your rescuers to that pond in the river."

Sean leaned forward in his chair. "Now I have a question for you Kaela. How did you know there was a cave behind the waterfall? All the people I know that have gone to the falls since I was a small boy never mentioned a cave."

Shelby and Kaela looked at each other. "Tell them," Shelby said.

Kaela looked embarrassed and shifted her body around. "Okay. It was Feathers. He ..."

Shelby cut in. "What? You told me it was an elder."

"I didn't tell you the whole dream, Shelby, 'cause I knew you wouldn't believe me." She looked down and picked at the comforter.

Georgia and Sean looked at each other in confusion. "Go on, honey. Tell us." Georgia said.

"Well, the first night we slept by a stream on some pine boughs. I woke up in the night and there was a dark shadow on the path. It came closer and turned white. The shape changed and it became a man with a whitish mist around him ..." she stopped and looked around.

"Continue, sweetheart," Georgia said, softly.

"He looked really old, like a Tahltan elder ..."

Sean laughed out loud. Kaela stopped talking. "Sorry, it sounded funny," he said.

Shelby shrugged. "He told me he was an Ancestor and this was really weird, 'cause he told me that he and Shelby and me would become blood and he was there to protect us. I didn't know what that meant and he wouldn't say anything. He kept telling me to go to the waterfall and we'd be safe."

"So he *was* a native. What's Feathers have to do with it?" Shelby pushed.

"Don't rush me."

"Sorry."

"He told me about the cave behind the waterfall. There's a hole in the big rocks. You can swim through it and come out the other side under the waterfall into a smaller pond. The cave is behind it. The elder told us to go into the cave at night and sleep there. During the day we swam and ate blackberries."

Shelby interjected. "She never told me about the cave and she disappeared under the water. I thought she'd drowned."

"I'm sorry, Shelby. I wanted to check it out before I said anything."

"Thus is eerie. Everything he told you happened in my dreams. You've given me goose bumps," Georgia said.

"There's more. When he said goodbye, he walked down the path and turned into white again. I ran after him. The white shadow became smaller and smaller and turned black. The black shape became a raven. He was Feathers."

Shelby's mouth dropped open. "How do you know it was Feathers?"

"Cause he made that sound in his throat. You know the one, Mommy. I asked him not to leave and he came down and did those dives above my head, like he did with you." Her eyes were big and full of wonder.

"What's an Ancestor, Auntie G?" Shelby asked.

Georgia knew her daughter had experienced a vision and said, "An ancestor is the spirit of an elder that's passed over to the other side."

"So Feathers is a spirit?" Shelby asked, her eyes now big like saucers.

"Sounds like it." Georgia said. She glanced at Sean who was leaning on his elbows, looking quite pensive.

Shelby turned to her sister. "Was the native naked with one of those leather thingies from the waist down and a feather in his hair?"

Kaela looked disgusted. "No. He wore blue jeans and sneakers."

"What? Who ever heard of a native spirit wearing blue jeans and sneakers?"

"Well mine did. He had long gray hair in braids and a leather vest with those thingies hanging all over it."

Georgia was amused at the interplay between the two girls. "Thingies, Kaela?"

"I bet she means leather fringes," Sean interjected.

"Yeah, *those* thingies." Kaela said.

Sean jumped up and left the loft. Georgia almost called out to him, but she noticed Shelby's face clouded over. The child stared down at the comforter. "Shelby? What's wrong?"

Shelby raised her eyes and dropped them again. "Oh Auntie G, I'm sorry I said you were crazy."

"I didn't know you did, sweetheart."

"When Kaela told me about the Ancestor dream, I told her she was crazy and you were too because you said you had visits from a spirit."

"It's okay. It's not easy believing in something spiritual when you haven't experienced it yourself."

"But I did believe it deep down. That's why I was so upset. When Mommy died, I prayed for her to come and visit me. She never did. So when you and Kaela had visits and I didn't, I was mad and said bad things."

Sean returned to the room carrying something, but Georgia ignored him. She patted the bed beside her. "Come, sit here with me. I want to share something with you." Shelby moved up beside her and waited. "The night your mommy passed, you and I were curled up together in the armchair sleeping. At the point she left us, I woke up. All I could do was open my eyes. I had no feeling in my body and I couldn't move. Your mommy was standing beside us. She looked so beautiful, like before she became ill. She leaned down and pushed your hair away from your face and kissed you on the forehead. She reached for your hand and touched the birthstone ring she gave you for your birthday. Then, she stood and spoke to you."

Shelby's eyes filled with tears and her mouth dropped open. In barely a whisper, she asked, "What did she say?"

"She said, 'I love you, Shelby. Be good and have a great life'."

Shelby beamed. "So she did come but I was sleeping? Why didn't you tell me?"

"Because it wouldn't have meant anything then when you were so full of pain. I decided to wait for the right time. I think today was that time."

"Thank you, Auntie G." Shelby put her arms around her neck and gave her a hug.

Sean sat in his chair with a picture frame in his hand. "Kaela, take a look at this photo." He handed the frame to Kaela.

She stared at the picture and gasped. "Uhh ... that's him." Her finger tapped excitedly on the face in the photo. She looked at Sean in utter amazement. "That's him, Sean, my native Ancestor."

The frame was passed around. When Georgia's turn came, she found herself looking at a man in blue jeans and runners, wearing a suede fringed vest, with long gray braids hanging down the front of his vest. "Who is he?"

They all looked at Sean.

"My grandfather. He built the original part of this cabin."

"Do you think your grandfather's spirit is in Feathers?" Georgia said. "I knew there was something spiritual about him and this place six years ago. That's why he stays here."

"I do and you girls are lucky to have an Ancestor looking out for you," Sean said.

"We have our own spirit, Shelby." The girls clapped their hands and laughed.

"Yay!" Shelby added.

Georgia started to laugh. "Oww ... I want to laugh and it hurts." But once she started she couldn't stop. Of course, that led to her infamous snort, and they all laughed with her. Finally, aching and out of breath, she stopped.

"How about sharing with us what's so funny." Sean said, grinning wide.

"I was thinking about when I wrote my story six years ago and the detractors, especially about Nonnock. If I do a sequel, what do you think they'd say this time?" Sean laughed and the girls giggled. Georgia continued. "This time it won't only be me they'll say is crazy."

Sean sat on the bed beside Georgia. "Well, every story needs a happy ending, and this one isn't finished yet." He took Georgia's hand in his. "Georgia Mavis Charles, will you marry me?"

Georgia heard the girls gasp, but her eyes never left Sean's face. Her heart pounded and her breath caught in her throat. This was it: the moment of truth. All she'd been through, the emotional and physical pain, came down to this moment. No one said a word. Three faces stared at her. It was a simple question with a simple yes or no answer, from a complicated woman who came from a place filled with complications. Georgia looked from one to the other. Through everything they'd experienced together , love had brought them together. They were a family—her family. She looked deep into Sean's eyes and smiled. "Yes."

Kaela squealed and Shelby giggled and put her hand over her mouth. Sean leaned over and kissed his new fiancé.

"I love you." Georgia said.

Sean beamed. "I love you too."

"We have to choose a date. When do you think?" Georgia asked.

"Like tomorrow. But I don't think you want a wedding album with that multi-coloured face. How about here at the cabin, towards the end of August."

Her eyebrows shot up. *Oh my, not a lot of time, especially with me recovering.* "That soon?"

"You can stay right here in bed. I'll give you lots of pen and paper. You plan what you want and the girls and I will see it's done. What do you say girls?"

Kaela and Shelby echoed Sean. "Yes, Mommy. It's going to be so much fun." Kaela said. Shelby nodded.

She looked at the happy faces of the girls and realized how important it was to them. She turned to Sean. "I'd love to have the wedding here at the cabin. But what about your book?"

"So I'll have to extend my deadline. John will understand. Family's more important."

"End of August it is," she said.

The girls squealed for the umpteenth time and Sean beamed.

"I think this is a time for celebration. How about you girls go get some glasses and that fresh jug of lemonade we made this morning?" Sean asked.

"And the chocolate chip cookies?" Kaela asked.

"Can't drink lemonade with cookies. Those too," he said.

After the girls left, Sean turned his attention back to Georgia. "How do you feel about me adopting the girls? I love them as if they were my own daughters. Why not make it legal?"

Georgia was feeling overwhelmed with his proposal and now this. "Oh Sean, I don't know if the girls will totally understand the implications of that right now but they will in time. It's a beautiful gesture and I love you even more for it."

The girls returned with their party food and drink and Sean poured them all a glass of lemonade.

"I was thinking that when your mother and I marry, maybe we could adopt each other's last name and become the Charles-Dixon family. What do you all think?"

"Oh Sean...yes," Georgia answered.

The girls repeated their names.

"Kaela Charles-Dixon. I love it."

"Shelby Charles-Dixon. Me too."

Sean lifted his glass. "To the Charles-Dixon family."

They all clinked their glasses and took a sip.

Shelby leaned towards Kaela and poked her with her elbow. "Let's tell Sean his name."

Kaela giggled and turned to Sean. "Once Shelby and I talked about you and Mommy getting married. We hoped you would and if you did, we would call you Poppy. Is that okay?"

Two expectant faces stared at Sean. He turned towards them on the bed. "Come here, you two." He put his arms out and they moved over and into his arms. "Poppy it is. I love my new name."

Chapter 36

August 29th, Cabin in Dease Lake

The helicopter flew over the cabin. As it turned in a circle to land, John and Betty Carr looked down at the scene on the ground. The cabin sat at the edge of a meadow where tons of people were busy working. Most people drove in, but he and Betty chose to fly in from Dease Lake. This was Tom's fifth trip in today.

"My God, it's in the middle of nowhere," John gasped. "When she escaped those kidnappers, I can't imagine her living here alone though the winter."

Betty shuddered in agreement. John was filled with a sense of pride when he thought of what his granddaughter endured for the duration of her stay in this remote area six years previous and what she had recently survived at the hands of her stalker.

They landed in a field on the other side of the stream. Tom Glass helped them down and led them with their bags across the wooden bridge and into the cabin. There were as many people inside as outside.

"Nan, Granddad, you're here." Georgia ran to her grandparents and threw her arms around each of them. "Follow me." She led them to the back of the cabin and into a bedroom with a queen-sized bed and dresser. "You two are in this room. No stairs for you."

Betty placed her suitcase on the bed. "My goodness, dear, where are all these people going to sleep?"

"Mom and Dad are upstairs in the loft. Grams is bunking with the kids across the hall from you. Frank's on the pullout couch in the living room. Sean's parents chose to sleep in a tent and the other guests are in tents. Easy." Georgia stopped for a breath. "Oh, and some of the Tahltan members coming are putting up Teepees on the other side of the gazebo. Why don't you settle in and join us?" She left them alone in the room.

Twenty minutes later, John Carr looked through the picture window at the workers in the meadow. It was a beautiful August morning. Although the temperatures were unusually hot for the time of year, a cool breeze made the day tolerable. That was good for the men who were busy setting up more tents in rows down each side of the field. In the centre, a newly constructed gazebo, freshly stained in a natural tone, was being decorated with hanging baskets of multi-coloured trailing flowers. Two huge peach bows were placed on the front of the railings on each side of the three steps that lead up to the hexagonal floor.

Betty joined the women in the open kitchen behind him. They were cooking up a storm and gabbing like hens in a chicken house. John hadn't had much of a chance to talk to anyone. They all seemed to be busy with one chore or another. He decided to wander outside and offer his services to the tent raisers. At eighty, he wasn't too steady on his feet, but he could hold up a pole.

On the veranda, he found his great-granddaughter sitting on the front steps alone. A ball cap pulled down low over her eyes, her face resting in her palms, elbows on her knees, she looked a little dejected. With a tug of her pony tail, extruding from the back of the cap, he sat down beside her. "Hi, pumpkin! What's up?"

"Nothin'…"

"You seem a little distracted. Want some company?"

"Sure!" she replied, with a shrug, "I was thinking."

"Would you like to share your thoughts with your old Grampa?"

She glanced sideways at him from beneath the visor of the ball cap, but she didn't respond. John saw the semblance of a smile tug at the corner of her mouth.

"Sure a lot of excitement going on around here today. Lots of people, coming and going. It's a happy day—the start of happier times to come, I think," he said.

He saw her face soften and a full grin broke through the grimness of her expression.

"Yeah! I think so too."

John slipped his arm around her shoulders. "You've been though a lot this past year, sweetheart. Time to look to the future and be happy. You're about to have a new family, a new sister and a lot of people that love and care about you. We all want you to be happy. You're entitled to that."

"But I'm scared," she said flatly, her body stiffening under his touch.

"Of what, pumpkin?"

She looked up into his eyes, her own blue eyes wide and full of tears. It broke his heart to see her cry. He hadn't realized how much she suffered at the loss of her natural father. *After all, Colin wasn't a big part of her life.*

"I'm scared something will happen to my new family—someone will die again."

"Child, that's not going to happen."

"Promise?"

John stared down at his great-granddaughter in silence. She was looking at him with such expectation.

"You have your whole life ahead of you with many great experiences waiting to happen. Life can be unfair sometimes, sweetheart. I can't guarantee there won't be some sad times again but you have to meet life head on, one day at a time. Look at me, I'm eighty years old. I've had many sad times over the years. But today is a happy time for me and do you know where the biggest part of my happiness comes from?"

"Where?"

"From you that's where—you and the love of my family," John said, tweaking her nose.

Giving him a long stare, suddenly she burst into tears. She jumped up and ran down the stairs.

John stood up unsteady on his feet. "Oh dear." He turned to see Georgia standing silently in the doorway, arms full of ribbons. "I don't think I handled that well."

Stepping onto the porch, she approached him. "No, Granddad. You did great. It's an emotional day for all of us. I'll go to her."

"She's too young and innocent to have to suffer so much pain," John said.

"Youth is on her side. Children can be more resilient than adults."

"I didn't expect Colin's death to have such a big impact on her." He missed the perplexed look on Georgia's face. "You've done a great job raising her, honey. I'm proud of you." He watched the child run across the meadow. "I can't believe how much taller she is since the last time I saw her. She's developed a quiet intensity, not so hyper. I suppose it's because of her loss."

Georgia's confusion gave way to a fit of the giggles. "No, Granddad, it's because she's not Kaela."

"What do mean, she isn't Kaela?"

Dropping the ribbons onto the wooden bench, Georgia planted a kiss on his cheek as she slipped past him. Once down the steps, she turned to face him and started walking backwards away from him.

"Kaela's out back with Sean. She's the other one," Georgia said, nodding towards the one who'd run away in tears. With a pause and a wink, she whispered, "You know—the bastard child?" With a giggle and a snort, she turned and ran across the field in pursuit of Shelby.

John stared after her in amazement. He watched as she caught up with the child, slipping an arm around her shoulders. "Well, I'll be damned."

He headed towards a group of men unfolding another tent canvas. His son was busy untangling tent ropes, chatting and laughing with none other than Frank Charles. Colin's father? *Who'd a thought he'd live to see the day this happened.*

Robert Carr looked up and saw his father heading towards them. "Hi, Dad. Come join us."

The two men hugged and Robert turned to Frank. "Dad, you remember Frank?"

"Sure do. How are you?"

Frank smiled and gave him a nod and offered his hand. "I could use some help sorting these poles, John."

"Tell me what you need." John chuckled. *This family becomes more and more complicated as time goes on. We could be a television reality show.*

Georgia led Shelby away from the group towards the wooden bridge over the stream. Finding a private spot on the bank, she sat and pulled the weeping girl on her lap. "Let it out, sweetie." Holding her head against her breast, she cooed and rocked back and forth, encouraging her to cry. This was the moment Georgia had waited for. She'd cried before, but not like this. Since Julie had passed, Shelby held the memory of her mother inside and held Georgia at a distance. Now, as she clung to Georgia, she finally gave in to her grief.

Eventually, she was spent and she sat quietly in Georgia's lap. "I'm sorry."

"No need for apologies."

"But today is your special day. Everyone's so happy and I'm ruining it."

She gently pushed Shelby's head back and turned her face to hers. "Sweetheart, never apologize for expressing grief. It's a strange thing. You never know when it will grab hold, or where. But when it happens, go with it. I'm quite happy you finally released your pain. It takes time, but if you can let it go, each day will be brighter and brighter."

"I want to be happy too, but whenever I am I feel bad."

"Bad in what way?" Georgia coaxed softly.

"I don't know. I guess 'cause … I'm supposed to be sad."

Georgia suddenly understood. "You mean you feel guilty about feeling happy?"

Shelby wiped her face with the back of her arm. "Yeah…sort of."

Georgia started to talk but hesitated. She knew she needed to say something to help Shelby but was afraid of losing the moment. "Do you remember when Auntie Mabel died?"

"Not really … I was too little"

"Well, she raised your mommy and they were close. When she became ill and went into the nursing home, you're mommy was sad. Then Auntie passed away and she was devastated. Honey, she knew she had to be strong for you and that you deserved to be happy. That couldn't happen if your mommy didn't let herself be happy too." She paused to take a Kleenex out of her pocket and gave it to Shelby to blow her nose.

"What I'm saying is that your parents are gone but you're still here. They would want you to be happy and enjoy life. It's okay for you to enjoy good times like today. It makes you strong to handle the sad times when they come."

Shelby lifted her face up and stared at Georgia. "So I'm not being bad if I feel happy sometimes?"

"No, sweetheart, you're not being bad. You know you're mom gave a lot of thought to where she wanted you to live after she passed on. She chose your sister, Kaela and me to be your family and now we all have Sean. She wanted you to be safe and to be part of a family full of love so you could have a happy childhood."

"She told me that once. That she wanted me to be happy, but sometimes I'm afraid I'll forget what my parents look like. Isn't that bad?"

Georgia watched the tears well up in her eyes once more. "No, it's not. And that's why you have an album of pictures. Whenever you want to, you can look at those pictures and any forgotten memories will come back."

The girl climbed out of her lap and sat down beside her. Together, they stared into the creek, hypnotized by the running water, each lost to their own thoughts. A little curl of the lip tugged at the corner of Shelby's mouth and grew into a crooked smile. "Mr. Carr thought I was Kaela, didn't he?"

Georgia smiled. "Yes, he did. But even though he believed he was talking to your sister, he would have said those same words to you too."

"He's a nice man." She gave Georgia a shy glance. "Do you think after you're married, I could call him Granddad?"

Tears filled Georgia's eyes. "Of course." Shelby didn't know it, but she'd allowed her guardian to finally believe they could become a real family. This was the best wedding gift of all.

"Know what? This is a special day for all of us. I think it's time we went inside and started getting ready."

Chapter 37

Brenda Dixon helped Georgia on with her dress. She pulled it over her head guiding her arms through the sleeveless two inch straps, turned her around and zipped up the back. "What a lovely dress," her future mother-in-law said. Georgia looked in the full-length mirror pleased with her choice. The ivory glass beaded shoulder straps followed the v-neckline to a circled pattern that swirled down the front of the beige flapper-style dress, with a flared skirt that fell in folds to the scalloped mid-calf hemline.

Her mother then helped her on with a cotton housecoat to protect the dress. "Brenda and I will help the flower girls dress. See you soon." She turned to Marion who sat on the bed watching. "She's all yours." The two women left the loft and went downstairs.

Georgia sat in a chair in front of the mirrored dresser. Marion started to brush her long hair. "What do you want me to do with your hair?"

"I thought we could pull it back into a bun on the nape of my neck, swoop my bangs to the right with the hair pulled back over my right ear, but on the left we pull it back behind my ear. There's a peach scrunchy in the top drawer to wrap around the bun"

"Ooh, sophisticated." Marion worked her magic and before long her hair was done. "What do you think?"

Georgia stared at her image in the mirror. "Maybe a little severe. What do you think?"

"Hmmm ..." Marion took the end of a rat's tail comb and pulled out a few wisps of curly hair at the nape of Georgia's neck and down each side of her face, adding a softening touch. "Better?"

"I love it." She smiled at her best friend through the mirror, who stood behind with her hands on Georgia's shoulders. She reached up and gave Marion's hand a squeeze. "Thank you."

After the two women shared a quiet moment, Marion asked, "So what's next?"

"It's time for you to dress. I'm going to do my make-up and take a few minutes to calm my nerves."

"I don't know why you're nervous. You're only about to marry the most handsome man in the whole world, who also happens to be loving and generous, not to mention, he loves your kids to death."

Georgia giggled. "I feel like the luckiest woman in the world."

"So you should."

She gave Marion a crooked grin. "I'm so glad you like my choice this time."

"What's not to like? If I wasn't a happily married woman, I might give you a run for your money. But, then, he's so head over heels crazy for you, no other woman stands a chance." Marion gave her a quick kiss on the cheek. "I'll be back shortly. Relax."

Georgia turned back to the mirror and applied the dry skin lotion to her face and neck. The familiar smell of lanolin reminded her of her childhood. There was something comforting about practicing such a simplistic daily ritual spanning three generations and some sixty years.

She carefully applied her make-up, while musing about her last six years with Sean. In her mind's eye, she could see the mud-caked man who'd found her in his cabin the spring after she'd escaped her kidnappers. And then, there were the warm spring days they spent at his favourite fishing holes. Last of all, came the movie and the book tours, the talk shows, and helping him write a screenplay on his book series. *How I love this wonderfully smart, witty man. We work well together.*

Against all this was her life with Colin; his lack of respect, his controlling attitude, and her feelings of inadequacy and lack of focus. *My God. It suddenly all makes sense. Sean respects me as a woman and as a working partner. He brings out the best out in me and encourages my ambitions. How could I let myself slip back into old thinking? This man understands me, accepts me, and truly loves me as I am.*

A smile of contentment stared back at her from the mirror and a quiet feeling of happiness surged through her body, replacing all the fears and doubts that had engulfed her the past twelve months. With a newfound confidence, Georgia removed the robe over her dress. She put on the white pearl drop earrings her mother lent her and slipped on peach open-toed sandals with a wedge heel. *No point breaking my ankles trying to wear high heels in the grass.* They looked attractive with a beaded strap that ran up the centre of her foot and wrapped around her ankle.

The look was completed with the crystal Nonnock gave her at the cabin many years previously, mounted on a white gold chain. She placed it around her neck and rubbed it between her fingers, lost in thought. *Wish you were here to see this. Can you believe Kaela is six years old? So much has changed.*

"Oh my God, look at you." Marion entered the loft with Georgia's mom and Brenda, Sean's mother. "Turn around, let's see."

Georgia stood and put her hands out, completing a turn. Her mother gasped. "You look beautiful."

Brenda shook her head from side to side. "Lovely."

Marion gasped. "Wow, Sean's eyes will bulge out of his head when he sees you."

Georgia took in Marion's maid of honour dress. "You look lovely, too, dear friend. Peach really suits you."

Marion smiled. "Thanks."

Georgia released a deep sigh and headed to the top of the loft stairs. "It's time."

"Oh bridal one ... hold on. You need this." Marion held a long hair comb covered with flowers. A single peach rose sat in the centre, encircled with white baby's breath and lilac daisies running the length of the comb. Marion placed it behind Georgia's left ear and pushed it in place.

"Perfect." The other women nodded in approval and the four of them headed down the stairs.

Waiting on the lower level, Shelby and Kaela looked adorable in their matching dresses, one in peach and one in lilac.

"Look at you girls, aren't you gorgeous," Georgia said.

"Oh Mommy, you look like a movie star," Kaela squealed.

Shelby clapped her hands. "You're so beautiful."

"Thank you."

"Are we ready?" Marion asked.

When they all nodded, Georgia's mother gave her a hug and a kiss on the cheek. "I'm so proud of you. Love you." She stepped back.

"You're about to become a member of my family and I couldn't be prouder," Brenda said, stepping forward and placing a kiss on her other cheek. "We'll go out and have everyone stand around the gazebo."

Marion picked up two baskets full of flower petals and gave one to each of the girls.

As soon as the girls stepped onto the cabin deck, Frank started the music. The two girls looked at each other and started to giggle. Marion and Georgia watched through the window. Shelby and Kaela made their way down the stairs to the grass and both glanced shyly at Sean and Tom who stood at the edge of the path. Sean gave them a wink and a thumbs up. They moved slowly along the track throwing their petals in front of them. Once in a while, one would giggle and the other would follow suit.

Marion turned to Georgia with a big smile. "They're doing great. Almost halfway. See you on the podium." She stepped out onto the porch. Georgia moved into place by the door and stole a glance outside. She watched Marion meet the two men at the bottom of the stairs. Tom stepped forward and offered Marion his arm. Georgia's heart fluttered when she looked at Sean. He was handsomer than ever in beige slacks, and his grandfather's fringed suede vest over a long-sleeved mauve shirt.

She took a deep breath, picked up a bouquet that matched the flowers in her hair and proceeded out of the door. Her eyes met Sean's, his face lit up with that wide boyish grin she'd come to love and her nervous jitters disappeared instantly. She gave him a huge smile. Instead of waiting for her to meet him on the grass, he bounded up the stairs two at a time and took her arm in his. "You look absolutely ravishing. Do we have time for a quickie?" he whispered.

Georgia felt her face redden as she laughed. "Behave yourself, Mr. Dixon." They took their time walking to the gazebo, whispering sweet nothings to each other.

The couple joined the others on the gazebo and stood before Lydia Smith, the marriage commissioner. A member of the Tahltan band, she was a highly respected elder. To Georgia's left, Marion stood with Kaela. Tom and Shelby stood to Sean's right.

Lydia smiled and nodded to them both. She looked around the outside of the gazebo and addressed the crowd of people.

"Welcome, family and friends. We gather here today to celebrate the union of Georgia and Sean. You have come here to share in this formal commitment they make to one another, to offer love and support as they start their married life together. They thank you for travelling to this remote location where their story first began."

She turned her attention back to the bride and groom. "Marriage is more than a ceremony. It is more than a commitment. There must be a communion. Through love, patience, dedication, and respect, talking and most importantly, listening, you can solidify your choice to be partners."

Georgia heard her mother crying softly. She braced herself. *Oh mom, don't get me started. Tune it out, girl.*

Lydia turned to Sean. "Do you, Sean Mitchell Dixon, take this woman to be your wedded wife?"

"I do."

She turned to Georgia. "Do you, Georgia Lynne Charles, take this man to be your wedded husband?"

"I do."

Lydia addressed their guests once more: "In the spirit of their love, Georgia and Sean have written their own vows." Once again, she spoke to the couple before her. "Before you share your vows, please remember if you are able to be true to the vows you take here today, not because of any religious or civic law, but out of your commitment to each other, you will establish a home in which you will both find the direction of your growth, your freedom, and your responsibility. Georgia?"

Georgia handed her flowers to Marion and turned to face Sean. Taking hold of his hands in hers, she looked deeply into his eyes. "Sean, I take you to be my husband, my friend, my partner, my love, and the father of my children. You've shown me the power of a love that is honest and supportive. Trusting in what we know and what is yet to come, whether in success or failure, I give you my love unconditionally." Her mother's soft crying turned to sobs. Georgia sucked in her lips.

"Sean?" Lydia said.

"Georgia, I take you to be my wife, my friend, my partner, my love, and embrace the responsibility of being a father to your children. From the first moment I saw you, I knew you were the one for me. Your beauty, heart, and mind inspire me. I promise to be honest and faithful—and as the only man in a household with three females, I promise to put the toilet seat down." Sounds of laughter echoed around the clearing.

Lydia turned to Shelby. "May I have the ring, please?" The child undid a piece of lace tied into a bow on the waistband of her dress and retrieved a ring. Lydia gave it to Sean. "Please place the ring on Georgia's finger as a seal of your love for each other and repeat after me. "I give you this ring to remind you each day of my love and devotion." Sean repeated the words as he placed a wide, white gold band, embossed with a yellow gold raven on Georgia's finger. A glitter of light sparkled from the small diamond set in the eye of the raven.

Lydia then turned to Kaela and made the same request for the ring. She gave it to Georgia.

Georgia placed an identical band on his finger. "Sean, I give you this ring to remind you each day of my love and devotion."

The marriage commissioner spoke to the guests. "Sean and Georgia chose a white gold band, embossed with a raven for their rings. They chose the raven because he is an important creature to the northwest people. He's the creator and represents prestige and knowledge. But it is more than that. They wish to honour, Feathers, their ancestral raven, who became Georgia's companion during her time alone at the cabin and later, a guide and protector to Kaela and Shelby."

Georgia couldn't believe the ceremony was almost finished. It went so smoothly. They were about to be named husband and wife. She waited for Lydia to say her final words but instead she nodded to Sean. He passed in front of Georgia and Marion and kneeled down before Kaela. He reached into his right pocket and took something out. *This wasn't part of what we rehearsed. What's he doing?* She glanced back at Lydia confused, but she was staring at Sean with a smile on her face.

Sean took a hold of Kaela's hand. "The first time I saw you, you were this tiny little bundle of joy. You opened my heart and taught me a different kind of love. I promise to be there for you, to guide you, and protect you." Sean opened his hand to reveal a white gold amulet on a white gold chain. He placed the pendant around her neck. "I give you this amulet engraved with the wolf. Like the wolf, you're strong and intelligent, and have proven yourself as a great protector. The wolf represents family and togetherness. Welcome to my family." He put his arms around her and she gave him a tight hug.

Oh boy. The tears were too big to hold back now. Through blurred vision, Georgia looked at her guests. All the women were crying or near tears, some of the men looked like they were having a hard time holding back. Sean rose, and this time, as he passed in front of Georgia, he squeezed her hand. His touch was electrifying and she fought hard to keep from sobbing. He knelt down in front of Shelby. Georgia watched the child's eyes enlarge as his hand went into his other pocket. "My dear, sweet Shelby, I thought I was blessed to gain one daughter, and now I have two. You're the quiet one–thank God." Another laugh echoed through the trees. Sean looked over at Kaela and gave her a wink. He placed the second pendant around her neck. "You're a deep thinker and an old soul. I promise to be there for you, to guide you, and protect you. I give you this amulet engraved with the hummingbird, not only because you love this bird, but because when you see a hummingbird during a time of pain or sorrow, a healing will soon follow. This bird also represents love and joy. Welcome to our family." Sean raised both of Shelby's hands and kissed each one.

That was it. The sobs started. Georgia couldn't believe the sensitivity of this man who knew Shelby may not be ready to hug him in such an intimate moment, so he kissed her hands. She felt so blessed to have such a man in her life and that of her children. Sean started to rise and to Georgia's surprise, Shelby reached up to stop him. She put her arms up and he picked her up. As she slipped her arms around his neck and held him tight , Georgia saw Sean's throat tighten and a tear fall down his cheek.

Georgia's chest was so tight, she thought it would burst as she took Kaela's small hand and leaned down to kiss her forehead. Wiping her eyes with a tissue Marion passed to her, she turned to Sean who was still holding Shelby and mouthed the words, 'you will always live in my heart'.

Finally, they all turned back to Lydia, who said, "This celebration represents an inward union of hearts. It's been created by and will be continued by the love of Georgia, Sean, Kaela, and Shelby, as they begin their new life together. Inasmuch, as Sean and Georgia have consented together in the bond of marriage, and have pledged their love to one another and to their children—by the joining of hands, the exchanging of rings, and the presentation of gifts—I declare them husband and wife. Congratulations, you may kiss the bride."

Sean put Shelby down and turned to Georgia. The love she saw in his eyes and all she had witnessed through this ceremony confirmed the belief in their union. She felt the heat of his hands on her face and closed her eyes as his lips touched hers. A quick, simple kiss, but one that sealed them together, as one, and as a family.

They turned to leave the gazebo, her arm linked through his and her daughter Kaela's hand in her right, as Sean held Shelby's on his left. Tom and Marion left first. As they started down the steps, Lydia spoke to the crowd.

"It is my great honour and pleasure to present to you, Mr. and Mrs. Charles-Dixon and family."

THE END

Epilogue

It was a cold, but beautiful New Year's Day. Georgia pulled her scarf a little tighter around her neck to block out the chill of the wind that blew in over the ocean. She observed the crowd of about two hundred people circling a beach fire. A man with a guitar was strumming and singing, *What a Beautiful World.* Some of the people sang along, other's closed their eyes while swaying to the music. Others cried softly.

Georgia watched Shelby and Kaela walk hand-in-hand towards the fire. Shelby leaned forward and threw a white card into the fire pit. The two girls stood side-by-side with their arms around each other, watching it burn. They had been a family for four months now. *How the girls have grown. Soon they'll be turning seven.* She felt Sean's arm slip across her shoulders and heard him whisper, "Are you alright?"

"Yes..." She replied softly, placing her hand over his.

A month earlier they had all gone to the mall in Gibsons to celebrate the *Lights of Life.* An annual event for some twenty-two years put on by the Coast Hospice Society, it was an opportunity to remember the life of a lost loved one.

Shelby had written a personal message to her mother and placed the card in a white envelope embossed with two hands intertwined and a burning candle embossed on the front. She placed the envelope on a tree in the mall next to a blue light. At that point the blue light was changed to a white one, a symbol of remembrance.

Today's *Lighting the Memories* completed the ceremony by burning the cards in a common fire on the beach. It was a special and moving event that welcomed all to participate.

Volunteers handed out hot apple cider and cookies and people began to mingle. Georgia sat on a log to watch Sean and Kaela throw rocks into the sea. Shelby sat beside her sipping her cider, deep in thought. *Always the thinker.* Georgia stayed silent, leaving Shelby to her thoughts.

"I think Mommy's happy that we remembered her today," Shelby finally said.

Georgia smiled down into the innocent eyes that stared back at her. "I'm sure she is." She placed an arm around the child and drew her closer into her side. She stared across the water and watched the sunlight dance across the waves.

"Poppy's cheating."

Georgia glanced towards the two and knew Shelby was right. Their game was to see who could throw rocks the furthest into the water.

"He's letting her win," Shelby said.

Georgia looked back down into Shelby's face and the serious expression in her eyes. *The child sees things so black and white.* "Is that a bad thing?"

Shelby gave her that famous crooked grin she'd come to love. "Nooo... 'cause he's only teasing." They resumed their silence, each moving back into their own thoughts.

After a time, she felt Shelby shift, cuddling a little closer. "Auntie G?"

"Yes, sweetheart?"

"Mommy told me once that when the adoption papers were final, you would legally be my other mommy."

Georgia wasn't quite sure where this conversation was heading so she spoke carefully, "That's right. The papers have been through the courts and legally Sean and I are your parents."

More silence. Georgia waited and resumed watching the waves churn up the sand. Finally, she heard Shelby sigh. "Auntie G?"

"Mmm...?"

"Do...do you think Mommy would be upset if I called you Mommy too?"

Georgia's throat constricted and tears rolled down her cheeks.

Shelby stood up in alarm and faced her. As she wiped Georgia's face with her woollen gloves, a stricken look came over her face. "Oh Auntie G...are you mad at me?"

"No...no," Georgia croaked, trying to regain her composure. She put her arms around Shelby and pulled her against her chest. "You've made me so happy. And no, your mother wouldn't be upset and yes ... you can call me Mommy too."

Acknowledgements

It was my sole intention to dedicate this book to the children in my extended family circle, as the story encompasses the difficulties and complexities of blended families and my family fits this profile.

After I'd finished writing a section in the book where one of the characters dies of an inoperable brain tumour, my friend and neighbour was diagnosed with a similar condition. This news devastated me and I put the book away unfinished because it was too close to home. My feeling at the time was that I should change my character's health issue. The time lapse between my friend Sharon's diagnosis and her passing was a short three month period. At the memorial service for Sharon, as I listened to her family and friends speak, it occurred to me that she was a definitive example of the subject of my story; a dedicated mother, wife, grandmother, mentor, and friend in her own very large, blended family. With this in mind, I decided to keep my story line intact. Along with the dedication to the children in my family circle, I chose to dedicate the book in part to the memory of my friend and neighbour, Sharon Marchant.

I must acknowledge the efforts of Heidi Frank and Anne Marsh for their input and support, as well as, Carol Cajigas for her creative insight. The members of my writing circle, Patricia Puddle, Chrissy Pebbles, and Irene Kueh for their continued support on a personal and professional level.

On the research side, special thanks to the Royal Canadian Mounted Police, E Division, Clinton Detachment for their valued contribution of police procedures, the Sunshine Coast Hospice Society for kindly answering all my questions on end of life care. And to Margery Loverin, for her input as a Tahltan Elder and Marriage Commissioner.